I0584959

Rosamund (Ball) Marriott Watson

Ballads of the North Countrie

Edited with introd. and notes by Graham R. Tomson

Rosamund (Ball) Marriott Watson

Ballads of the North Countrie
Edited with introd. and notes by Graham R. Tomson

ISBN/EAN: 9783744766173

Printed in Europe, USA, Canada, Australia, Japan

Cover: Foto ©Andreas Hilbeck / pixelio.de

More available books at **www.hansebooks.com**

BALLADS OF THE NORTH COUNTRIE

BALLADS

OF THE

NORTH COUNTRIE

EDITED,

WITH INTRODUCTION AND NOTES

BY

GRAHAM R. TOMSON

———◆———

WALTER SCOTT

LONDON: 24 WARWICK LANE

PATERNOSTER ROW

1888

To A. G. T.

CONTENTS.

CONTENTS.

CONTENTS.

INTRODUCTORY NOTE.

I N making this Book of Ballads the Editor has chiefly relied on the admirable collection of Professor Child. —(Boston, U.S., four volumes published out of eight.) Professor Child has had access to Motherwell's and other MSS., and his Notes and Variants are of the utmost value. His earlier work, *English and Scottish Ballads* (London, 1861, 8 vols.), has also been consulted.

Of older collections the Editor owes most to *The Border Minstrelsy* (4th Ed., 1810), to Motherwell's *Minstrelsy* (Glasgow, 1827), Aytoun's *Ballads of Scotland* (Edinburgh, 1859), Pinkerton's *Select Scottish Ballads* (London, 1783), Jamieson's *Popular Ballads* (Edinburgh, 1806), Chambers's *Popular Rhymes of Scotland* (Edinburgh, 1842), Messrs. Hales and Furnivall's reprint of the Percy Folio, the Edinburgh reprint of Charles Kirkpatrick Sharpe's *Ballad Book* (1823-1880), and Mr. Allingham's *Ballad Book* in the *Golden Treasury* series.

The Notes are intended to illustrate the diffusion of ballads in Europe, and to clear up some points of Border topography. They are by another hand.

The Ballads in this collection are, for the more part, English and Scotch narrative *Volks-lieder*.

Lyrics, even when "popular" and of ancient and unknown authorship, are seldom introduced. An example of the popular lyric is *Helen of Kirkconnel Lee*, where the lover deplores his own personal sorrow, and proclaims his desire of revenge. The ballad, as distinguished from the lyric, is a *story* of "old, unhappy, far off things," handed on by tradition, based on real events, or on some situation of primitive invention. A ballad of a real event is *Kinmont Willie;* a ballad on some primitive invention is *Fair Annie of Loch Ryan,* or *The Bonny Hind.* As to comic ballads, but few are given. Nothing is more trying than a difference of opinion about jokes, and it appears that there is a difference about the fun of the *Dragon of Wantley.* For other reasons the *Jollie Beggar* is left out with regret. *Volks-lieder* naturally fall into certain categories; from these it is the purpose of this collection to offer a choice.

There are (1) Ballads of the Supernatural: as a rule either *Ghostly,* or based on the belief in *Fairies* and Fairyland. There are *Romantic* ballads; these deal with some powerful situations of successful or thwarted love, of tragic death, of unhappy recognition.

(2, 3, and 4.) There are ballads of wild *Historical Adventure,* of Border raids, of battles long ago, and of the exploits of outlaws, like Robin Hood.

(5.) There are Humorous Ballads, usually a rendering into verse of some old *schwank* or popular jest, such as *Hame cam our Gudeman at E'en,* of wide diffusion.

(6.) There are *Nursery* ballads, suited to the tastes of children, and there are *Lullabies.*

These are the chief divisions of *Volks-lieder.* All these songs were essentially the poetry of the people, the articulate expression of peasant life. Long before literature was, they were.

In most countries, certainly in all European countries where narrative ballads are sung, the stories differ in many ways in plot and incident, but in essentials are much alike.

For they deal with the strong primal elements of human nature while it still remained unsoftened, unveiled by the neutral tints, the perhaps more delicate influences, of civilisation. Love and Hate—Joy and Despair—Birth and Death—sometimes a robust licentiousness, more frequently a certain savage purity, form the chief elements and characteristics of this poetry.

In all likelihood ballad-poetry is a development of that primitive impulse to sing whatever may be said, in a moment of emotion, that still exists among savage tribes. For instance, Lamech (Gen. iv., 23) bursts into a sorrowful recitative when he has "slain a man to my wounding, and a young man to my hurt." This habit of expression did not escape the notice of Aristotle (Poetics I., iv. 6), who remarks that "all poetry springs from improvisations." Good examples in fiction are the song of *Jacky*, the Australian black, in *Never Too Late to Mend*, and the song of Alan Breck, after the battle, in *Kidnapped*. The primitive chant was also used for magical purposes, and as an accompaniment to work, and the dance, a survival of which latter custom exists in children's games, such as "Round the Merry May-tanzie." Again, as when Achilles sang "the deeds renowned of men" in his hut, song was employed as a method of beguiling hours of leisure and inaction.

Not infrequently the story was both sung and said, as described by Mr. Motherwell in his "Preliminary Essay on Scotch Ballad Literature." "Some pieces, too, are prose and rhyme intermixed; the dialogue and those parts purely lyrical are in metre, while the narrative and descriptive portions are given in such humble prose as the reciter can furnish." The Cantefable of *Aucassin and Nicolete* (Nutt, London, 1887) is an example of this in old France; and Mr. Motherwell also makes mention of a precisely similar form which was known in Scotland in his time. According to him there is a Scotch version (told in much the same fashion) of a story very like *Aucassin and Nicolete* itself.

The traditional *formulæ*, such as "Up and spake the Popinjay," "An ill death may ye die," and others too many to enumerate, found in all ballad poetry, were, not improbably, used partially as an aid to memory, or rather like à mould into which the molten metal might be poured. Homer continually employs a like method. The constant use of these *formulæ*, as Motherwell noticed, makes the ballad really an *artificial* poetry. Popular as it is, the people have their own recognised rules of composition. The ballads, thus considered, have passed beyond the stage of impulsive improvisation; they have their own laws, and are, in fact, very abstract in expression. No one *naturally* expresses himself in stereotyped forms, like the ballad poets. Theirs are conventions, though they be popular conventions.

The age of our ballads is unknown, but they are antique. This is proved by their wide diffusion, from Iceland to the Peloponnesus. It is notable that Shakespeare was so familiar with the old popular songs, old even in his day, that he wove snatches of them into his plays—*Hamlet* and *Othello* for example. Goethe also makes Gretchen, in the prison scene, sing part of an old folk-song, which, again, is known to the remote Bechuanas of South Africa. While the authors of the ballads are unknown, the mode of their preservation is understood. The wandering singer—minstrel—*jongleur—minnesinger*—(in Finland the *Runoia,* or relater of old runes)—in fine, the frequently hereditary preserver and reciter of oral traditions, was common to most countries and communities. By the Runoias—old men who, clasping hands, would challenge each the other to feats of memory—the Kalevala, the great Finnish collection of popular songs, was preserved for posterity (La Finlande, par Leouzon Leduc, 1845). When the professed minstrel's vocation ceased to exist, the songs, of which he had been the temporary vehicle, were remembered and still sung among the peasantry (from whose forefathers they had sprung), passing from generation to generation, and finally (all that have escaped from destruction and mischance) being taken down from the recitation of some old peasant, or from the lips of those who had learned them, in childhood, from their nurses and mothers. Unhappily, many ballads must have been purged, collated, and altogether "improved" by enthusiastic editors (Allan Ramsay for example), well-nigh past the recognition of the original singers, could they but hear them in their renovated state. Many, however, have been preserved in their pristine strength and simplicity, and many others, before unknown, were unearthed by the admirably learned and conscientious efforts of such men as Mr. Motherwell, Sir Walter Scott, Charles Kirkpatrick Sharpe, Jamieson, Kinloch, and other original collectors.

The history of ballad-collecting may be briefly stated thus :—In England the songs of the people were very early printed in the shape of broadsheets, such as were sold in Shakespeare's time—" stall-copies," as Scott styles them.

Autolycus, with his wares, is a study of a ballad-monger. In the time of Charles II. these broadsheets were eagerly collected by the famous Mr. Pepys, of the *Diary*, and by Lord Dorset. Addison speaks of the custom of papering the walls of rooms with these ballad broadsheets, and his criticism of *Chevy Chase* shows the literary interest in these poems. Many were printed in collections by Tom Durfey, over whose shoulder the Merry Monarch would lean to read them, by Allan Ramsay, and others. The most notable edition is the three volume collection of 1721.

Then came Percy's publication of his old folio, and Burns recast many popular lyrics. The first useful collection from oral tradition in the north was Herd's (1769). Then came Ritson, then Scott with *The Border Minstrelsy* (1804). Compared with his predecessors, Sir Walter was a conscientious collector. But he probably patched up many ballads with lines of his own : he was assuredly hoaxed by Surtees of Mainsforth : *Auld Maitland,* chanted to him by Hogg's mother, was, perhaps, by the Shepherd himself. *Tamlane* (which Sir Walter used to sing to a mysterious tune) is full of modern interpolations, and there are pieces in *Kinmont Willie* and *Jamie Telfer* which seem suspicious.

Motherwell (1827) was a more exact antiquarian, and hated interpolations. Later collections are chiefly based on these, and on Messrs. Hales and Furnivall's reprint of Percy's genuine folio. The best of all collections will be Professor Child's of Harvard, whereof four volumes are now published.

We have spoken of the wide diffusion of the plots of Ballads. This first became known when Jamieson examined the popular poetry of the Scandinavian and Teutonic North. Ballads from France, Greece, Italy, and Spain now prove to be "all in the same tale." Between the traditional ballads, then, as between the *märchen,* or *contes populaires,* of European countries, from Finland to Portugal and Greece, there is a marked similarity and often identity of plot and incident, but this diffusion does not appear to extend so uniformly beyond the European range. In a short introduction to a group of Ballads in Mr. Ward's *English Poets,* it is remarked that "there are certain incidents, like that of the return of the dead mother to her oppressed children ; like the sudden recovery of a fickle bridegroom's heart by the patient affection of his first love ; like the adventure of May Colvin with a lover who has slain seven women, and tries to slay her ; like the story of the bride who pretends to be dead, that she may escape from a detested marriage, which are in all European countries the theme of popular song."—(Ward's *English Poets*, London, ·1880, p. 203.) Of this Professor Child, in his *English and Scottish Popular Ballads* (Boston, 1884), points out instances too many to enumerate, but it may not be out of place to give a few examples. The interest of these parallels may be rather scientific than literary, but it is distinctly curious.

In the case of *The Gay Goss-Hawk*, wherein a maid counterfeits death in order to escape from her father's keeping to a lover whom she is forbidden to espouse. A ballad closely resembling this in its most salient features exists in France, having been printed as early as 1607. As Professor Child remarks, " in the development of the story there is no likeness," but it will readily be seen that the leading ideas are identical.

" The king wishes to give Fair Isambourg a husband, but her heart is fixed on a handsome knight, whom she loves more than all her kin together, though he is poor. The king shuts her up in a dark tower, thinking that this treatment will bring about a change, but it does not. Isambourg sees her lover riding towards or by the tower at full speed. She calls to him to stop, and says :—

> " 'Malade et morte m'y feray,
> Porter en terre m'y lairray,
> Pourtant morte je ne seray.
>
> Puis après je vous prie amy,
> Qu' à ma chapelle à Sainct-Denis
> Ne m'y laissez pas enfouir.' "

(Which may be roughly translated as,

> " Sick and dead I'll seem to be,
> To the grave they'll carry me,
> Yet my life-breath shall not flee.

b

> Then, sweet friend, I pray of thee,
> At my chapel in St. Denis,
> See that no man bury me.")

"Isambourg is now proclaimed to be dead, and is carried to burial by three princes and a knight. Her lover hearing the knelling and chanting, puts himself in the way and bids the bearers stop. Since she has died for loving him too well, he wishes to say a De Profundis. He rips open a little of the shroud, and she darts a loving smile at him. Everybody is astonished."—(*English and Scottish Ballads*, part iv., p. 355.) Of this ballad there are many other popular traditional versions in France; and the story of a girl under stress of need counterfeiting death exists in Roumania, Italy, Bohemia, and Germany.

Willie's Lady, wherein the young wife is bewitched by her mother-in-law, and only restored to health and hope of life by the ingenious advice of the household familiar, has almost exact counterparts in Denmark; and very similar versions have been printed in Sweden. Professor Child calls attention to the myths regarding the malicious suspension of child-birth in classic mythology—namely, those of Latona and Alcmena; he also says, "Apuleius, in his Metamorphoses, mentions a case of suspended child-birth, which, curiously enough, had lasted eight years, as in the Danish and Swedish ballads. The witch is a mistress of her victim's husband, as in Grundtvig, 85, and as in a story cited by Scott from Heywood's 'Hierarchy of the Blessed Angels,' p. 474."

"There is a curious tale about a Count of Westeravia [Vestravia, in diocesi Argentoratensi], whom a deserted concubine bewitched upon his marriage, so as to preclude all hopes of his becoming a father. The spell continued to operate for three years, till one day, the Count happening to meet with his former mistress, she maliciously asked him about the increase of his family. The Count, conceiving some suspicion from her manner, craftily answered that God had blessed him with three fine children ; on which she exclaimed, like Willie's mother in the ballad, 'May Heaven confound the old hag by whose counsel I threw an enchanted pitcher into the draw-well of your palace !' The spell being found and destroyed, the Count became the father of a numerous family."—(*English and Scottish Ballads*, i., p. 84.)*

In a Roumanian tale, as also in some of the Danish and Swedish versions, the children immediately upon being brought into the world avenge the mother.

Of the story of May Colvin there are Polish, German (Low and High), Dutch, Flemish, Danish, Swedish, Norwegian, Icelandic, Swiss, Bohemian, Servian, French, Italian, Spanish, Portuguese, and Magyar versions, this being, apparently, the most widely circulated ballad in existence. It seems not unlikely that Mr. T. L. Beddoes might have been partly influenced in his *Bride's Tragedy* by the gloomy suggestions in the beginning of this tale.

Again, of the ballad of *Lord Randal* (of which Professor Child gives no less than fifteen variants) we find versions in German, Dutch, Danish, Swedish and Italian. The last-

---

* An analogous instance is the story of Iphiclus. Iphiclus had no children. He asked Melampus, the soothsayer, to relieve him of the spell. Melampus set out meat for all the fowls of the air, and they all came, but they knew nothing of the matter. However, they consulted the vulture, who said that, when Iphiclus was a boy, his brother Phylacus threw a knife at him. It stuck in a tree, and till it was extracted Iphiclus would be childless.

Melampus took out the knife, and gave Iphiclus a daily dose of the sap of the tree, and presently a little girl was added to the family of Iphiclus.—(Scholiast on Odyssey, xi. 287.)

named is entitled *L' Avvelenato,* and was popular in Italy more than two hundred years ago. The story is thus epitomised in the first stanza :—

> " Io vo' finire con questa d'un amante
>   *Tradito dall' amata.*
>   Oh che l'è sì garbata
>   A cantarla in ischiera :
>   ' *Dov 'andastu iersera,*
>   *Figliuol mio ricco, savio e gentile?*
>   *Dov 'andastu iersera' ?* "

and commences thus—

> " Dôve sì stâ jersira,
>   *Figliuol mio caro, fiorito e gentil?*
>   *Dôve sì stâ jersira ?*
>   Sôn stâ dalla mia dama ;
>   *Signôra Mama, mio core sta mal!*
>   Son stâ dalla mia dama ;
>   *Ohimè! ch'io moro, ohimè!* "

There is a Bohemian (and also a Catalan) ballad bearing in several points a close resemblance to this story. The "*Wee Croodlen Doo*" is a nursery variant of *Lord Randal.*

Of the piteous story ot *The Lass of Lochroyan* (or Roch Royal) Professor Child gives eleven variants. The incident of the proofs of identification asked for and given is found in the French ballad of *Germaine;* but in *The Lass of Lochroyan,* it is the mother-in-law (feigning to be the husband or lover) who demands them from the lady who implores admittance; and in *Germaine* the wife, who receives convincing evidence that the man who asserts himself to be her long-absent husband is indeed speaking the truth.

" 'Ouvre ta port', Germin', c'est moi qu'est ton mari'.
'Donnez-moi des indic's de la première nuit,
Et par lá je croirai que vous êt's mon mari.'

" ' T'en souviens-tu, Germin', de la première nuit,
Où tu étais monté' sur un beau cheval gris,
Placée entre tes frèr's et moi ton favori ? '

" ' Donnez-moi des indic's de la deuxième nuit,
Et par là je croirai que vous êt's mon mari,
Et par lá je croirai que vous êt's mon mari.'

" ' T'en souviens-tu, Germin', de la deuxième nuit ?
En te serrant les doigts ton anneau y cassa,
Tu en as la moitié, et l'autre la voilá.' "

—CHAMPFLEURY, *Chansons Populaires
des Provinces*, p. 196.

Marcellus, in his *Chants du Peuple en Grèce* (Paris, 1851,
vol. i., p. 351), gives an almost parallel case. The legend is
entitled *L' Épouse Fidele ;* as in *Germaine,* the husband has
been absent for an unreasonable length of time, and the
wife is entirely ignorant of his movements, or whether he be
alive or dead. "Si tu es mon mari, si tu es mon amant,
montre que tu connais la maison, avant que je te l'ouvre."—
Il y a un pommier près de la porte, et dans la cour une
vigne qui donne des raisins roses et un vin doux comme le
miel. Les janissaires qui le boivent s' animent au combat ;
et le pauvre qui le goûte oublie sa misère. "Cela, tout le
voisinage le sait, et c'est connu à la ronde. Montre que tu
connais ma personne, avant que je t'ouvre." Tu as un signe
sur la joue, un autre sous l' aisselle, et une petite morsure
sur le sein droit.—" Courez, mes bonnes ; ouvrez, ouvrez !
c'est bien mon amant et mon mari."

This is all so old that it has its counterpart in the

Odyssey, where Odysseus gives the tokens of his identity to Penelope.—(xxiii. 183-206.)

The central idea of the fine old Scottish ballad of *Tamlane*—where the lady holds her lover fast despite his being changed into an ask, an adder, a bear, and a lion in turn, and finally into red-hot iron, before he regains his normal shape—occurs in the winning of Thetis, in the tale of Proteus in the Odyssey (iv. 155), and also in a Cretan fairy-tale. But in the Cretan case, and that of Thetis, the parts are reversed, and the lover detains the lady, who undergoes various alarming metamorphoses in his grasp, but eventually turns into a nereid again.

A curious example of the diffusion of folk-song is given by Herodotus (Herodotus, ii. 79), who, in speaking of the marvels of Egypt, relates that he was especially astonished at their singing the Linus song (a lament) in Egypt, in Cyprus, Phœnicia, and elsewhere, the name varying in the different countries.

To descend to, comparatively speaking, modern times, it may be interesting to compare the refrain of *The Jollie Beggar*—

"And we'll gang nae mair a roving,"

with the French popular rhyme—

" Nous n'irons plus au bois,"

woven by Musset and Banville into regretful verse, and the favourite of the childhood of George Sand.

Although the plots and incidents of popular song are much the same in different peoples, the literary qualities and characteristics vary considerably.

The modern Greek are the most literary and sentimental; witness the marvellously beautiful *Volks-lieder* in the collections of Passow, Fauriel, and Marcellus. The following "*Plainte Amoureuse,*" translated by Marcellus, might almost have been sung by Moschus :—

" L'amour ne va jamais sans chagrins, sans douleurs et sans soupirs.
" Nuit et jour, ô ma lumière je te désire ; et je n'ai pas d'ami fidèle à qui dire mes peines.
" J'étais autrefois un petit oiseau sans raisonement ; je suis tombé en amour, et en bien des maux a la fois.
"Petits oiseaux qui êtes libres, n'entrez pas en cage ! fuyez les embûches de l'amour !"
                                        (MARCELLUS, ii. 135.)

As for the French "anciennes chansons populaires," their prevailing tone is a species of light gaiety; not infrequently they are cheap and meaningless, but occasionally tragic ; *La Chasse,* for example (translated by Andrew Lang in *Ballads and Lyrics of Old France*), and *C'est sur le pont de Nantes.* Here is Mr. Lang's translation of *La Chasse :*—

THE MILK WHITE DOE.

" It was a mother and a maid
    That walked the woods among,
And still the maid went slow and sad,
    And still the mother sung.

'What ails you, daughter Margaret ?
    Why go you pale and wan ?
Is it for a cast of bitter love,
    Or for a false leman ? '

' It is not for a false lover
    That I go sad to see,
But it is for a weary life
    Beneath the greenwood tree.

'For ever in the good daylight
 A maiden may I go,
But always on the ninth midnight
 I change to a milk white doe.

'They hunt me through the green forest
 With hounds and hunting men ;
And ever it is my fair brother
 That is so fierce and keen.'

 . . . . . .

'Good morrow, mother.' 'Good morrow, son ;
 Where are your hounds so good ?'
'Oh, they are hunting a white doe
 Within the glad greenwood.

'And three times have they hunted her,
 And thrice she's won away ;
The fourth time that they follow her
 That white doe they shall slay.'

 . . . . . .

Then out and spake the forester,
 As he came from the wood,
'Nor never saw I maid's gold hair
 Among the wild deer's blood.

'And I have hunted the wild deer
 In east lands and in west ;
And never saw I white doe yet
 That had a maiden's breast.'

Then up and spake her fair brother,
 Between the wine and bread,
'Behold, I had but one sister,
 And I have been her dead.

'But ye must bury my sweet sister
 With a stone at her foot and her head,
And ye must cover her fair body
 With the white roses and red.

'And I must out to the greenwood,
The roof shall never shelter me ;
And I shall lie for seven long years
On the grass below the hawthorn tree.'"

But in French, with few exceptions, what Artemus Ward
would have termed the "gay and festive" element pre-
dominates.

To account for the prosaic triteness, the whining morality,
and absence of poetic qualities in the English traditional
ballads, Mr. Lang suggests the following hypothesis, in
defence of the natural imagination of the English people:—
"The English ballads are not, or are very rarely, pure *volks-
lieder.* The vast majority of them have not been collected
straight from oral tradition, like the ballads of the Scotch
Border, of Italy, and of Greece. As soon as printing was
firmly established in England, the traditional songs were
distributed in cheap broadsheets. The people 'love a
ballad but even too well; if it be doleful matter, merrily set
down, or a very pleasant thing indeed, and sung lamentably.'
Pedlars, like Shakespeare's Autolycus, 'had songs for man or
woman of all sizes.' These songs may originally have been
true *volks-lieder*—many of them, indeed, can have been
nothing else. In passing, however, through the hands of
the printers and poor scholars who prepared them for the
press, they became dull, long-drawn, and didactic.

"The loyalty, good-humour, and love of the free air and
the greenwood remain, but the clerks have spoiled the praise
of 'Robin Hood, the good outlaw.' The ballads wandered
about the land, corrupted from the simplicity that pleased
the untaught, into harmony with the roughest educated
taste."—(Ward's *English Poets*, p. 207.)

But were the original English *volks-lieder* ever possessed
of much poetical merit? and may one not also form a

surmise as to whether the characteristics of the English rustic had not (in conjunction with garbled transcription) *something* to do with the inferiority of his traditionary ballads?

Surely no transcriber, however dull and illiterate, could have enfeebled the terse, tense tragedy of *Glasgerion*, or spoiled the laconic beauty of *The Bonny Hind*.

The English peasantry are a phlegmatic and unimaginative folk, living amidst scenery as unromantic as themselves. They breathe an unstimulating atmosphere. Soft air, rich pasture-lands, and expanses of mild, undulating country seldom produce a singing people. This country may have possessed many a "mute, inglorious Milton," but it must be admitted that no great singer has arisen from her agricultural population.

On the other hand, consider the influences that surround, and form, the peasant of the Northern Border—the keen air, the heather-clad beauty of mountain and moor, the mysteries of loch and correi. The very spirit of the country, stern, and full of romantic possibilities, must it not transmit to its offspring the poetic imagination, the fire and vigour that characterise the mythologies and folk-lore of the Northern races? However this may be, the ballads of the North are so infinitely superior to those of the South, that English ballads only obtain a place by favour in a collection chosen for poetical and not for scientific and archæological interest.

It is now ascertained that ballads are not, as some patriots have supposed, the peculiar property of the North. The Scottish Border, with Denmark, and Sweden, and Germany, has perhaps the richest wealth of narrative ballad. But France has far more of gaiety, and modern Greece excels in a Southern profusion of beautiful pictures, and touches imitated, but not excelled, by Theocritus.

The merits of our Northern ballads is to be " passionate, sensuous, and simple." It is a commonplace of criticism to show how those qualities of the ballad awakened the drowsy Muse of England, lulled by the monotonous cadences of the heroic couplets. She awoke at the sound of the Border songs ; she awoke with Burns, with Scott ; and *The Lay of the Last Minstrel, Christabel,* and Wordsworth's earlier ballads, are all inspired, though in very various measure, by peasant song and by Border Minstrelsy. Ghosts and Fairies, banished by *la Raison,* by " common sense " came back, as the rural measures returned, and Romance was re-born and restored.

All this we owe to our ballads, more than to any one cause. No man can read the ballads and fail to understand their influence. In the realm of the supernatural, where Romance so willingly dwells, take lines like these from *Thomas the Rhymer :—*

> "O they rade on, and farther on,
>   And they waded thro' rivers aboon the knee,
> And they saw neither sun nor moon,
>   But they heard the roaring of the sea.
>
> ` It was mirk, mirk night, and there was nae stern light,
>   And they waded thro' red blude to the knee,
> For a' the blude that's shed on earth
>   Rins through the springs o' that countrie."

This is an echo from a lost world in English poetry, and hence comes *Christabel,* and hence the night-ride of William òf Deloraine. How would the verses have sounded, one may ask, in Dr. Johnson's ear ? To him a ballad meant something like his parody—

> " I put my hat upon my head
>   And walked into the Strand,
> And there I met another man
>   With his hat in his hand."

In this performance, to be sure, Johnson was only carica
turing modern imitations of the ballads.   But it was not in
the heart of the generation of the Cock Lane Ghost to feel
the true thrill of the supernatural.   Mallet's ballad of the
ghost has none of the eeriness of

> " It fell·about the Martinmas,
>   When nights are lang and mirk,
> The carline wife's three sons cam' hame,
>   And their hats were o' the birk.
>
> It neither grew in syke nor ditch,
>   Nor yet in ony sheugh ;
> But at the gates o' Paradise
>   That birk grew fair eneugh."

There is in the ballads a certain haste to be done with
dishonourable or intolerable life that was not less alien
than the supernatural element from the moderate Muse of
the eighteenth century.   Hearts break at a word, swords
are drawn for an angry look ; they are the poems of a hot-
blooded people.   Richardson's Clarissa might as well have
followed the path of Glenkindie's lady :

> " ' Forbid it, forbid it,' says that lady,
>   ' That ever sic shame betide,
> That I should first be a wild loon's lass,
>   And then a young knight's bride.' "

But Clarissa was a Christian lady, and the ladies of
ballad are frank heathens, however they may cross themselves.   The Nut-brown Bride is as ready with a knife for
her rival as any one of them with a stab for herself.   They
neither hesitate in love nor in hate, and dance the measure
that is to be their last, with the bridegroom they loathe, or
the lover they have lost, as gaily as though their bridal were
prosperous and peaceful.

This fervour, this sudden heat of affection or resentment, sounded strangely to the age that diluted *Glasgerion* into Home's *Douglas.* Nor was the time quite come for the Riding Ballads, for *Kinmont Willie* and *Jamie Telfer*, and the rest that stir a Border listener as Sidney was moved by the blind Crowder's *Chevy Chase.* It needed the touch of Scott to take from men's ears the wax with which the Circe of the eighteenth century had stopped them, lest they should hear the music of the Border Sirens. We can all hear it now, and follow in fancy the rising of the fray, down Borthwick water, up Teviotdale to Branxholme, across the passes into Liddesdale, and so to Bewcastle, where the plunder is won back with more to boot; or see the wan water, the angry Eden, running white from lip to lip, that was swum by Buccleuch and his men. On every side, from every quarter, the ballads brought back the sighs of lovers long buried between briar-bush and rose-tree, the echoes of Border trumpets, the sound of the slogan, *Rise for Branx-holme readily.* The world heard them, and was young again, as in each revival of Romance. The day of Hayley's *Triumph of Temper* was over: Temper triumphed over everything in the ballads.

People listened no longer to cold-blooded satire endeavouring to be angry, nor to didactic treatises in verse. They woke again to the pleasure of a good fight, of a grim ghost, of a tragic sudden close to a wild love. The moon shone on the Douglas Burn, red with the knight's heart's blood, on the burning of the Bonny House of Airlie, on Janet waiting at Carterhaugh for the sound of the bells of Faery. The invincible youth of poetry, the charm of dreams, the delight in the impossible, revived at the sound of the ballads.

A new age of poetry began, not for long to dwindle again into versified photographs of middle-class life. This was the merit of ballads; they were not only poetical, but the cause of poetry in others. In restoring Romance they brought mankind into touch with its wild past, with its youth, with the days of hot blood, strong beliefs, and high resolves. In the history of Literature this revival has happened again and again, now at the touch of recovered Greek art, now at the sound of the forgotten music of the North. To lose Romance is to lose the life of poetry and of art.

BALLADS
OF THE NORTH COUNTRIE

Romantic and Supernatural.

Thou who for ballads gapest aye,
 Or printed, sung, or cried;
Thy mouth I'll fill abundantlye,
 Do thou it open wide.

—SIR WALTER SCOTT:
To Charles Kirkpatrick Sharpe.

BALLADS.

THOMAS THE RHYMER.

(Child, Part ii., p. 317.)

TRUE Thomas lay on Huntlie bank ;
A ferlie he spied wi' his e'e ;
And there he saw a lady bright,
Come riding down by the Eildon Tree.

Her skirt was o' the grass-green silk,
Her mantle o' the velvet fyne,
At ilka tett of her horse's mane
Hang fifty siller bells and nine.

True Thomas he pull'd aff his cap,
And louted low down to his knee :
'All hail, thou mighty Queen of Heaven !
For thy peer on earth I never did see.'

'O no, O no, Thomas,' she said,
'That name does not belang to me ;
I am but the queen of fair Elfland,
That am hither come to visit thee.

'Harp and carp, Thomas,' she said,
  'Harp and carp, along wi' me,
And if ye dare to kiss my lips,
  Sure of your bodie I will be!'

'Betide me weal, betide me woe,
  That weird sall never daunton me;'
Syne he has kissed her rosy lips,
  All underneath the Eildon Tree.

'Now, ye maun go wi' me,' she said,
  'True Thomas, ye maun go wi' me,
And ye maun serve me seven years,
  Thro' weal or woe as may chance to be.'

She mounted on her milk-white steed,
  She's taen True Thomas up behind,
And aye whene'er her bridle rung,
  The steed flew swifter than the wind.

O they rade on, and farther on—
  The steed gaed swifter than the wind—
Until they reached a desart wide,
  And living land was left behind.

'Light down, light down, now, True Thomas,
  And lean your head upon my knee;
Abide and rest a little space,
  And I will shew you ferlies three.

'O see ye not yon narrow road,
  So thick beset with thorns and briers ?
That is the path of righteousness,
  Tho' after it but few enquires.

'And see ye not that braid braid road,
  That lies across that lily leven ?
That is the path of wickedness,
  Tho' some call it the road to heaven.

'And see not ye that bonny road,
  That winds about the fernie brae ?
That is the road to fair Elfland,
  Where thou and I this night maun gae.

'But, Thomas, ye maun hold your tongue,
  Whatever ye may hear or see,
For, if you speak word in Elflyn land,
  Ye'll ne'er get back to your ain countrie.'

O they rade on, and farther on,
  And they waded thro' rivers aboon the knee,
And they saw neither sun nor moon,
  But they heard the roaring of the sea.

It was mirk mirk night, and there was nae stern light,
  And they waded thro' red blude to the knee ;
For a' the blude that's shed on earth
  Rins thro' the springs o' that countrie.

Syne they came on to a garden green,
   And she pu'd an apple frae a tree:
' Take this for thy wages, True Thomas,
   It will give the tongue that can never lie.'

' My tongue is mine ain,' True Thomas said,
   ' A gudely gift ye wad gie to me !
I neither dought to buy nor sell,
   At fair or tryst where I may be.

' I dought neither speak to prince or peer,
   Nor ask of grace from fair ladye : '
' Now hold thy peace,' the lady said,
   ' For as I say, so must it be.'

He has gotten a coat of the even cloth,
   And a pair of shoes of velvet green,
And till seven years were gane and past
   True Thomas on earth was never seen.

TAMLANE.

(Child, Part ii., p. 340.)

O I FORBID you, maidens a',
  That wear gowd on your hair,
To come or gae by Carterhaugh,
  For young Tam Lin is there.

There's nane that gaes by Carterhaugh
  But they leave him a wad,
Either their rings, or green mantles,
  Or else their maidenhead.

Janet has kilted her green kirtle
  A little aboon her knee,
And she has braided her yellow hair
  A little aboon her bree,
And she's awa' to Carterhaugh,
  As fast as she can hie.

When she came to Carterhaugh
  Tam Lin was at the well,
And there she fand his steed standing,
  But away was himsel.

She had na pu'd a double rose,
  A rose but only twa,
Till up then started young Tam Lin,
  Says, 'Lady, thou's pu nae mae.

'Why pu's thou the rose, Janet,
  And why breaks thou the wand?
Or why comes thou to Carterhaugh,
  Withoutten my command?'

'Carterhaugh, it is my ain,
  My daddie gave it me;
I'll come and gang by Carterhaugh,
  And ask nae leave at thee.'

.   .   .   .

Janet has kilted her green kirtle
  A little aboon her knee,
And she has snooded her yellow hair
  A little aboon her bree,
And she is to her father's ha',
  As fast as she can hie.

Four and twenty ladies fair
  Were playing at the ba',
And out then cam the fair Janet,
  Ance the flower amang them a'.

Four and twenty ladies fair
  Were playing at the chess,
And out then cam the fair Janet,
  As green as onie grass.

Out then spak an auld grey knight,
  Lay o'er the castle wa',
And says, ' Alas, fair Janet, for thee
  But we'll be blamed a'.

' Haud your tongue, ye auld-fac'd knight,
  Some ill death may ye die !
Father my bairn on whom I will,
  I'll father nane on thee.'

Out then spak her father dear,
  And he spak meek and mild ;
'And ever alas, sweet Janet,' he says,
  ' I think thou gaes wi' child.'

' If that I gae wi' child, father,
  Mysel maun bear the blame ;
There's ne'er a laird about your ha'
  Shall get the bairn's name.

' If my love were an earthly knight,
  As he's an elfin grey,
I wad na gie my ain true-love
  For nae lord that ye hae.

'The steed that my true-love rides on
   Is lighter than the wind ;
Wi' siller he is shod before,
   Wi' burning gowd behind.'

Janet has kilted her green kirtle
   A little aboon her knee,
And she has snooded her yellow hair
   A little aboon her bree,
And she's awa' to Carterhaugh,
   As fast as she can hie.

When she cam' to Carterhaugh,
   Tam Lin was at the well,
And there she fand his steed standing,
   But away was himsel.

She had na pu'd a double rose,
   A rose but only twa,
Till up then started young Tam Lin,
   Says, 'Lady, thou pu's nae mae.

'Why pu's thou the rose, Janet,
   Amang the groves sae green,
And a' to kill the bonnie babe
   That we gat us between ?'

'O tell me, tell me, Tam Lin,' she says,
  'For's sake that died on tree,
If e'er ye was in holy chapel,
  Or christendom did see?'

'Roxburgh he was my grandfather,
  Took me with him to bide,
And ance it fell upon a day
  That wae did me betide.

'And ance it fell upon a day,
  A cauld day and a snell,
When we were frae the hunting come,
  That frae my horse I fell;
The Queen o' Fairies she caught me,
  In yon green hill to dwell.

'And pleasant is the fairy land,
  But, an eerie tale to tell,
Ay at the end of seven years
  We pay a tiend to hell;
I am sae fair and fu' o' flesh
  I'm fear'd it be mysel.

'But the night is Halloween, lady,
  The morn is Hallowday;
Then win me, win me, an ye will,
  For weel I wat ye may.

'Just at the mirk and midnight hour
  The fairy folk will ride,
And they that wad their true-love win,
  At Miles Cross they maun bide.'

'But how shall I thee ken, Tam Lin,
  Or how my true-love know,
Amang sae mony unco knights
  The like I never saw?'

'O first let pass the black, lady,
  And syne let pass the brown,
But quickly run to the milk-white steed,
  Pu' ye his rider down.

'For I'll ride on the milk-white steed,
  And ay nearest the town;
Because I was an earthly knight
  They gie me that renown.

'My right hand will be glovd, lady,
  My left hand will be bare,
Cockt up sall my bonnet be,
  And kaimd down sall my hair;
And thae's the takens I gie thee,
  Nae doubt I will be there.

'They'll turn me in your arms, lady,
  Into an ask and adder ;
But hold me fast, and fear me not,
  I'am your bairn's father.

'They'll turn me to a bear sae grim,
  And then a lion bold ;
But hold me fast, and fear me not,
  As ye sall love your child.

'Again they'll turn me in your arms
  To a red het gaud of airn ;
But hold me fast, and fear me not,
  I'll do to you nae harm.

'And last they'll turn me in your arms
  Into the burning gleed ;
Then throw me into well water,
  O throw me in wi' speed.

'And then I'll be your ain true-love,
  I'll turn a naked knight ;
Then cover me wi' your green mantle,
  And cover me out o' sight.'

Gloomy, gloomy was the night,
  And eerie was the way,
As fair Jenny in her green mantle
  To Miles Cross she did gae.

About the middle o' the night
  She heard the bridles ring ;
This lady was as glad at that
  As any earthly thing.

First she let the black pass by,
  And syne she let the brown ;
But quickly she ran to the milk-white steed,
  And pu'd the rider down.

Sae weel she minded whae he did say,
  And young Tam Lin did win ;
Syne cover'd him wi' her green mantle,
  As blythe's a bird in spring.

Out then spak the Queen o' Fairies,
  Out of a bush o' broom :
'Them that has gotten young Tam Lin
  Has gotten a stately groom.'

Out then spak the Queen o' Fairies,
  And an angry woman was she :
'Shame betide her ill-far'd face,
  And an ill death may she die,
For she's taen awa' the bonniest knight
  In a' my companie.

'But had I kend, Tam Lin,' she says,
  'What now this night I see,
I wad hae taen out thy twa grey e'en,
  And put in twa e'en o' tree.'

THE ELPHIN NOURICE.

(C. Kirkpatrick Sharpe.   *A Ballad Book*, p. 169 [1880].)

I HEARD a cow low, a bonnie cow low,
  An' a cow low doun in yon glen,
Lang, lang will my young son greet,
  Or his mither bid him come ben.

I heard a cow low, a bonnie cow low,
  An' a cow low doun in yon fauld,
Lang, lang will my young son greet
  Or his mither take him frae cauld.

Waken, Queen of Elfan,
  An' hear your Nourice moan.
O moan ye for your meat,
  Or moan ye for your fee,
Or moan ye for the ither bounties
  That ladies are wont to gie?

I moan na for my meat,
  Nor yet for my fee,
But I mourn for Christened land—
  It's there I fain would be.

O nurse my bairn, Nourice, she says,
    Till he stan' at your knee,
An' ye's win hame to Christen land,
    Whar fain it's ye wad be.

O keep my bairn, Nourice, .
    Till he gang by the hauld,
An ye's win hame to your young son,
    Ye left in four nights auld.'

      .   .   .   .

ALISON GROSS.

(Jamieson.)

O ALISON GROSS, that lives in yon tower,
    The ugliest witch in the north countrie,
She trysted me ae day up till her bower,
    And mony fair speeches she made to me.

She straiked my head and she kaimed my hair,
    And she set me doun saftly on her knee ;
Says, ' Gin ye will be my lemman sae true,
    Sae mony braw things as I would you gie !

She shaw'd me a mantle o' red scarlett,
    Wi' gouden flowers and fringes fine ;
Says, ' Gin ye will be my lemman sae true,
    This gudely gift it sall be thine.'

' Awa', awa', ye ugly witch,
    Haud far awa', and lat me be !
I never will be your lemman sae true,
    And I wish I were out o' your company.'

She neist brought a sark o' the saftest silk,
   Well wrought wi' pearls about the band ;
Says, 'Gin ye will be my ain trúe love,
   This gudely gift ye sall command.'

She shaw'd me a cup o' the gude red goud,
   Weel set in jewels sae fair to see ;
Says, 'Gin ye will be my lemman sae true, .
   This gudely gift I will ye gie.'

'Awa', awa', ye ugly witch,
   Haud far awa,' and lat me be !
For I wadna ance kiss your ugly mouth
   For a' the gifts that you could gie.'

She's turned her richt and round about,
   And thrice she blew on a grass-green horn ;
And she sware by the moon and the stars aboon
   That she'd gar me rue the day I was born.

Then out has she ta'en a silver wand,
   And she's turned her three times round and round ;
She's mutter'd sic words that my strength it fail'd,
   And I fell doun senseless on the ground.

She turned me into an ugly worm,
   And gar'd me twine about the tree;
And aye on ilka Saturday's night
   Alison Gross she cam' to me;

Wi' silver basin and silver kaim,
   To kaim my headie upon her knee;
But ere that I'd kiss her ugly mouth,
   I'd sooner gae twining around the tree.

But as it fell out, on last Hallowe'en,
   When the Seely Court cam' ridin' by,
The Queen lighted down on a gowan bank,
   Close by the tree where I wont to lie.

She took me up in her milkwhite hand,
   She straiked me three times o'er her knee;
She changed me back to my proper shape,
   And nae mair do I twine about the tree.

KEMPION.

(Border Minstrelsy.)

" CUM heir, cum heir, ye freely feed,
   And lay your head low on my knee;
The heaviest weird I will you read,
   That ever was read to gay ladye.

" O meikle dolour sall ye dree,
   And aye the salt seas o'er ye'se swim;
And far mair dolour sall ye dree,
   On Estmere crags, when ye them climb.

" I weird ye to a fiery beast,
   And relieved sall ye never be,
Till Kempion, the kingis son,
   Cum to the crag, and thrice kiss thee."—

O meikle dolour did she dree,
   And aye the salt seas o'er she swam;
And far mair dolour did she dree
   On Estmere crags, when she them clamb.

And aye she cried for Kempion,
   Gin he would but come to her hand:
Now word has gane to Kempion,
   That sicken a beast was in his land.

"Now, by my sooth," said Kempion,
  "This fiery beast I'll gang and see."—
"And by my sooth," said Segramour,
  "My ae brother, I'll gang wi' thee."

Then bigged hae they a bonny boat,
  And they hae set her to the sea ;
But a mile before they reach'd the shore,
  Around them she gar'd the red fire flee.

"O Segramour, keep the boat afloat,
  And let her na the land o'er near ;
For this wicked beast will sure gae mad,
  And set fire to a' the land and mair."—

Syne has he bent an arblast bow,
  And aim'd an arrow at her head ;
And swore if she didna quit the land,
  Wi' that same shaft to shoot her dead.

"O out of my stythe I winna rise,
  (And it is not for the awe o' thee,)
Till Kempion, the kingis son,
  Cum to the crag, and thrice kiss me."—

He has louted him o'er the dizzy crag,
  And gien the monster kisses ane ;
Awa she gaed, and again she cam,
  The fieriest beast that ever was seen.

"O out o' my stythe I winna rise,
(And not for a' thy bow nor thee),
Till Kempion, the kingis son, ‹
    Cum to the crag, and thrice kiss me."

He's louted him o'er the Estmere crags,
    And he has gi'en her kisses twa :
Awa she gaed, and again she cam,
    The fieriest beast that ever you saw.

"O out of my den I winna rise,
    Nor flee it for the fear o' thee,
Till Kempion, that courteous knight,
    Cum to the crag, and thrice kiss me.'

He's louted him o'er the lofty crag,
    And he has gi'en her kisses three :
Awa she gaed, and again she cam,
    The loveliest ladye e'er could be !

"And by my sooth," says Kempion,
    "My ain true love, (for this is she,)
They surely had a heart o' stane,
    Could put thee to such misery.

"O was it warwolf in the wood ?
    Or was it mermaid in the sea ?
Or was it man or vile woman,
    My ain true love, that misshaped thee ?"—

"It was na warwolf in the wood,
   Nor was it mermaid in the sea ;
But it was my wicked step-mother,
   And wae and weary may she be!

"O, a heavier weird shall light her on,
   Than ever fell on vile woman ;
Her hair sall grow rough, and her teeth grow
      lang,
   And on her forefeet sall she gang.

" None sall take pity her upon ;
   In Wormeswood she aye sall won ;
And relieved sall she never be,
   Till St. Mungo come over the sea."—
And, sighing, said that weary wight,
   " I doubt that day I'll never see ! "

THE WIFE OF USHER'S WELL.

(*Border Minstrelsy*, vol. iii., p. 46.)

THERE lived a wife at Usher's Well,
    And a wealthy wife was she ;
She had three stout and stalwart sons,
    And sent them o'er the sea.

They hadna been a week from her,
    A week but barely ane,
When word came to the carline wife,
    That her three sons were gane.

They hadna been a week from her,
    A week but barely three,
Whan word came to the carline wife,
    That her sons she'd never see.

" I wish the wind may never cease,
    Nor fish be in the flood,
Till my three sons come hame to me,
    In earthly flesh and blood ! "

It fell about the Martinmas,
  When nights are lang and mirk,
The carline wife's three sons came hame,
  And their hats were o' the birk.

It neither grew in syke nor ditch,
  Nor yet in ony sheugh ;
But at the gates o' Paradise
  That birk grew fair eneugh.

.   .   .   .   .

"Blow up the fire, my maidens !
  Bring water from the well !
For a' my house sall feast this night,
  Since my three sons are well."

And she has made to them a bed,
  She's made it large and wide ;
And she's ta'en her mantle her about,
  Sat down at the bedside.

.   .   .   .   .

Up then crew the red red cock,
  And up and crew the gray ;
The eldest to the youngest said,
  " 'Tis time we were away."

The cock he hadna craw'd but once,
  And clapp'd his wings at a',
When the youngest to the eldest said,
  " Brother, we must awa.

"The cock both craw, the day doth daw,
 The channerin' worm doth chide ;
Gin we be mist out o' our placé,
 A sair pain we maun bide.

"Fare-ye-weel, my mother dear !
 Fareweel to barn and byre !
And fare-ye-weel, the bonny lass
 That kindles my mother's fire."

.   .   .   .   .

CLERK SAUNDERS.

(*Border Minstrelsy*, vol. ii., p. 402.)

CLERK SAUNDERS and may Margaret
    Walked ower yon garden green ;
And sad and heavy was the love
    That fell thir twa between.

"A bed, a bed," Clerk Saunders said,
    "A bed for you and me !"
"Fye na, fye na," said may Margaret,
    "Till anes we married be.

"For in may come my seven bauld brothers,
    Wi' torches burning bright ;
They'll say,—'We hae but ae sister,
    And behold she's wi' a knight !'"

"Then take the sword frae my scabbard,
    And slowly lift the pin ;
And you may swear, and save your aith,
    Ye never let Clerk Saunders in.

" And take a napkin in your hand,
　And tie up baith your bonny een,
And you may swear, and save your aith,
　Ye saw me na since late yestreen."

It was about the midnight hour,
　When they asleep were laid,
When in and came her seven brothers,
　Wi' torches burning red.

When in and came her seven brothers,
　Wi' torches burning bright :
They said, " We hae but ae sister,
　And behold her lying with a knight I "

Then out and spake the first o' them,
　" I bear the sword shall gar him die I "
And out and spake the second o' them,
　" His father has nae mair than he I "

And out and spake the third o' them,
　" I wot that they are lovers dear ! "
And out and spake the fourth o' them,
　" They hae been in love this mony a year ! "

Then out and spake the fifth o' them,
　" It were great sin true love to twain ! "
And out and spake the sixth o' them,
　" It were shame to slay a sleeping man ! "

Then up and gat the seventh o' them,
   And never a word spake he ;
But he has striped his bright brown brand
   Out through Clerk Saunders' fair bodye.

Clerk Saunders he started, and Margaret she turned
   Into his arms as asleep she lay;
And sad and silent was the night
   That was atween thir twae.

And they lay still and sleeped sound
   Until the day began to daw;
And kindly to him she did say,
   "It is time, true love, you were awa'."

But he lay still, and sleeped sound,
   Albeit the sun began to sheen ;
She looked atween her and the wa',
   And dull and drowsie were his een.

Then in and came her father dear ;
   Said,—"Let a' your mourning be :
I'll carry the dead corpse to the clay,
   And I'll come back and comfort thee."

"Comfort weel your seven sons ;
   For comforted will I never be :
I ween 'twas neither knave nor loon
   Was in the bower last night wi' me."

The clinking bell gaed through the town,
   To carry the dead corse to the clay;
And Clerk Saunders stood at may Margaret's window,
   I wot, an hour before the day.

"Are ye sleeping, Margaret?" he says,
   "Or are ye waking presentlie?
Give me my faith and troth again,
   I wot, true love, I gied to thee."

"Your faith and troth ye sall never get,
   Nor our true love sall never twin,
Until ye come within my bower,
   And kiss me cheik and chin."

"My mouth it is full cold, Margaret,
   It has the smell, now, of the ground;
And if I kiss thy comely mouth,
   Thy days of life will not be lang.

"O, cocks are crowing a merry midnight,
   I wot the wild fowls are boding day;
Give me my faith and troth again,
   And let me fare me on my way."

"Thy faith and troth thou sall na get,
   And our true love sall never twin,
Until ye tell what comes of women,
   I wot, who die in strong traivelling?"

" Their beds are made in the heavens high,
    Down at the foot of our good lord's knee,
Weel set about wi' gillyflowers;
    I wot, sweet company for to see.

"O, cocks are crowing a merry midnight,
    I wot the wild fowl are boding day;
The psalms of heaven will soon be sung,
    And I, ere now, will be missed away."

Then she has ta'en a crystal wand,
    And she has stroken her troth thereon;
She has given it him out at the shot-window,
    Wi' mony a sad sigh, and heavy groan.

" I thank ye, Marg'ret; I thank ye, Marg'ret;
    And aye I thank ye heartilie;
Gin ever the dead come for the quick,
    Be sure, Marg'ret, I'll come for thee."

It's hosen and shoon, and gown alone,
    She climb'd the wall, and followed him,
. Until she came to the green forest,
    And there she lost the sight o' him.

" Is there ony room at your head, Saunders?
    Is there ony room at your feet?
Is there ony room at your side, Saunders,
    Where fain, fain I wad sleep?"

" There's nae room at my head, Marg'ret,
　There's nae room at my feet ;
My bed it is full lowly now,
　Amang the hungry worms I sleep.

" Cauld mould is my covering now,
　But and my winding-sheet ;
The dew it falls nae sooner down
　Than my resting-place is weet.

" But plait a wand o' bonnie birk,
　And lay it on my breast ;
And shed a tear upon my grave,
　And wish my saul gude rest.

"And fair Marg'ret, and rare Marg'ret,
　And Marg'ret, o' veritie,
Gin ere ye love another man,
　Ne'er love him as ye did me."

Then up and crew the milk-white cock,
　And up and crew the gray ;
Her lover vanish'd in the air,
　And she gaed weeping away.

WILLIE'S LADY.

(Child, Part i., p. 81.)

WILLIE has ta'en him o'er the fame,
He's woo'd a wife and brought her hame.

He's woo'd her for her yellow hair,
But his mother wrought her mickle care.

And mickle dolour gard her dree,
For lighter she can never be.

But in her bower she sits wi' pain,
And Willie mourns o'er her in vain.

And to his mother he has gone,
That vile rank witch of vilest kind.

He says : ' My ladie has a cup,
Wi' gowd and silver set about.

' This goodlie gift sall be your ain,
And let her be lighter o' her young bairn.

'O' her young bairn she'll ne'er be lighter,
Nor in her bower to shine the brighter.

' But she sall die and turn to clay,
And you sall wed another may.'

' Another may I'll never wed,
Another may I'll ne'er bring hame.'

But sighing says that weary wight,
' I wish my life were at an end.'

' Ye doe [ye] unto your mother again,
That vile rank witch of vilest kind.

' And say your ladie has a steed,
The like o' m's no in the lands of Leed.

' For he [i]s golden shod before,
And he [i]s golden shod behind.

' And at ilka tet of that horse's main,
There's a golden chess and a bell ringing.

' This goodlie gift sall be your ain,
And let me be lighter of my young bairn.'

'O' her young bairn she'll ne'er be lighter,
Nor in her bower to shine the brighter.

'But she sall die and turn to clay,
And you sall wed another may.'

'Another may I'[ll] never wed,
Another may I'[ll] ne'er bring hame.'

But sighing said that weary wight,
'I wish my life were at an end.'

'Ye doe [ye] unto your mother again,
That vile rank witch of vilest kind.

'And say your ladie has a girdle,
It's red gowd unto the middle.

'And ay at every silver hem,
Hangs fifty silver bells and ten.

'That goodlie gift sall be her ain,
And let me be lighter of my young bairn.'

'O' her young bairn she'll ne'er be lighter,
Nor in her bower to shine the brighter.

' But she sall die and turn to clay,
And you sall wed another may.',

' Another may I'll never wed,
Another may I'll ne'er bring hame.'

But sighing says that weary wight,
" I wish my life were at an end.'

Then out and spake the Billy Blind;
He spake aye in good time.

' Ye doe ye to the market place,
And there ye buy a loaf o' wax.

' Ye shape it bairn and bairnly like,
And in twa glassen e'en ye pit;

' And bid her come to your boy's christening;
Then notice weel what she shall do.

' And do you stand a little fore bye,
And listen weel what she shall say.'

' Oh wha has loosed the nine witch knots
That was amo' that ladie's locks ?

'And wha has ta'en out the kaims of care
That hangs amo' that ladie's hair?

'And wha's ta'en down the bush o' woodbine
That hang atween her bower and mine?

" And wha has kill'd the master kid
That ran beneath that ladie's bed?

'And wha has loosed her left-foot shee,
And letten that ladie lighter be?'

O Willie has loosed the nine witch knots
That was amo' that ladie's locks.

And Willie's ta'en out the kaims o' care
That hang amo' that ladie's hair.

And Willie's ta'en down the bush o' woodbine
That hang atween her bower and thine.

And Willie has killed the master kid
That ran beneath that ladie's bed.

And Willie has loosed her left-foot shee,
And letten his ladie lighter be.

And now he's gotten a bonny young son,
And mickle grace be him upon.

SIR ROLAND.

(Motherwell. *Legendary and Romantic Ballads of Scotland*, p. 124.)

.   .   .   .   .   .

WHAN he cam to his ain luve's bouir
He tirl'd at the pin,
And sae ready was his fair fause luve
To rise and let him in.

" O welcome, welcome, Sir Roland," she says,
" Thrice welcome thou art to me ;
For this night thou wilt feast in my secret bouir,
And to-morrow we'll wedded be."

" This night is hallow-eve," he said,
" And to-morrow is hallow-day ;
And I dreamed a drearie dream yestreen,
That has made my heart fu' wae.

" I dreamed a drearie dream yestreen,
And I wish it may cum to gude :
I dreamed that ye slew my best grew hound,
And gied me his lappered blude."

" Unbuckle your belt, Sir Roland," she said,
    " And set you safely down."
" O your chamber is very dark, fair maid,
    And the night is wondrous lown."

" Yes, dark dark is my secret bouir,
    And lown the midnight may be ;
For there is none waking in a' this tower
    But thou, my true love, and me."

      .   .   .   .   .

She has mounted on her true love's steed,
    By the ae light o' the moon ;
She has whipped him and spurred him,
    And roundly she rade frae the toun.

She hadna ridden a mile o' gate,
    Never a mile but ane,
Whan she was aware of a tall young man,
    Slow riding o'er the plain.

She turned her to the right about,
    Then to the left turn'd she ;
But aye 'tween her and the wan moonlight
    That tall knight did she see.

And he was riding burd alane,
    On a horse as black as jet,
But tho' she followed him fast and fell,
    No nearer could she get.

"O stop! O stop! young man," she said ;
  "For I in dule am dight ;
O stop, and win a fair lady's luve,
  If you be a leal true knight."

But nothing did the tall knight say,
  And nothing did he blin ;
Still slowly rode he on before,
  And fast she rade behind.

She whipped her steed, she spurred her steed,
  Till his breast was all a foam ;
But nearer unto that tall young knight,
  By our ladye she could not come.

"O if you be a gay young knight,
  As well I trow you be,
Pull tight your bridle reins, and stay
  Till I come up to thee."

But nothing did that tall knight say,
  And no whit did he blin,
Until he reached a broad river's side,
  And there he drew his rein.

"O is this water deep?" he said,
  "As it is wondrous dun ?
Or is it sic as a saikless maid,
  And a leal true knight may swim ?"

"The water it is deep," she said,
 "As it is wondrous dun ;
But it is sic as a saikless maid,
 And a leal true knight may swim."

The knight spurred on his tall black steed ;
 The lady spurred on her brown ;
And fast they rade unto the flood,
 And fast they baith swam down.

"The water weets my tae," she said ;
 "The water weets my knee,
And hold up my bridle reins, sir knight,
 For the sake of our ladye."

"If I would help thee now," he said,
 "It were a deadly sin,
For I've sworn neir to trust a fair may's word,
 Till the water weets her chin."

"Oh, the water weets my waist," she said,
 "Sae does it weet my skin,
And my aching heart rins round about,
 The burn maks sic a din.

"The water is waxing deeper still,
 Sae does it wax mair wide,
And aye the farther that we ride on,
 Farther off is the other side.

"O help me now, thou false, false knight,
  Have pity on my youth,
For now the water jawes owre my head,
  And it gurgles in my mouth."

The knight turned right and round about,
  All in the middle stream;
And he stretched out his hand to that lady,
  But loudly she did scream.

"O this is hallow-morn," he said,
  "And it is your bridal-day,
But sad would be that gay wedding,
  If bridegroom and bride were away.

"And ride on, ride on, proud Margaret!
  Till the water comes o'er your bree,
For the bride maun ride deep, and deeper yet,
  Wha rides this ford wi' me.

"Turn round, turn round, proud Margaret!
  Turn ye round, and look on me,
Thou hast killed a true knight under trust,
  And his ghost now links on with thee."

          .   .   .   .   .   .

EARL RICHARD.

(Border Minstrelsy.)

" O LADY, rock never your young son young,
    One hour langer for me;
For I have a sweetheart in Garlioch Wells
    I love far better than thee.

"The very sole o' that lady's foot
    Than thy face is far mair white."—
" But, nevertheless, now, erl Richard,
    Ye will bide in my bower a' night?"—

She birled him with the ale and wine,
    As they sat down to sup;
A living man he laid him down,
    But I wot he ne'er rose up.

Then up and spake the popinjay,
    That flew aboun her head;
"Lady! keep weel your green cleiding
    Frae gude erl Richard's bleid."—

" O better I'll keep my green cleiding
    Frae gude erl Richard's bleid,
Than thou canst keep thy clattering toung,
    That trattles in thy heid."

She has call'd upon her bower maidens,
  She has call'd them ane by ane ;
" There lies a dead man in my bower,
  I wish that he were gane ! "

They hae booted him, and spurred him,
  As he was wont to ride ;—
A hunting-horn tied round his waist,
  A sharpe sword by his side ;
And they hae had him to the wan water,
  For a' men call it Clyde.

Then up and spoke the popinjay
  That sat upon the tree—
"What hae ye done wi' erl Richard ?
  Yé were his gay ladye."—

"Come down, come down, my bonny bird,
  And sit upon my hand ;
And thou sall hae a cage o' gowd,
  Where thou hast but the wand."—

"Awa ! awa ! ye ill woman !
  Nae cage o' gowd for me ;
As ye hae done to erl Richard,
  Sae wad ye do to me."

She hadna cross'd a rigg o' land,
    A rigg but barely ane,
When she met wi' his auld father,
    Came riding all alane.

"Where hae ye been, now, ladye fair,
    Where hae ye been sae late?
We hae been seeking erl Richard,
    But him we canna get."—

"Erl Richard kens a' the fords in Clyde,
    He'll ride them ane by ane;
And though the night was ne'er sae mirk,
    Erl Richard will be hame."

O it fell anes, upon a day,
    The king was boun to ride;
And he has mist him, erl Richard,
    Should hae ridden on his right side.

The lady turn'd her round about,
    Wi' mickle mournfu' din—
"It fears me sair o' Clyde water,
    That he is drown'd therein."

"Gar douk, gar douk," the king he cried,
    "Gar douk for gold and fee;
O wha will douk for erl Richard's sake,
    Or wha will douk for me?"—

They douked in at ae weil-heid,
   And out aye at the other ;
" We can douk nae mair for erl Richard,
   Although he were our brother."—

It fell that, in that ladye's castle,
   The king was boun to bed ;
And up and spake the popinjay
   That flew abune his head,—

" Leave aff your douking on the day,
   And douk upon the night ;
And where that sackless knight lies slain,
   The candles will burn bright."—

" O there's a bird within this bower,
   That sings baith sad and sweet ;
O there's a bird within your bower,
   Keeps me fra my night's sleep."—

They left the douking on the day,
   And douked upon the night ;
And where that sackless knight lay slain,
   The candles burned bright.

The deepest pot in a' the linn,
   They fand erl Richard in ;
A green turf tyed across his breast,
   To keep that gude lord down.

THE PROPERTY OF SCARBORO MECHANIC INSTITUTE.

Then up and spake the king himsell,
   When he saw the deadly wound—
" O wha has slain my right-hand man,
   That held my hawk and hound ? "—

Then up and spake the popinjay,
   Says—" What needs a' this din ?
It was his light leman took his life,
   And hided him in the linn."

Sae swore her by the grass sae grene,
   Sae did she by the corn,
She had not seen him, erl Richard,
   Since Moninday at morn.

" Put na the wite on me," she said ;
   " It was my may Catherine."—
Then they hae cut baith fern and thorn,
   To burn that maiden in.

It wadna take upon her cheik,
   Nor yet upon her chin ;
Nor yet upon her yellow hair,
   To cleanse the deadly sin.

The maiden touch'd the clay-cauld corpse,
   A drap it never bled ;
The ladye laid her hand on him,
   And soon the ground was red.

Out they have ta'en her, may Catherine,
    And put her mistress in ;
The flame tuik fast upon her cheïk,
    Tuik fast upon her chin ;
Tuik fast upon her faire body—
    She burn'd like hollin green.

YOUNG BENJIE.

(Border Minstrelsy.)

OF a' the maids o' fair Scotland,
　The fairest was Marjorie;
And young Benjie was her ae true love,
　And a dear true love was he.

And wow but they were lovers dear,
　And loved fu' constantlie;
But aye the mair when they fell out,
　The sairer was their plea.

And they hae quarrell'd on a day,
　Till Marjorie's heart grew wae;
And she said she'd chuse another luve,
　And let young Benjie gae.

And he was stout, and proud-hearted,
　And thought o't bitterlie;
And he's gane by the wan moonlight,
　To meet his Marjorie.

"O open, open, my true love,
　O open, and let me in!"—
"I darena open, young Benjie,
　My three brothers are within."—

" Ye leed, ye leed, ye bonny burd
　Sae loud's I hear ye lee ;
As I came by the Lowden banks,
　They bade gude e'en to me.

" But fare ye weel, my ae fause love,
　That I have loved sae lang !
It sets ye chuse another love,
　And let young Benjie gang."—

Then Marjorie turn'd her round about,
　The tear blinding her ee—
" I darena, darena let thee in,
　But I'll come down to thee."—

Then saft she smiled, and said to him,
　" O what ill hae I done ? "—
He took her in his armis twa,
　And threw her o'er the linn.

The stream was strang, the maid was stout,
　And laith laith to be dang,
But, ere she wan the Lowden banks,
　Her fair colour was wan.

Then up bespak her eldest brother,
　" O see ye nae what I see ? "
And out then spak her second brother,
　" It's our sister Marjorie ! "—

Out then spak her eldest brother,
    "O how shall we her ken?"—
And out then spak her youngest brother,
    "There's a honey mark on her chin."—

Then they've ta'en up the comely corpse,
    And laid it on the ground—
"O wha has killed our ae sister,
    And how can he be found?

"The night it is her low lykewake,
    The morn her burial day,
And we maun watch at mirk midnight,
    And hear what she will say."—

Wi' doors ajar, and candle light,
    And torches burning clear,
The streikit corpse, till still midnight,
    They waked, but naething hear.

About the middle o' the night
    The cocks began to craw;
And at the dead hour o' the night
    The corpse began to thraw.

"O whae has done thee wrang, sister,
    Or dared the deadly sin?
Whae was sae stout, and fear'd nae dout,
    As thraw ye o'er the linn?"—

" Young Benjie was the first ae man
  I laid my love upon ;
He was sae stout, and proud-hearted,
  He threw me o'er the linn."—

" Sall we young Benjie head, sister,
  Sall we young Benjie hang,
Or sall we pike out his twa gray een,
  And punish him ere he gang?"—

" Ye maunna Benjie head, brothers,
  Ye maunna Benjie hang,
But ye maun pike out his twa gray een.
  And punish him ere he gang.

"Tie a green gravat round his neck,
  And lead him out and in,
And the best ae servant about your house
  To wait young Benjie on.

" And aye, at every seven years' end,
  Ye'll tak him to the linn ;
For that's the penance he maun dree,
  To scug his deadly sin."

PROUD LADY MARGARET.

(Border Minstrelsy.)

'Twas on a night, an evening bright,
   When the dew began to fa',
Lady Margaret was walking up and down
   Looking o'er her castle wa'.

She looked east, and she looked west,
   To see what she could spy,
When a gallant knight came in her sight,
   And to the gate drew nigh.

"You seem to be no gentleman,
   You wear your boots so wide;
But you seem to be some cunning hunter,
   You wear the horn so syde."—

"I am no cunning hunter," he said,
   "Nor ne'er intend to be:
But I am come to this castle
   To seek the love of thee;
And if you do not grant me love,
   This night for thee I'll dee."—

" If you should die for me, sir knight,
 · There's few for you will mane,
For mony a better has died for me,
 Whose graves are growing green.

" But ye maun read my riddle," she said,
 "And answer me questions three;
And but ye read them right," she said,
 " Gae stretch ye out and dee.

" Now what is the flower, the ae first flower,
 Springs either on moor or dale;
And what is the bird, the bonnie bonnie bird,
 Sings on the evening gale ? "

" The primrose is the ae first flower
 Springs either on moor or dale;
And the thistlecock is the bonniest bird
 Sings on the evening gale."—

" But what's the little coin," she said,
 Wad buy my castle bound?
And what's the little boat," she said,
 Can sail the world all round ? "—

" O hey, how mony small pennies
 Make thrice three thousand pound?
Or hey, how mony small fishes
 Swim a' the salt sea round ? "—

" I think ye maun be my match," she said
  My match and something mair,
You are the first e'er got the grant
  Of love frae my father's heir.

" My father was lord of nine castles,
  My mother lady of three ;
My father was lord of nine castles,
  And there's nane to heir but me.

" And round about a' thae castles,
  You may baith plow and saw,
And on the fifteenth day of May
  The meadows they will maw."—

" O hald your tongue, lady Margaret," he said,
  "For loud I hear you lee !
Your father was lord of nine castles,
  Your mother was lady of three ;
Your father was lord of nine castles,
  But ye fa' heir to but three.

" And round about a' thae castles,
  You may baith plow and saw,
But on the fifteenth day of May
  The meadows will not maw.

"I am your brother Willie," he said,
　"I trow ye ken na me;
I came to humble your haughty heart,
　Has gar'd sae mony dee."—

"If ye be my brother Willie," she said,
　"As I trow well ye be,
This night I'll neither eat nor drink,
　But gae alang wi' thee."—

"O hald your tongue, lady Margaret," he said,
　"Again I hear you lee;
For ye've unwashen hands, and ye've unwashen
　　feet,
　To gae to clay wi' me.

"For the wee worms are my bedfellows,
　And cauld clay is my sheets;
And when the stormy winds do blow,
　My body lies and sleeps."

FINE FLOWERS IN THE VALLEY.

(Allingham.)

SHE sat down below a thorn,
  Fine flowers in the valley;
And there she has her sweet babe born,
  And the green leaves they grow rarely.

'Smile na sae sweet, my bonny babe,
  Fine flowers in the valley;
An ye smile sae sweet, ye'll smile me dead,'
  And the green leaves they grow rarely.

She's ta'en out her little penknife,
  Fine flowers in the valley;
And twinn'd the sweet babe o' its life,
  And the green leaves they grow rarely.

She's howket a grave by the light o' the moon,
  Fine flowers in the valley;
And there she's buried her sweet babe in,
  And the green leaves they grow rarely.

As she was going to the church,
  Fine flowers in the valley,
She saw a sweet babe in the porch,
  And the green leaves they grow rarely.

' O sweet babe, if thou wert mine,
  Fine flowers in the valley,
I wad cleed thee in silk and sabelline,
  And the green leaves they grow rarely.

' O mother mine, when I was thine,
  Fine flowers in the valley ;
You did na prove to me sae kind,'
  And the green leaves they grow rarely.

' But now I'm in the heavens hie,
  Fine flowers in the valley ;
And ye have the pains o' hell to dree'—
  And the green leaves they grow rarely.

THE TWA BROTHERS.

(Motherwell's *Minstrelsy, Ancient and Modern.*)

THERE were twa brothers at the schule,
    And when they got awa',
It's "Will ye play at the stane-chucking,
    Or will ye play at the ba',
Or will ye gae up to yon hill head,
    And there we'll warsle a fa'?"

"I winna play at the stane-chucking,
    Nor will I play at the ba',
But I'll gae up to yon bonnie green hill,
    And there we'll warsle a fa.'"

They warsled up, they warsled down,
    Till John fell to the ground;
A dirk fell out of William's pouch,
    And gave John a deadly wound.

"O lift me up upon your back,
    Take me to yon well fair;
And wash my bluidy wounds o'er and o'er,
    And they'll ne'er bleed nae mair."

He's lifted his brother upon his back,
   Ta'en him to yon well fair ;
He's washed his bluidy wounds o'er and o'er,
   But they bleed ay mair and mair.

" Tak' ye aff my Holland sark,
   And rive it gair by gair ;
And row it in my bluidy wounds,
   And they'll ne'er bleed nae mair."

He's taken aff his Holland sark,
   And torn it gair by gair ;
He's rowit it in his bluidy wounds,
   But they bleed ay mair and mair.

" Tak' now aff my green cleiding,
   And row me saftly in ;
And tak' me up to yon kirk style,
   Where the grass grows fair and green."

He's taken aff the green cleiding,
   And rowed him saftly in ;
He's laid him down by yon kirk style,
   Where the grass grows fair and green.

" What will ye say to your father dear
   When ye gae hame at e'en ? "
" I'll say ye're lying at yon kirk style,
   Where the grass grows fair and green."

"O no, O no, my brother dear,
  O you must not say so;
But say that I'm gane to a foreign land,
  Where nae man does me know."

When he sat in his father's chair,
  He grew baith pale and wan,
"O' what blude's that upon your brow?
  O dear son, tell to me."
"It is the blude o' my good grey steed—
  He wadna ride wi' me."

"O thy steed's blude was ne'er sae red,
  Nor e'er sae dear to me,
O what blude's this upon your cheek?
  O dear son, tell to me."
It is the blude o' my greyhound—
  He wadna hunt for me."

"O thy hound's blude was ne'er sae red,
  Nor e'er sae dear to me,
O what blude's this upon your hand?
  O dear son, tell to me."
It is the blude o' my gay goshawk—
  He wadna flee for me."

"O thy hawk's blude was ne'er sae red,
  Nor e'er sae dear to me;
O what blude's this upon your dirk?
  Dear Willie, tell to me."
"It is the blude o' my a'e brother—
  O dule and wae is me!"

"O what will ye say to your father?
  Dear Willie, tell to me,"
" I'll saddle my steed, and awa I'll ride,
  To dwell in some far countrie."

"O when will ye come hame again?
  Dear Willie, tell to me."
"When sun and mune leap on yon hill,
  And that will never be."

She turned hersel' right round about,
  And her heart burst into three :
" My a'e best son is deid and gane,
  And my tother ane I'll ne'er see."

THE DEMON LOVER.

(Motherwell, 1827, p. 92.)

" O WHERE have you been, my long, long love,
  This long seven years and mair? "
" O I'm come to seek my former vows,
  Ye granted me before.."

" O hold your tongue of your former vows.
  For they will breed sad strife ;
O hold your tongue of your former vows,
  For I am become a wife."

He turned him right and round about,
  And the tear blinded his e'e :
" I wad never hae trodden on Irish ground,
  If it had not been for thee.

" I might have had a king's daughter,
  Far, far beyond the sea ;
I might have had a king's daughter,
  Had it not been for love o' thee."

"If ye might have had a king's daughter,
　Yer sel ye had to blame ;
Ye might have taken the king's daughter,
　For ye kend that I was nane."

" O faulse are the vows o' womankind,
　But fair is their faulse bodie ;
I never wad hae trodden on Irish ground,
　Had it not been for love o' thee."

" If I was to leave my husband dear,
　And my two babes also,
O what have you to take me to,
　If with you I should go ? "

" I have seven ships upon the sea,
　The eïghth brought me to land ;
With four-and-twenty bold mariners,
　And music on every hand."

She has taken up her two little babes,
　Kissed them baith cheek and chin ;
" O fare ye weel, my ain twa babes,
　For I'll never see you again."

She set her foot upon the ship,
　No mariners could she behold ;
But the sails were o' the taffetie,
　And the masts o' the beaten gold.

5

They had not sailed a league, a league,
  A league but barely three,
Until she espied his cloven foot,
  And she wept right bitterlie.

"O hold your tongue of your weeping," says he,
  "Of your weeping now let me be ;
I will show you how the lilies grow
  On the banks of Italy."

"O what hills are yon, yon pleasant hills,
  That the sun shines sweetly on ?"
"O yon are the hills of heaven," he said,
  "Where you will never win."

"O whaten a mountain is yon," she said,
  "All so dreary wi' frost and snow ?"
"O yon is the mountain of hell," he cried,
  "Where you and I will go." .

And aye when she turned her round about,
  Aye taller he seemed to be ;
Until that the tops o' the gallant ship
  Nae taller were than he.

He strack the tapmast wi' his hand,
  The foremast wi' his knee ;
And he brake that gallant ship in twain,
  And sank her in the sea.

LOVE GREGOR; OR, THE LASS OF LOCH-ROYAN.

(Child, Part iii., page 220.)

'O WHA will shoe my fu' fair foot?
   And wha will glove my hand?
And wha will lace my middle jimp,
   Wi' the new-made London band?

'And wha will kaim my yellow hair,
   Wi' the new-made silver kaim?
And wha will father my young son,
   Till Love Gregor come hame?'

'Your father will shoe your fu' fair foot,
   Your mother will glove your hand;
Your sister will lace your middle jimp
   Wi' the new-made London band.

'Your brother will kaim your yellow hair
   Wi' the new-made silver kaim?
And the king of heaven will father your bairn,
   Till Love Gregor come haim.'

'But I will get a bonny boat,
　And I will sail the sea,
For I maun gang to Love Gregor,
　Since he canno come hame to me.'

O she has gotten a bonny boat,
　And sailld the sa't sea fame ;
She langd to see her ain true-love,
　Since he could no come hame.

'O row your boat, my mariners,
　And bring me to the land,
For yonder I see my love's castle,
　Close by the sa't sea strand.'

She has ta'en her young son in her arms,
　And to the door she's gone,
And lang she's knocked and sair she ca'd,
　But answer got she none.

'O open the door, Love Gregor,' she says,
　'O open, and let me in ;
For the wind blaws thro' my yellow hair,
　And the rain draps o'er my chin.'

'Awa, awa, ye ill woman,
　You'r nae come here for good ;
You'r but some witch, or wile warlock,
　Or mer-maid of the flood.'

' I am neither a witch nor a wile warlock,
  Nor mer-maid of the sea,
I am Fair Annie of Rough Royal ;
  O open the door to me.'

' Gin ye be Annie of Rough Royal—
  And I trust ye are not she—
Now tell me some of the love-tokens
  That past between you and me.'

' O dinna ye mind now, Love Gregor,
  When we sat at the wine,
How we changed the rings frae our fingers ?
  And I can show thee thine.

' O yours was good, and good eneugh,
  But ay the best was mine ;
For yours was o' the good red goud,
  But mine o' the dimonds fine.

' But open the door now, Love Gregor,
  O open the door I pray,
For your young son that is in my arms
  Will be dead ere it be day.'

' Awa, awa, ye ill woman,
  For here ye shanno win in ;
Gae drown ye in the raging sea,
  Or hang on the gallows-pin.'

When the cock had crawn, and day did dawn,
    And the sun began to peep,
Then up he rose him, Love Gregor,
    And sair, sair did he weep.

'O I dreamed a dream, my mother dear,
    The thoughts o' it gars me greet,
That Fair Annie of Rough Royal
    Lay cauld dead at my feet.'

'Gin it be for Annie of Rough Royal
    That ye make a' this din,
She stood a' last night at this door,
    But I trow she wan no in.'

'O wae betide ye, ill woman,
    An ill deed may ye die !
That ye woudno open the door to her,
    Nor yet woud waken me.'

O he has gone down to yon shore-side,
    As fast as he could fare ;
He saw Fair Annie in her boat,
    But the wind it tossd her sair.

And 'Hey, Annie !' and 'How, Annie !
    O Annie, winna ye bide ?'
But ay the mair that he cried, 'Annie,'
    The braider grew the tide.

And 'Hey, Annie!' and 'How, Annie!
   Dear Annie, speak to me!'
But ay the louder he cried 'Annie,'
   The louder roard the sea.

The wind blew loud, the sea grew rough,
   And dashd the boat on shore;
Fair Annie floats on the raging sea,
   But her young son rose no more.

Love Gregor tare his yellow hair,
   And made a heavy moan;
Fair Annie's corpse lay at his feet,
   But his bonny young son was gone.

O cherry, cherry was her cheek,
   And gowden was her hair,
But clay cold were her rosey lips,
   Nae spark of life was there.

And first he's kissd her cherry cheek,
   And neist he's kissed her chin;
And saftly pressd her rosey lips,
   But there was nae breath within.

'O wae betide my cruel mother,
   And an ill dead may she die!
For she turn'd my true-love frae my door,
   When she came sae far to me.'

THE DOWIE DENS O' YARROW.

(Motherwell. *Legendary and Romantic Ballads of Scotland*, p. 252.)

THERE were three lords birling at the wine,
  On the Dowie Dens o' Yarrow,
They made a compact them between
  They would go fecht to-morrow.

"Thou took our sister to be thy wife,
  And thou ne'er thocht her thy marrow,
Thou stealed her frae her Daddy's back,
  When she was the Rose o' Yarrow."

" Yes, I took your sister to be my wife,
  And I made her my marrow ;
I stealed her frae her Daddy's back,
  And she's still the Rose o' Yarrow."

He is hame to his lady gane,
  As he had done before, O ;
Says, " Madam, I must go and fecht
  On the Dowie Downs o' Yarrow.

"Stay at hame, my lord," she said,
  "For that will breed much sorrow;
For my three brethren will slay thee
  On the Dowie Downs o' Yarrow."

"Hold your tongue, my lady fair,
  For what needs a' this sorrow,
For I'll be hame gin the clock strikes nine,
  From the Dowie Downs o' Yarrow."

He wush his face and she combed his hair,
  As she had done before, O;
She dressed him up in his armour clear,
  Sent him forth to fecht on Yarrow.

"Come ye here to hawk or hound?
  Or drink the wine that's sae clear, O;
Or come ye here to eat in your words,
  That you're not the Rose o' Yarrow.

"I came not here to hawk or hound,
  Nor to drink the wine that's sae clear, O;
Nor I cam' not here to eat in my words,
  For I'm still the Rose o' Yarrow.

Then they all begoud to fecht,
  I wad they focht richt sore, O;
Till a cowardly man cam' behind his back,
  And pierced his body through.

"Gae hame, gae hame, its my man John,
    As ye have done before, O;
And tell it to my gay ladye,
    That I soundly sleep on Yarrow."

His man John, he has gane hame,
    As he had done before, O;
And told it to his gay ladye,
    That he soundly slept on Yarrow.

" I dream'd a dream now since yestreen,
    God keep us a' frae sorrow;
That my lord and I was pu'ing the heather green,
    From the dowie downs o' Yarrow."

Sometimes she rade, sometimes she gade,
    As she had done before, O;
And aye between she fell in a swoon,
    Lang or she cam to Yarrow.

Her hair it was five quarters lang,
    'Twas like the gold for yellow;
She twisted it round his milk-white hand,
    And she's drawn her hame frae Yarrow.

Out and spak her father dear,
    Says, " What needs a' this sorrow,
For I'll get you a far better lord,
    Than ever died on Yarrow."

" O hold your tongue, father," she said,
  " For you've bred a' my sorrow ; '
For that Rose 'll ne'er spring so sweet in May
  As that Rose I lost on Yarrow ! "

LORD THOMAS AND FAIR ANNET.

(Child, Part iii., p. 182.)

Lord Thomas and Fair Annet
  Sate a' day on a hill;
Whan night was cum, and sun was sett,
  They had not talkt their fill.

Lord Thomas said a word in jest,
  Fair Annet took it ill:
'A, I will nevir wed a wife
  Against my ain friends' will.'

'Gif ye wull nevir wed a wife,
  A wife wull neir wed yee;'
Sae he is hame to tell his mither,
  And knelt upon his knee.

'O rede, O rede, mither,' he says,
  'A gude rede gie to mee;
Or sall I tak the nut-browne bride,
  And let Faire Annet bee?'

'The nut-browne bride haes gowd and gear,
  Fair Annet she has gat nane;
And the little beauty Fair Annet haes,
  O it wull soon be gane.'

And he has till his brother gane :
  'Now, brother, rede ye mee;
A, sall I marrie the nut-browne bride,
  And let fair Annet bee?'

'The nut-browne bride has oxen, brother,
  The nut-browne bride has kye;
I wad hae ye marrie the nut-browne maid,
  And cast Fair Annet bye.'

'Her oxen may dye i' the house, billie,
  And her kye into the byre;
And I sall hae nothing to mysell
  But a fat fadge by the fyre.'

And he has till his sister gane;
  'Now, sister, rede ye mee;
O sall I marrie the nut-browne bride,
  And set Fair Annet free?'

'I'se rede ye tak Fair Annet, Thomas,
  And let the browne bride alane;
Lest ye sould sigh, and say, Alace,
  What is this we brought hame!'

'No, I will tak my mither's counsel,
　And marrie me owt o' hand;
And I will tak the nut-browne bride,
　Fair Annet may leive the land.'

Up then rose Fair Annet's father,
　Twa hours or it wer day,
And he is gane unto the bower
　Wherein fair Annet lay.

'Rise up, rise up, Fair Annet,' he says,
　'Put on your silken sheene;
Let us gae to St. Marie's Kirke,
　And see that rich weddeen.'

'My maides, gae to my dressing-roome,
　And dress to me my hair;
Whaireir yee laid a plait before,
　See yee lay ten times mair.

'My maids, gae to my dressing-room,
　And dress to me my smock;
The one half is o' the holland fine,
　The other o' needle-work.'

The horse Fair Annet rade upon,
　He amblit like the wind;
Wi' siller he was shod before,
　Wi' burning gowd behind.

Four and twanty siller bells
    Wer a' tyed till his mane,
And yae tilt o' the norland wind,
    They tinkled ane by ane.

Four and twanty gay gude knichts
    Rade by Fair Annet's side,
And four and twanty fair ladies,
    As gin she had bin a bride.

And whan she cam to Marie's Kirk,
    She sat on Marie's stean :
The cleading that Fair Annet had on
    It skinkled in their een.

And whan she cam into the kirk,
    She shimmered like the sun ;
The belt that was about her waist
    Was a' wi pearles bedone.

She sat her by the nut-browne bride,
    And her e'en they wer sae clear,
Lord Thomas he clean forgat the bride,
    When Fair Annet drew near.

He had a rose into his hand,
    He gae it kisses three,
And reaching by the nut-browne bride,
    Laid it on Fair Annet's knee.

Up then spak the nut-browne bride,
   She spak wi' meikle spite :
'And whair gat ye that rose-water,
   That does mak yee sae white ? '

'O I did get the rose-water
   Whair ye wull neir get nane,
For I did get that very rose-water
   Into my mither's wame.'

The bride she drew a long bodkin
   Frae out her gay head-gear,
And strake Fair Annet unto the heart,
   That word spak nevir mair.

Lord Thomas he saw Fair Annet wex pale,
   And marvelit what mote bee ;
But whan he saw her dear heart's blude,
   A' wood-wroth wexed hee.

He drew his dagger that was sae sharp,
   That was sae sharp and meet,
And drave it into the nut-browne bride,
   That fell deid at his feit.

'Now stay for me, dear Annet,' he sed,
   'Now stay, my dear,' he cry'd ;
Then strake the dagger untill his heart,
   And fell deid by her side.

Lord Thomas was buried without kirk-wa,
 Fair Annet within the quiere,
And o' the ane thair grew a birk,
 The other a bonny briere.

And ay they grew, and ay they threw,
 As they wad faine be neare;
And by this ye may ken right weil
 They were twa luvers dear.

LORD THOMASINE AND FAIR ELLINNOR.

(From a MS. in possession of Mrs. Rider Haggard.)

LORD THOMASINE was a bold forrester,
    A chaser of our king's deer;
And Ellinnor she was a fair ladye,
    And Lord Thomasine lov'd her dear.

"Come, riddle my riddle, dear mother," says he,
    "Come riddle us both in one,
Whether I shall wed fair Ellinnor
    Or bring the brown girl home?"

"The brown girl she has house and lands,
    And Fair Ellinnor has none,
So I charge thee, child, upon my blessing,
    To bring the brown girl home."

O then he called his merry men all,
    He clothed them all in white,
And the very next borough they did come thorough
    They thought it had been some great knight.

The very first town they did come at,
   The bells did merrily ring ;
The very next borough they did go thorough
   They thought it had been a wedding,

He rode till he came to fair Ellinnor's bower,
   And knockèd at the ring,
And who so ready as fair Ellinnor
   To let Lord Thomasine in ?

"What news, what news, Lord Thomas," she said,
   "What news do you bring unto me ?"
"I am come to invite you to my wedding,
   And that is ill news for thee."

"To your wedding, Lord Thomas," she said,
   "Methinks it is wondrous soon ;
I thought to have been your bride myself,
   And you to have been my bridegroom.

"Come riddle, come riddle, dear mother," said she,
   "Come riddle us both in one,
Whether I go to Lord Thomas's wedding,
   Or whether I shall stay at home."

" Friends few, dear daughter, have we,
   And many more foes I know,
So I charge thee, child, upon my blessing,
   To Lord Thomasine's wedding don't go."

"Friends few, dear mother, have we,
  And many more foes I know,
But betide me life, or betide me death,
  To Lord Thomasine's wedding I'll go."

O then she called her merry maids all,
  She clothed them all in green,
And the very next borough she did come thorough
  They thought it had been a great queen.

The very next town she did come at,
  The bells did merrily ring;
The very next borough they did go thorough
  They thought it had been a wedding.

She rode till she came to Lord Thomasine's hall,
  And knockèd at the ring,
And who so ready as Lord Thomasine
  To let fair Ellinnor in.

He took her by her lily-white hand,
  And led her through the hall,
Where there were ladies of great sort,
  But she was the flower of them all

He took her by her little finger
  And placed her by the bride,
Like a lily and a poppy flower
  Growing side by side.

"Is this your bride, Lord Thomas?" she said,
  "Methinks she looks wondrous brown;
You might have had as fair a lady
  As ever set foot on the ground."

"Dispraise her not, fair Ellinnor,
  Dispraise her not to me,
For better I love your little finger
  Than I do her whole bodie."

The brown girl she had a knife by her side,
  It was both long and sharp,
And betwixt the small ribs and the great
  She pierced fair Ellinnor's heart.

"What ails thee now?" Lord Thomasine said,
  "Methinks you look wondrous wan;
You used to have as fair a colour
  As ever the sun shone on."

"Now, are you blind, Lord Thomas," she said,
  "Or can't you very well see,
My own heart's blood, so clear and red,
  Runs trickling down to my knee?"

Lord Thomasine had a sword by his side,
  As he walked up and down the hall,
And with it he cut off the brown girl's head
  And dashed it against the wall.

He set the hilt again the floor,
　　The point upon his heart,
And never three lovers so soon did meet,
　　Nor sooner did they part.

"A grave, a grave let there be made,
　　And let it be wide and deep;
And fair Ellinnor shall rest by my side,
　　And the brown girl at my feet."

A grave, a grave there then was made,
　　And it was both wide and deep;
And fair Ellinnor was laid by his side,
　　And the brown girl at his feet.*

---

* This poem was, with the tune to which it is sung, learnt by my grandmother from an old woman named Becky Duck, who was my great-grandmother's nurse.—M. L. HAGGARD, 1888.

THE TWA SISTERS O' BINNORIE.

(Allingham, p. 132.)

THERE were twa sisters sat in a bow'r
(Binnorie, O Binnorie !) ;
A knight cam' there, a noble wooer,   ᶜ
By the bonny mill-dams o' Binnorie.

He courted the eldest wi' glove and ring
(Binnorie, O Binnorie !),
But he lo'ed the youngest aboon a' thing,
By the bonny mill-dams o' Binnorie.

The eldest she was vexed sair
(Binnorie, O Binnorie !),
And sair envied her sister fair,
By the bonny mill-dams o' Binnorie.

Upon a morning fair and clear
(Binnorie, O Binnorie !),
She cried upon her sister dear,
By the bonny mill-dams o' Binnorie.

'O sister, sister, tak' my hand'
   (Binnorie, O Binnorie !),
'And let's go down to the river-strand,
   By the bonny mill-dams o' Binnorie.'

She's ta'en her by the lily hand
   (Binnorie, O Binnorie !),
And down they went to the river-strand,
   By the bonny mill-dams o' Binnorie.

The youngest stood upon a stane,
   (Binnorie, O Binnorie !)
The eldest cam' and pushed her in,
   By the bonny mill-dams o' Binnorie.

'O sister, sister, reach your hand !'
   (Binnorie, O Binnorie !)
'And ye sall be heir o' half my land'—
   By the bonny mill-dams o' Binnorie.

'O sister, reach me but your glove !'
   (Binnorie, O Binnorie !)
'And sweet William sall be your love'—
   By the bonny mill-dams o' Binnorie.

Sometimes she sank, sometimes she swam,
   (Binnorie, O Binnorie !)
Till she cam' to the mouth o' yon mill-dam,
   By the bonny mill-dams o' Binnorie.

Out then cam' the miller's son,
  (Binnorie, O Binnorie !)
And saw the fair maid soummin' in,
  By the bonny mill-dams o' Binnorie.

'O father, father, draw your dam !'
  (Binnorie, O Binnorie !)
'There's either a mermaid or a swan,'
  By the bonny mill-dams o' Binnorie.

The miller quickly drew the dam,
  (Binnorie, O Binnorie !)
And there he found a drown'd womàn,
  By the bonny mill-dams o' Binnorie.

Round about her middle sma'
  (Binnorie, O Binnorie !)
There were a gouden girdle bra',
  By the bonny mill-dams o' Binnorie !

All amang her yellow hair
  (Binnorie, O Binnorie !)
A string o' pearls was twisted rare,
  By the bonny mill-dams o' Binnorie.

On her fingers lily-white
  (Binnorie, O Binnorie !)
The jewel-rings were shining bright,
  By the bonny mill-dams o' Binnorie.

And by there cam' a harper fine,
  (Binnorie, O Binnorie !)
Harpèd to nobles when they dine,
  By the bonny mill-dams o' Binnorie.

And when he looked that lady on,
  (Binnorie, O Binnorie !)
He sigh'd and made a heavy moan,
  By the bonny mill-dams o' Binnorie.

He's ta'en three locks o' her yellow hair,
  (Binnorie, O Binnorie !)
And wi' them strung his harp sae rare,
  By the bonny mill-dams o' Binnorie.

He went into her father's hall,
  (Binnorie, O Binnorie !)
And played his harp before them all,
  By the bonny mill-dams o' Binnorie.

And sune the harp sang loud and clear,
  (Binnorie, O Binnorie !)
'Fareweel, my father and mither dear!'
  By the bonny mill-dams o' Binnorie.

And neist when the harp began to sing,
  (Binnorie, O Binnorie !)
'Twas 'Fareweel, sweetheart!' said the string,
  By the bonny mill-dams o' Binnorie.

And then as plain as plain could be,
    (Binnorie, O Binnorie !)
'There sits my sister wha drownèd me'
    By the bonny mill-dams o' Binnorie !

BESSIE BELL AND MARY GRAY.

(C. K. Sharpe, *Ballad Book*, p. 62.)

O BESSIE BELL and Mary Gray,
   They war twa bonny lasses !
They bigget a bower on yon burn-brae,
   And theekit it o'er wi' rashes.

They theekit it o'er wi' rashes green,
   They theekit it o'er wi' heather,
But the pest cam frae the burrows town,
   And slew them baith thegither.

They thought to lie in Methven kirk-yard,
   Amang their noble kin ;
But they maun lye in Stronach Haugh,
   To beik forenent the sin.

And Bessie Bell and Mary Gray,
   They were twa bonny lasses !
They bigget a bower on yon burn-brae,
   And theekit it o'er wi' rashes.

BARTHRAM'S DIRGE.

(Border Minstrelsy, vol. i., p. 267.—*Apocryphal.*)

THEY shot him dead on the Nine-Stone Rig,
   Beside the Headless Cross,
And they left him lying in his blood,
   Upon the moor and moss.

.   .   .   .   .   '

They made a bier of the broken bough,
   The sauch and the aspin gray,
And they bore him to the Lady Chapel,
   And waked him there all day.

A lady came to that lonely bower,
   And threw her robes aside,
She tore her ling (long) yellow hair,
   And knelt at Barthram's side.

She bath'd him in the Lady-Well
   His wounds so deep and sair,
And she plaited a garland for his breast,
   And a garland for his hair.

They rowed him in a lily-sheet,
   And bare him to his earth
(And the Grey Friars sung the dead man's mass,
   As they passed the Chapel Garth).

They buried him at (the mirk) midnight,
   (When the dew fell cold and still,
When the aspin gray forgot to play
   And the mist clung to the hill).

They dug his grave but a bare foot deep,
   By the edge of the Nine-Stone Burn,
And they covered him (o'er with the heather-flower)
   The moss and the (Lady) fern.

A Gray Friar staid upon the grave,
   And sang till the morning tide,
And a friar shall sing for Bartram's soul,
   While Headless Cross shall bide.

A LYKE-WAKE DIRGE.

(*Border Minstrelsy*, vol. ii., p. 357.)

THIS ae nighte, this ae nighte,
   Every nighte and alle,
Fire, and sleet, and candle-lighte,
   And Christe receive thye saule.

When thou from hence away art paste,
   Every nighte and alle,
To Whinny-muir thou comest at laste ;
   And Christe receive thye saule.

If ever thou gavest hosen and shoon,
   Every nighte and alle,
Sit thee down and put them on ;
   And Christe receive thye saule.

If hosen and shoon thou ne'er gavest nane,
   Every nighte and alle,
The whinnes sall pricke thee to the bare bane ;
   And Christe receive thye saule.

From Whinny-muir when thou mayst passe,
　Every nighte and alle,
To Brigg o' Dread thou comest at laste,
　And Christe receive thye saule.

.　　　.　　　.　　　.　　.　　　.

From Brigg o' Dread when thou mayst passe,
　Every nighte and alle,
To Purgatory fire thou comest at last,
　And Christe receive thye saule.

If ever thou gavest meat or drink,
　Every nighte and alle,
The fire sall never make thee shrinke;
　And Christe receive thye saule.

If meate or drinke thou never gavest nane,
　Every nighte and alle,
The fire will burn thee to the bare bane;
　And Christe receive thye saule.

This ae nighte, this ae nighte,
　Every nighte and alle,
Fire, and sleet, and candle-lighte,
　And Christe receive thye saule.

THE DOUGLAS TRAGEDY.

(*Border Minstrelsy*, vol. ii., p. 214.)

"RISE up, rise up now, Lord Douglas," she says,
 " And put on your armour so bright ;
Let it never be said, that a daughter of thine
 Was married to a lord under night.

" Rise up, rise up, my seven bold sons,
 And put on your armour so bright ;
And take better care of your youngest sister,
 For your eldest's awa the last night."

He's mounted her on a milk-white steed,
 And himself on a dapple grey,
With a bugelet horn hung down by his side,
 And lightly they rode away.

Lord William lookit o'er his left shoulder,
 To see what he could see.
And there he spy'd her seven brethren bold,
 Come riding over the lee.

" Light down, light down, Lady Marg'ret," he said,
    " And hold my steed in your hand,
Until that against your seven brothers bold,
    And your father I mak a stand."

She held his steed in her milk-white hand,
    And never shed one tear,
Until that she saw her seven brethren fa',
    And her father hard fighting, who lov'd her so dear.

" O hold your hand, Lord William," she said,
    " For your strokes they are wond'rous sair ;
True lovers I can get many a ane,
    But a father I can never get mair."

O she's ta'en out her handkerchief,
    It was o' the holland sae fine,
And aye she dighted her father's bloody wounds,
    That were redder than the wine.

" O chuse, O chuse, Lady Marg'ret," he said,
    " Or whether will ye gang or bide ? "
" I'll gang, I'll gang, Lord William," she said,
    " For ye have left me no other guide."

He's lifted her on a milk-white steed,
    And himself on a dapple grey,
With a bugelet horn hung down by his side,
    And slowly they baith rade away.

O they rade on, and on they rade,
  And a' by the light of the moon,
Until they came to yon wan water,
  And there they lighted down.

They lighted down to tak a drink
  Of the spring that ran sae clear:
And down the stream ran his gude heart's blood,
  And sair she gan to fear.

"Hold up, hold up, Lord William," she says,
  "For I fear that you are slain!"
"'Tis naething but the shadow of my scarlet cloak
  That shines in the water sae plain."

O they rade on, and on they rade,
  And a' by the light of the moon,
Until they cam' to his mother's ha' door,
  And there they lighted down.

"Get up, get up, lady mother," he says,
  "Get up, and let me in!—
Get up, get up, lady mother," he says,
  "For this night my fair ladye I've win.

"O make my bed, lady mother," he says,
  "O mak it braid and deep!
And lay Lady Marg'ret close at my back,
  And the sounder I will sleep."

Lord William was dead lang ere midnight,
    Lady Marg'ret lang ere day—
And all true lovers that go thegither,
    May they have mair luck than they!

Lord William was buried in St. Mary's kirk,
    Lady Margaret in Mary's quire;
Out o' the lady's grave grew a bonny red rose,
    And out o' the knight's a brier.

And they twa met, and they twa plat,
    And fain they wad be near;
And a' the warld might ken right weel,
    They were twa lovers dear.

But by and rade the Black Douglas,
    And wow but he was rough!
For he pull'd up the bonny brier,
    And flang't in St. Mary's Loch.

THE GAY GOSS-HAWK.

(*Border Minstrelsy*, vol. ii., p. 373.)

"O WALY, waly, my gay goss-hawk,
    Gin your feathering be sheen ; "
"And waly, waly, my master dear,
    Gin ye look pale and lean.

"O have ye tint at tournament,
    Your sword, or yet your spear ?
Or mourn ye for the southern lass,
    Whom you may not win near ? "

" I have not tint at tournament,
    My sword nor yet my spear ;
But sair I mourn for my true love,
    Wi' mony a bitter tear.

"But weel's me on ye, my gay goss-hawk,
    Ye can baith speak and flee ;
Ye sall carry a letter to my love,
    Bring an answer back to me."

"But how sall I your true love find,
    Or how suld I her know?
I bear a tongue ne'er wi' her spake,
    An eye that ne'er her saw."

"O weel sall ye my true love ken,
    Sae sune as ye her see;
For, of a' the flowers of fair England,
    The fairest flower is she.

"The red that's on my true love's cheik
    Is like blood draps on the snaw;
The white that is on her bare breast,
    Like the down o' the white sea-maw.

"And even at my love's bour door,
    There grows a flowering birk;
And ye maun sit and sing thereon,
    As she gangs to the kirk.

"And four-and-twenty fair ladyes
    Will to the mass repair,
But weel may ye my ladye ken,
    The fairest lady there."

Lord William has written a love-letter,
    Put it under his pinion gray;
And the bird is awa' to Southern land,
    As fast as wings can gae.

And even at that ladye's bour,
　There grew a flowering birk ;
And he sat down and sung thereon,
　As she gaed to the kirk.

And weel he kent that ladye fair
　Amang her maidens free ;
For the flower that springs in May mornin;
　Was not sae sweet as she.

He lighted at the ladye's yate,
　And sat him on a pin,
And sang fu' sweet the notes o' love,
　Till a' was cosh within.

And first he sang a low low note,
　And syne he sang a clear ;
And aye the o'erword o' the sang
　Was—"Your love can no win here."

"Feast on, feast on, my maidens a',
　The wine flows you amang ;
While I gang to my shot-window,
　And hear yon bonnie bird's sang.

"Sing on, sing on, my bonnie bird,
　The sang ye sung yestreen ;
For weel I ken by your sweet singing,
　Ye are frae my true love sen."

Oh, first he sang a merry sang,
　And. syne he sang a grave ;
And syne he peck'd his feathers gray,
　To her the letter gave.

.

" Have there a letter from Lord William,
　He says he's sent ye three ;
He canna wait your love langer,
　But for your sake he'll die."

"Gae bid him bake his bridal bread,
　And brew his bridal ale ;
And I sall meet him at Mary's Kirk,
　Lang, lang ere it be stale."

The lady's gane to her chamber,
　And a moanfu' woman was she,
As gin she had ta'en a sudden brash,
　And were about to die.

" A boon, a boon, my father deir,
　A boon I beg of thee ! "
" Ask not that paughty Scottish lord,
　For him you ne'er shall see.

" But for your honest asking else,
　Weel granted it shall be ; "
" Then gin I die in Southern land,
　In Scotland gar bury me.

"And the first kirk that ye come to,
    Ye's gar the mass be sung ;
And the neist kirk that ye come to,
    Ye's gar the bells be rung.

"And when ye come to St. Mary's Kirk,
    Ye's tarry there till night."
And so her father pledged his word,
    And so his promise plight.

She has ta'en her to her bigly bower,
    As fast as she could fare ;
And she has drank a sleepy draught,
    That she had mixed wi' care.

And pale, pale grew her rosy cheek,
    That was sae bright of blee ;
And she seemed to be as surely dead
    As any one could be.

Then spak her cruel step-minnie :
    "Take ye the burning lead,
And drap a drap on her bosome,
    To try if she be dead."

They took a drap o' boiling lead,
    They drapp'd it on her breast ;
"Alas ! alas !" her father cried,
    "She's dead without the priest !"

She neither chatter'd with her teeth,
　　Nor shiver'd with her chin ;
" Alas ! alas ! " her father cried,
　　" There is nae breath within."

Then up arose her seven brethren,
　　And hew'd to her a bier ;
They hew'd it frae the solid aik,
　　Laid it o'er wi' silver clear.

Then up and gat her seven sisters,
　　And sewed to her a kell ;
And every steek that they put in,
　　Sewed to a siller bell.

The first Scots kirk that they cam' to,
　　They garr'd the bells be rung ;
The neist Scots kirk that they cam' to,
　　They garr'd the mass be sung.

But when they cam' to St. Mary's Kirk,
　　There stude spearmen all on a raw ;
And up and started Lord William,
　　The chieftane amang them a'.

"Set down, set down the bier," he said,
　　"Let me look her upon : "
But as soon as Lord William touched her hand,
　　Her colour began to come.

She brightened like the lily flower,
   Till her pale colour was gone ;
With rosy cheik and ruby lip,
   She smiled her love upon.

" A morsel of your bread, my lord,
   And one glass of your wine ;
For I hae fasted these three lang days,
   All for your sake and mine.

"Gae hame, gae hame, my seven bauld brothers,
   Gae hame and blaw your horn !
I trow ye wad ha'e gi'en me the skaith,
   But I've gi'en you the scorn.

"Commend me to my grey father,
   That wish'd my saul gude rest ;
But wae be to my cruel step-dame,
   Gar'd burn me on the breast."

"Ah ! woe to you, you light woman !
   An ill death may you die !
For we left father and sisters at hame,
   Breaking their hearts for thee."

CHILDE MAURICE.

(Bishop Percy's Folio MS.—Hales and Furnivall.)

CHILDE MAURICE hunted i' the Silver wood,
He hunted it round about,
And noebody that he found therein,
Nor none there was without.

And he tooke his silver combe in his hand,
To comb his yellow locks ;
He sayes, " Come hither thou little foot-page,
That runneth lowlye by my knee ;
For thou shalt goe to John Steward's wiffe
And pray her speake with me.

" And as it falls out as many times,
As knotts beene knit on a kell,
Or Marchant men gone to leave London
Either to buy ware or sell,

"Aye, and greete thou doe that Ladye well,
Ever so well froe me,—
And as it falles out many times
As any heart can thinke,
As schoole-masters are in any schoole-house

Writing with pen and inke,—
For if I might, as well she may,
This night I would with her speake.

"And here I send her a mantle of greene,
As greene as any grasse,
And bid her come to the Silver wood
To hunt with Child Maurice;

"And there I send her a ring of gold,
A ring of precious stone,
And bid her come to the Silver wood
Let for no kind of man."

One while this little boy he rode,
Another while he ran;
Untill he came to John Steward's hall,
I-wis he never blan.

And of nurture the child had good;
He ran up hall and bower free,
And when he came to this Lady faire,
Sayes, "God you save and see!

"I am come from Childe Maurice,
A message unto thee;
And Child Maurice, he greetes you well,
And ever soe well from me.

"And as it falls out oftentimes
As knotts beene knit on a kell,
Or Marchant men gone to leave London,
Either for to buy ware or sell,

"And as oftentimes he greetes you well
As any heart can thinke,
Or schoole-masters in any schoole
Writing with pen and inke;

"And here he sends a mantle of greene,
As greene as any grasse,
And he bids you come to the Silver wood,
To hunt with Childe Maurice.

"And here he sends you a ring of gold,
A ring of the precious stone,
He prays you to come to the Silver wood,
Let for no kind of man."

"Now peace, now peace, thou little foot-page,
For Christ's sake, I pray thee!
For if my lord heare one of these words,
Thou must be hanged hye!"

John Steward stood under the Castle wall,
And he wrote the words every one,
And he called unto his horsekeeper,
" Make readye you my steede ! "
Aye, and soe he did to his Chamberlaine,
" Make readye then my weede ! "

And he cast a leash upon his back,
And he rode to the Silver wood ;
And there he sought all about,
About the Silver wood.

And there he found him Child Maurice
Sitting upon a blocke,
With a silver combe in his hand
Combing his yellow locke.

He sayes, " How now, how now, Child Maurice,
Alacke ! how may this be ? "
But then stood up him Childe Maurice,
And sayd these words trulye :

" I doe not know your Ladye," he said,
" If that I doe her see."
" For thou hast sent her love tokens,
More now than two or three ;

" For thou hast sent her a mantle of greene,
As green as any grasse,
And bade her come to the Silver wood
To hunt with Childe Maurice;

" And thou hast sent her a ring of gold,
A ring of precious stone,
And bade her come to the Silver wood,
Let for noe kind of man.

" And by my faith, now, Childe Maurice,
The one of us shall dye ! "
" Now by my troth," sayd Childe Maurice,
" And that shall not be I."

But he pulled forth his bright browne sword,
And dryed it on the grasse,
And soe fast he smote at John Steward,
I-wis he never rest.

Then he pulled forth his bright browne sword,
And dryed it on his sleeve;
And the first good stroke John Steward stroke,
Child Maurice head he did cleave;

And he pricked it on his sword's poynt,
Went singing there beside,
And he rode till he came to that Ladye faire
Whereas this Ladye lyed;

And sayes, "Dost thou know Childe Maurice
    head
If that thou dost it see?
And lapp it soft, and kisse it oft,
For thou lovdst him better than me."

But when she looked on Child Maurice head,
She never spake words but three,
"I never bare no child but one,
And you have slaine him trulye."

Sayes, "Wicked be my merrymen all,
I gave meate, drinke, and clothe!
But could they not have holden me
When I was in all that wrath?

"For I have slaine one of the courteousest Knights
That ever bestrode a steed!
Soe have I done one of the fairest Ladyes
That ever wore woman's weede!"

FAIR ANNIE.

(Child, Part iii., p. 69.)

" I⊤'s narrow, narrow, make your bed,
   And learn to lie your lane ;
For I'm ga'n o'er the sea, Fair Annie,
   A braw bride to bring hame.
Wi' her I will get gowd and gear ;
   Wi' you I ne'er got nane.

" But wha will bake my bridal bread,
   Or brew my bridal ale ?
And wha will welcome my brisk bride,
   That I bring o'er the dale."

"It's I will bake your bridal bread,
   And brew your bridal ale,
And I will welcome your brisk bride,
   That you bring o'er the dale."

" But she that welcomes my brisk bride
   Maun gang like maiden fair ;
She maun lace on her robe sae jimp,
   And braid her yellow hair."

" But how can I gang maiden-like,
    When maiden I am nane?
Have I not born seven sons to thee,
    And am with child again?"

She's taen her young son in her arms,
    Another in her hand,
And she's up to the highest tower,
    To see him come to land.

"Come up, come up, my eldest son,
    And look o'er yon sea-strand,
And see your father's new-come bride,
    Before she comes to land."

"Come down, come down, my mother dear,
    Come frae the castle wa!
I fear, if langer ye stand there,
    Ye'll let yoursell down fa."

And she gaed down, and farther down,
    Her love's ship for to see,
And the topmast and the mainmast
    Shone like the silver free.

And she's gane down, and farther down,
    The bride's ship to behold,
And the topmast and the mainmast
    They shone just like the gold.

She's taen her seven sons in her hand,
    I wot she didna fail ;
She met Lord Thomas and his bride,
    As they came o'er the dale.

" You're welcome to your house, Lord Thomas,
    You're welcome to your land ;
Your welcome with your fair ladye,
    That you lead by the hand.

" You're welcome to your ha's, ladye,
    Your welcome to your bowers ;
Your welcome to your hame, ladye,
    For a' that's here is yours."

" I thank thee, Annie ; I thank thee, Annie,
    Sae dearly as I thank thee ;
You're the likest to my sister, Annie,
    That ever I did see.

" There came a knight out o'er the sea,
    And steald my sister away ;
The shame scoup in his company,
    The land where'er he gae ! "

She hang ae napkin at the door,
    Another in the ha',
And a' to wipe the trickling tears,
    Sae fast as they did fa'.

And aye she served the lang tables,
    With white bread and with wine,
And aye she drank the wan water,
    To haud her colour fine.

And aye she served the lang tables,
    With white bread and with brown ;
And aye she turned her round about,
    Sae fast the tears fell down.

And he's taen down the silk napkin,
    Hung on a silver pin,
And aye he wipes the tear trickling
    A'down her cheek and chin.

And aye he turn'd him round about,
    And smiled amang his men ;
Says, "Like ye best the old ladye,
    Or her that's new come hame ?"

When bells were rung, and mass was sung,
    And a' men bound to bed,
Lord Thomas and his new-come bride
    To their chamber they were gaed.

Annie made her bed a little forbye,
    To hear what they might say ;
"And ever alas !" Fair Annie cried,
    "That I should see this day !

" Gin my seven sons were seven young rats,
    Running on the castle wa',
And I were a grey cat mysell,
    I soon would worry them a'.

" Gin my young sons were seven young hares,
    Running o'er yon lilly lee,
And I were a grew hound mysell,
    Soon worried they a' should be."

And wae and sad Fair Annie sat,
    And drearie was her sang,
And ever, as she sobbd and grat,
    " Wae to the man that did the wrang ! "

" My gown is on," said the new-come bride,
    " My shoes are on my feet,
And I will to Fair Annie's chamber,
    And see what gars her greet.

" What ails ye, what ails ye, Fair Annie,
    That ye make sic a moan ?
. Has your wine barrels cast the girds,
    Or is your white bread gone ?

" O wha was't was your father, Annie,
    Or wha was't was your mother ?
And had ye ony sister, Annie,
    Or had ye ony brother ? "

"The Earl of Wemyss was my father,
    The Countess of Wemyss my mother;
And a' the folk about the house
    To me were sister and brother."

"If the Earl of Wemyss was your father,
    I wot sae was he mine;
And it sall not be for lack o' gowd
    That ye your love sall tyne.

" For I have seven ships o' mine ain,
    A' loaded to the brim,
And I will gie them a' to thee,
    Wi' four to thine eldest son:
But thanks to a' the powers in heaven
    That I gae maiden hame!"

WALY, WALY.

(Allingham, p. 41.)

O WALY, waly, up the bank,
 O waly, waly, doun the brae,
And waly, waly, yon burn-side,
 Where I and my love were wont to gae !
I lean'd my back unto an aik,
 I thocht it was a trustie tree,
But first it bow'd and syne it brak',—
 Sae my true love did lichtlie me.

O waly, waly, but love be bonnie
 A little time while it is new !
But when it's auld it waxeth cauld,
 And fadeth awa' like the morning dew.
O wherefore should I busk my heid,
 O wherefore should I kame my hair ?
For my true love has me forsook,
 And says he'll never lo'e me mair.

Noo Arthur's Seat sall be my bed,
 The sheets sall ne'er be press'd by me ;
Saint Anton's well sall be my drink ;
 Since my true love's forsaken me.

Martinmas wind, when wilt thou blaw,
    And shake the green leaves off the tree?
O gentle death, when wilt thou come?
    For of my life I am wearie.

'Tis not the frost that freezes fell,
    Nor blawing snaw's inclemencie,
'Tis not sic cauld that makes me cry;
    But my love's heart grown cauld to me.
When we cam' in by Glasgow toun,
    We were a comely sicht to see;
My love was clad in the black velvet,
    An' I mysel' in cramasie.

But had I wist before I kiss'd
    That love had been so ill to win,
I'd lock'd my heart in a case o' gould,
    And pinn'd it wi' a siller pin.
Oh, oh! if my young babe were born,
    And set upon the nurse's knee;
And I mysel' were dead and gane,
    And the green grass growing over me!*

* Variant—"For a maid again I'll never be."

THE LAWLANDS O' HOLLAND.

(Allingham, p. 131.)

" THE love that I hae chosen,
 I'll therewith be content ;
The saut sea sall be frozen
 Before that I repent.
Repent it sall I never
 Until the day I dee ;
But the Lawlands o' Holland
 Hae twinn'd my love and me.

" My love he built a bonny ship
 And set her to the main,
Wi' twenty-four brave mariners
 To sail her out and hame.
But the weary wind began to rise,
 The sea began to rout,
And my love and his bonny ship
 Turned withershins about.

" There sall nae mantle cross my back,
 No kaim gae in my hair,
Neither sall coal nor candle-light
 Shine in my bower mair ;

Nor sall I choose anither love
   Until the day I dee,
Sin' the Lawlands o' Holland
   Hae twinn'd my love and me."

"Noo haud your tongue, my daughter dear,
   Be still and bide content; .
There's ither lads in Galloway;
   Ye needna sair lament."
"O there is nane in Galloway,
   There's nane at a' for me.
I never lo'ed a lad but ane,
   And he's drown'd in the sea."

GLASGERION.

(Percy's *Reliques.*)

GLASGERION was a kings owne sonne,
    And a harper he was goode ;
He harped in the kings chambere,
    Where cuppe and caudle stoode.

And soe did hee in the queens chambere,
    Till ladies waxed glad,
And then bespake the kings daughter,
    And these wordes thus shee sayd :

"Strike on, strike on, Glasgerion,
    Of thy striking doe not blinne ;
There's never a stroke comes o'er thy harpe,
    But it glads my hart withinne."

"Faire might he fall, ladye," quoth he,
    "Who taught you nowe to speake !
I have loved you, ladye, seven longe yeere,
    My mind I neere durst breake."

"But come to my bower, my Glasgerion,
    When all men are att rest;
As I am a ladye true of my promise,
    Thou shalt be a welcome guest."

Home then came Glasgerion,
    A glad man, lord! was hee:
"And, come thou hither, Jacke my boy,
    Come hither unto mee.

"For the kinge's daughter of Normandye
    Hath granted mee my boone;
And att her chambere must I bee
    Beffore the cocke have crowen."

"O master, master," then quoth hee,
    "Lay your head downe on this stone;
For I will waken you, master deere,
    Afore it be time to gone."

But up then rose that lither ladd,
    And hose and shoon did on;
A coller he cast upon his necke,
    He seemed a gentleman.

And when he came to the ladyes chamber,
    He tirl'd upon the pinn;
The lady was true of her promise,
    And rose and lett him inn.

He did not take the lady gaye
  To boulster nor to bed:
Nor thoughe he had his wicked wille,
  A single word he sed.

He did not kiss that ladyes mouthe,
  Nor when he came, nor yode:
And sore that ladye did mistrust
  He was of some churls bloud.

But home then came that lither ladd,
  And did off his hose and shoone;
And cast the coller from off his necke:
  He was but a churles sonne.

"Awake, awake, my deere mastèr,
  The cock hath well-nigh crowen:
Awake, awake, my master deere,
  I hold it time to be gone.

For I have saddled your horse, master,
  Well bridled I have your steede,
And I have served you a good breakfast,
  For therefore ye have need."

Up then rose good Glasgerion,
  And did on hose and shoone,
And cast a coller about his neck:
  For he was a king his sonne.

And when he came to the ladyes chambere,
    He tirl'd upon the pinne;
The lady was more than true of promise,
    And rose and let him inn.

"O whether have you left with me
    Your bracelet or your glove ?
Or are you returned back againe
    To know more of my love ? "

Glasgerion swore a full great othe,
    By oake, and ashe, and thorne;
"Ladye, I was never in your chambere,
    Sith the time that I was borne."

"O then it was your lither-foot page,
    He hath beguiled me ;"
Then shee pulled forth a little pen-kniffe,
    That hanged by her knee.

Sayes, "There shall never noe churlès blood
    Within my bodye spring :
No churlès blood shall eer defile
    The daughter of a kinge."

Home then went Glasgerion,
    And woe, good lord l was hee :
Sayes, "Come thou hither, Jacke my boy,
    Come hither unto mee.

"If I had killed a man to-night,
  Jacke, I would tell it thee :
But if I have not killed a man to-night,
  Jacke, thou hast killed three."

And he puld out his bright browne sword,
  And dryed it on his sleeve,
And he smote off that lither ladds head,
  Who did his ladye grieve.

He sett the swords poynt till his brest,
  The pummil until a stone :
Throw the falsenesse of that lither ladd,
  These three lives were all gone.

HELEN OF KIRKCONNELL.

(*Border Minstrelsy*, vol. ii., p. 325.)

I wish I were where Helen lies !
Night and day on me she cries ;
O that I were where Helen lies,
   On fair Kirkconnell Lee !

Curst be the heart that thought the thought,
And curst the hand, that fired the shot,
When in my arms burd Helen dropt,
   And died to succour me !

O think na ye my heart was sair,
When my love dropt down and spak nae mair !
There did she swoon wi' meikle care,
   On fair Kirkconnell Lee.

As I went down the water side,
None but my foe to be my guide,
None but my foe to be my guide,
   On fair Kirkconnell Lee.

9

I lighted down, my sword did draw,
I hack'd him into pieces sma',
I hack'd him into pieces sma',
    For her sake that died for me.

O Helen fair, beyond compare !
I'll make a garland of thy hair,
Shall bind my heart for evermair,
    Until the day I die !

O that I were where Helen lies !
Night and day on me she cries ;
Out of my bed she bids me rise,
    Says, " Haste, and come to me ! "

O Helen fair ! O Helen chaste !
If I were with thee, I were blest,
Where thou lies low, and takes thy rest,
    On fair Kirkconnell Lee.

I wish my grave were growing green,
A winding-sheet drawn ower my een,
And I in Helen's arms lying,
    On fair Kirkconnell Lee.

I wish I were where Helen lies !
Night and day on me she cries,
And I am weary of the skies,
    For her sake that died for me.

LADY MAISRY.

(Child, Part iii., p. 114.)

THE young lords o' the north country
    Have all a wooing gone,
To win the love of Lady Maisry,
    But o' them she woud hae none.

O they hae courted Lady Maisry
    Wi' a' kin kind of things ;
An they hae sought her Lady Maisry
    Wi' brotches an wi' rings.

An' they ha sought her Lady Maisry
    Frae father and frae mother ;
An' they ha sought her Lady Maisry
    Frae sister and frae brother.

An' they ha followd her Lady Maisry
    Thro' chamber and thro' ha' ;
But a' that they coud say to her,
    Her answer still was Na.

"O had your tongues, young men," she says,
  "An' think nae mair o' me ;
For I've gien my love to an English lord,
  An' think nae mair o' me."

Her father's kitchy-boy heard that,
  An ill death may he dee !
An' he is on to her brother,
  As fast as gang coud he.

"O is my father an' my mother well,
  But an my brothers three ?
Gin my sister Lady Maisry be well,
  There's naething can ail me."

"Your father and your mother is well,
  But an your brothers three,
Your sister Lady Maisry's well,
  So big wi' bairn gangs she."

"Gin' this be true you tell to me,
  My mailison light on thee !
But gin it be a lie you tell,
  You sal be hangit hie."

He's done him to his sister's bowr,
  Wi' meikle doole an care ;
An there he saw her Lady Maisry,
  Kembing her yallow hair.

"O wha is aught that bairn," he says,
   "That ye sae big are wi'?
And gin' ye winna own the truth,
   This moment ye sall dee."

She turnd her right an round about,
   An the kem fell frae her han ;
A trembling seizd her fair body,
   An her rosy cheek grew wan.

"O pardon me, my brother dear,
   An the truth I'll tell to thee ;
My bairn it is to Lord William,
   An he is betrothed to me."

"O coud na ye gotten dukes, or lords
   Intill your ain country,
That ye draw up wi' an English dog
   To bring this shame on me?

"But ye maun gi' up the English lord,
   Whan your younge babe is born ;
For, gin you keep by him an hour langer
   Your life sall be forlorn."

"I will gi' up this English blood,
   Till my young babe be born ;
But never a day nor hour langer,
   Tho my life should be forlorn."

O whare is a' my merry young men,
    Whom I gi' meat and fee,
To pu' the thistle and the thorn,
    To burn this vile whore wi'?"

"O whare will I get a bonny boy,
    To help me in my need,
To rin wi' hast to Lord William,
    And bid him come wi' speed?"

O out it spake a bonny boy,
    Stood by her brother's side:
"O I would rin your errand, lady,
    O'er a' the world wide.

"Aft have I run your errands, lady,
    Whan blawn baith wind and weet;
But now I'll rin your errand, lady,
    Wi' saut tears on my cheek."

O whan he came to broken briggs,
    He bent his bow and swam,
An whan he came to the green grass growin,
    He slacked his shoone and ran.

O whan he came to Lord William's gates,
    He baed na to chap or ca',
But set his bent bow till his breast,
    An lightly lap the wa;
An', or the porter was at the gate,
    The boy was i' the ha'.

"O is my biggins broken, boy?
   Or is my towers won?
Or is my lady lighter yet,
   Of a dear daughter or son?"

"Your biggin is na broken, sir,
   Nor is your towers won;
But the fairest lady in a' the land
   For you this day maun burn."

"O saddle me the black, the black,
   Or saddle me the brown;
O saddle me the swiftest steed
   That ever rade frae a town."

Or he was near a mile awa,
   She heard his wild horse sneeze:
"Mend up the fire, my false brother,
   Its na come to my knees."

O whan he lighted at the gate,
   She heard his brid'e ring:
"Mend up the fire, my false brother,
   Its far yet frae my chin.

"Mend up the fire to me, brother,
   Mend up the fire to me;
For I see him comin' hard an' fast
   Will soon men't up to thee.

"O gin my hands had been loose, Willy,
　　Sae hard as they are boun,
I would have turn'd me frae the gleed,
　　And castin' out your young son."

"O I'll gar burn for you, Maisry,
　　Your father an' your mother ;
An I'll gar burn for you, Maisry,
　　Your sister an' your brother.

"An I'll gar burn for you, Maisry,
　　The chief of a' your kin ;
An the last bon-fire that I come to,
　　Mysel I will cast in."

THE BONNY HIND.

COPIED IN 1771 FROM THE MOUTH OF A MILKMAID.

(*Border Minstrelsy.*)

O MAY she comes, and May she goes,
　Down by yon gardens green;
And there she spied a gallant squire,
　As squire had ever been.

And May she comes, and May she goes,
　Down by yon hollin tree;
And there she spied a brisk young squire,
　And a brisk young squire was he.

"Give me your green manteel, fair maid;
　Give me your maidenhead!
Gin ye winna give me your green manteel,
　Give me your maidenhead!"—

　　.　　.　　.　　.　　.

"Perhaps there may be bairns, kind sir:
　Perhaps there may be nane;
But if you be a courtier,
　You'll tell me soon your name."—

"I am nae courtier, fair maid,
　　But new come frae the sea ;
I am nae courtier, fair maid,
　　But when I court with thee.

"They call me Jack, when I'm abroad ;
　　Sometimes they call me John ;
But, when I'm in my father's bower,
　　Jock Randal is my name."—

"Ye lee, ye lee, ye bonny lad !
　　Sae loud's I hear ye lee !
For I'm lord Randal's ae daughter,
　　He has nae mair nor me."

"Ye lee, ye lee, ye bonny May !
　　Sae loud's I hear ye lee !
For I'm lord Randal's ae ae son,
　　Just now come o'er the sea."—

She's putten her hand down by her gare,
　　And out she's ta'en a knife ;
And she has put it in her heart's bleed,
　　And ta'en away her life.

And he has ta'en up his bonny sister,
　　With the big tear in his een ;
And he has buried his bonny sister
　　Amang the hollins green.

And syne he's hied him o'er the dale,
   His father dear to see—
"Sing, Oh! and Oh! for my bonny hind,
   Beneath yon hollin tree!"—

" What needs you care for your bonny hind?
   For it you needna care;
There's aught score hinds in yonder park,
   And five score hinds to spare.

" Four score of them are siller-shod,
   Of thae ye may get three;
But oh! and oh! for my bonny hind,
   Beneath yon hollin tree.

" What needs you care for your bonny hind?
   For it you needna care;
Take you the best, gie me the warst,
   Since plenty is to spare."—

" I carena for your hinds, my lord,
   I carena for your fee;
But oh! and oh! for my bonny hind
   Beneath the hollin tree!"

"O were ye at your sister's bower,
   Your sister fair to see,
You'll think nae mair o' your bonny hind
   Beneath the hollin tree."—

HYND HORN.

(Allingham.)

NEAR the King's court was a young child born,
With a hey lillelu and a how lo lan;
And his name it was called Young Hynd Horn,
And the birk and the broom blooms bonnie.

Seven lang years he served the King,
With a hey lillelu and a how lo lan;
And it's a' for the sake o' his daughter Jean,
And the birk and the broom blooms bonnie.

The King an angry man was he,
With a hey lillelu and a how lo lan;
He sent Young Hynd Horn to the sea,
And the birk and the broom blooms bonnie.

O his love gave him a gay gold ring,
With a hey lillelu and a how lo lan;
With three shining diamonds set therein,
And the birk and the broom blooms bonnie.

'As lang as these diamonds keep their hue,
  With a hey lillelu and a how lo lan,
Ye'll know I am a lover true,
  And the birk and the broom blooms bonnie.

'But when your ring turns pale and wan,
  . *With a hey lillelu and a how lo lan,*
Then I'm in love with another man,
  And the birk and the broom blooms bonnie.'

He's gone to the sea and far away,
  With a hey lillelu and a how lo lan ;
And he's stayed for seven lang years and a day,
  And the birk and the broom blooms bonnie :

Seven lang years by land and sea,
  With a hey lillelu and a how lo lan;
And he's aften look'd how his ring may be,
  And the birk and the broom blooms bonnie.

One day when he look'd this ring upon,
  With a hey lillelu and a how lo lan ;
The shining diamonds were pale and wan,
  And the birk and the broom blooms bonnie.

He hoisted sails, and hame cam' he,
  With a hey lillelu and a how lo lan ;
Hame unto his ain countrie,
  And the birk and the broom blooms bonnie.

He's left the sea and he's come to land,
  With a hey lillelu and a how lo lan;
And the first he met was an auld beggar-man,
  And the birk and the broom blooms bonnie.

'What news, what news, my silly auld man?
  With a hey lillelu and a how lo lan;
For it's seven lang years since I saw this land,
  And the birk and the broom blooms bonnie.

'No news, no news,' doth the beggar-man say,
  With a hey lillelu and a how lo lan;
'But our King's ae Daughter she's wedded to-day,
  And the birk and the broom blooms bonnie.'

'Wilt thou give to me thy begging coat?
  With a hey lillelu and a how lo lan;
And I'll give to thee my scarlet cloak,
  And the birk and the broom blooms bonnie.

'Give me your auld pike-staff and hat,
  With a hey lillelu and a how lo lan;
And ye sall be right weel paid for that,
  And the birk and the broom blooms bonnic.

The auld beggar-man cast off his coat,
  With a hey lillelu and a how lo lan,
And he's ta'en up the scarlet cloak,
  And the birk and the broom blooms bonnie.

He's gi'en him his auld pike-staff and hat,
  With a hey lillelu and a how lo lan ;
And he was right weel paid for that,
  And the birk and the broom blooms bonnie.

The auld beggar-man was bound for the mill,
  With a hey lillelu and a how lo lan ;
But Young Hynd Horn for the King's ain hall,
  And the birk and the broom blooms bonnie.

When he came to the King's ain gate,
  With a hey lillelu and a how lo lan,
He asked a drink for Young Hynd Horn's sake,
  And the birk and the broom blooms bonnie.

These news unto the bonnie bride cam',
  With a hey lillelu and a how lo lan ;
That at the gate there stands an auld man,
  And the birk and the broom blooms bonnie.

There stands an auld man at the King's gate,
  With a hey lillelu and a how lo lan ;
He asketh a drink for Young Hynd Horn's sake,
  And the birk and the broom blooms bonnie.

The Bride cam' tripping down the stair,
  With a hey lillelu and a how lo lan ;
The combs o' fine goud in her hair,
  And the birk and the broom blooms bonnie ;

A cup o' the red wine in her hand,
 With a hey lillelu and a how lo lan;
And that she gave to the beggar-man,
 And the birk and the broom blooms bonnie.

Out o' the cup he drank the wine,
 With a hey lillelu and a how lo lan;
And into the cup he dropt the ring,
 And the birk and the broom blooms bonnie.

'O gat thou this by sea or by land?
 With a hey lillelu and a how lo lan,
Or gat thou it aff a dead man's hand?
 And the birk and the broom blooms bonnie.'

'I gat it neither by sea nor land,
 With a hey lillelu and a how lo lan,
Nor gat I it from a dead man's hand,
 And the birk and the broom blooms bonnie.

'But I gat it at my wooing gay,
 With a hey lillelu and a how lo lan;
And I gie it to you on your wedding-day,
 And the birk and the broom blooms bonnie.'

'I'll cast aside my satin goun,
 With a hey lillelu and a how lo lan,
And I'll follow you frae toun to toun,
 And the birk and the broom blooms bonnie.

'I'll tak' the fine goud frae my hair,
  With a hey lillelu and a how lo lan;
And follow you for evermair,
  And the birk and the broom blooms bonnie.'

He let his cloutie cloak doun fa',
  With a hey lillelu and a how lo lan;
Young Hynd Horn shone above them a',
  And the birk and the broom blooms bonnie.

The Bridegroom thought he had her wed,
  With a hey lillelu and a how lo lan;
But she is Young Hynd Horn's instead,
  And the birk and the broom blooms bonnie.

LADY ELSPAT.

(Jamieson.)

'BRENT's your brow, my Lady Elspat;
　　Gouden yellow is your hair !
O' a' the maids o' fair Scotland,
　　There's no anither half sae fair.'

'O keep your vows, sweet William,' she says,
　　'The vows which ye ha' made to me ;
And at the back o' my mither's castell,
　　This night I'll surely meet wi' thee.'

But wae be to her brother's page,
　　That heard the words thir twa did say ;
He's tauld them to her lady mither,
　　Wha wrought sweet William mickle wae.

For she's ta'en him, sweet William,
　　And she's gar'd bind him wi' his bow-string,
Till the red bluid o' his fair bodie
　　Frae ilka nail o' his hand did spring.

She kept him in a tower o' strength,
   Till the Lord-justice came to town ;
Out has she ta'en him, sweet William,
   Brought him before the Lord-justice boun'.

'And what is the crime, now, lady,' he says,
   'That has by this young man been dane ?"
'O he has broken my bonny castell,
   That was weel biggit wi' lime and stane.

'And he has broken my bonny coffers,
   That was weel bandit wi' aiken ban' ;
And he has stown my rich jewels ;
   I wot he has stown them every ane.'

Then out it spak her Lady Elspat,
   As she sat by Lord-justice's knee;
'Now ye hae tauld your tale, mither,
   I pray, Lord-justice, ye'll now hear me.

'He hasna broken her bonny castell,
   That was weel biggit wi' lime and stane ;
Nor has he stown her rich jewels,
   For I wat she has them every ane.

'But though he was my first true-love,
   And though I had sworn to be his bride,
Because he hadna a great estate,
   She would this way our loves divide.'

Syne out and spak the Lord-justice,
 I wat the tear was in his e'e ;
' I see nae faut in this young man ;
 Sae loose his bands, and set him free.

' And tak your love, now, Lady Elspat,
 And my best blessin' you baith upon ;
For gin he be your first true love,
 He is my eldest sister's son.

' There stands a steed in my stable,
 Cost me baith gold and white monie ;
Ye's get as mickle o' my free land
 As he'll ride about in a summer's day.'

YOUNG REDIN.

(Buchan.)

FAIR CATHERINE from her bower-window
.Look'd over heath and wood ;
She heard a smit o' bridle-reins,
And the sound did her heart good.

'Welcome, young Redin, welcome !
And welcome again, my dear !
Light down, light down from your horse,' she says,
'It's long since you were here.'

'O good morrow, lady, good morrow, lady ;
God make you safe and free !
I'm come to take my last farewell,
And pay my last visit to thee.

'I mustna light, and I canna light,
. I winna stay at a' ;
For a fairer lady than ten of thee
Is waiting at Castleswa'.'

'O if your love be changed, my dear,
    Since better may not be,
Yet, ne'ertheless for auld lang syne,
    Ye'll stay this night wi' me.'

She birl'd him wi' the ale and wine,
    As they sat doun to sup;
A living man he laid him down,
    But I wot he ne'er rose up.

'Now lie ye there, young Redin,' she says,
    'O lie ye there till morn—
Though a fairer lady than ten of me
    Is waiting till you come home!

'O lang, lang is the winter night,
    Till day begins to daw;
There is a dead man in my bower,
    And I would he were awa'.'

She cried upon her bower-maiden,
    Aye ready at her ca':
'There is a knight into my bower,
    'Tis time he were awa'.'

They've booted-him and spurred him,
　As he was wont to ride,
A hunting-horn tied round his waist,
　A sharp sword by his side ;
And they've flung him into the wan water,
　The deepest pool in Clyde.

Then up bespake a little bird
　That sat upon a tree,
'Gae hame, gae hame, ye fause lady,
　And pay your maid her fee.'

'Come down, come down, my pretty bird,
　That sits upon the tree ;
I have a cage of beaten gold,
　I'll gie it unto thee.'

'Gae hame, gae hame, ye fause lady ;
　I winna come down to thee ;
For as ye have done to young Redin,
　Ye'd do the like to me.'

O there came seeking young Redin
　Mony a lord and knight,
And there came seeking young Redin
　Mony a lady bright.

They've call'd on Lady Catherine,
    But she sware by oak and thorn
That she saw him not, young Redin,
    Since yesterday at morn.

The lady turn'd her round about,
    Wi' mickle mournfu' din:
'It fears me sair o' Clyde water
    That he is drown'd therein.'

Then up spake young Redin's mother,
    The while she made her mane:
'My son kenn'd a' the fords o' Clyde,
    He'd ride them ane by ane.'

'Gar dive, gar dive!' his father he cried,
    'Gar dive for gold and fee!
O wha will dive for young Redin's sake,
    And wha will dive for me?'

They dived in at ae pool-side,
    And out again at the other:
'We'll dive nae mair for young Redin,
    Although he were our brother.'

Then out it spake a little bird
    That flew above their head:
'Dive on, dive on, ye divers all,
    For there he lies indeed.

'But leave off your day diving,
  And dive at dark of night ;
In the pool where young Redin lies in
  The candles they'll burn bright.'

They left off their day diving,
  And dived at dark of night ;
In the pool where young Redin lay
  The candles they burn'd bright.

The deepest pool in a' the stream
  They found young Redin in ;
Wi' a great stone tied across the breast
  To keep his body down.

Then up and spake the little bird,
  Says, 'What needs a' this din ?
It was his light leman took his life,
  And hided him in the linn.'

She sware her by the sun and moon,
  She sware by grass and corn,
She hadna seen him, young Redin,
  Since Monanday at morn.

It's surely been my bower-woman—
  O ill may her betide !
I ne'er wad hae slain my young Redin,
  And thrown him in the Clyde.'

Now they hae cut baith fern and thorn,
  The bower-woman to brin;
And they hae made a big balefire,
  And put this maiden in;
But the fire it took na on her cheek,
  It took na on her chin.

Out they hae ta'en the bower-woman,
  And put her mistress in;
The flame took fast upon her cheek,
  Took fast upon her chin,
Took fast upon her fair body,
  Because of her deadly sin.

THE CRUEL BROTHER.

(Jamieson.)

'O FAIREST lady ever seen,
  With a heigh-ho! and a lily gay,
Give consent to be my queen,'
  As the primrose spreads so sweetly.

'O you must ask my father dear,
  With a heigh-ho! and a lily gay,
And the mother, too, that did me bear,'
  As the primrose spreads so sweetly.

'And you must ask my sister Anne,
  With a heigh-ho! and a lily gay,
And not forget my brother John,'
  As the primrose spreads so sweetly.

'To anger him it were not good,
  With a heigh-ho! and a lily gay,
For he is of a heavy mood,'
  As the primrose spreads so sweetly.

Now he has asked her father dear,
  With a heigh-ho ! and a lily gay,
And the mother, too, that did her bear,
  As the primrose spreads so sweetly.

And he has asked her sister Anne,
  With a heigh-ho ! and a lily gay,
But he left out her brother John,
  As the primrose spreads so sweetly.

Her father handed her down the stair,
  With a heigh-ho ! and a lily gay ;
Her mother kindly kiss'd her there,
  As the primrose spreads so sweetly.

Her sister Anne through the close her led,
  With a heigh-ho ! and a lily gay ;
Her brother John put her upon her steed,
  As the primrose spreads so sweetly.

' You are high and I am low,
  With a heigh-ho ! and a lily gay ;
Let me have a kiss before you go,'
  As the primrose spreads so sweetly.

She was louting down to kiss him sweet,
  With a heigh-ho ! and a lily gay ;
Wi' his penknife he wounded her deep,
  As the primrose spreads so sweetly.

' Ride saftly on,' said the best young man,
With a heigh-ho ! and a lily gay;
' I think our bride looks pale and wan,'
As the primrose spreads so sweetly.

' O take me from my horse, I pray,
With a heigh-ho ! and a lily gay,
And let me breathe, if so I may,'
As the primrose spreads so sweetly.

' O lean me on my true love's breast,
With a heigh-ho ! and a lily gay;
I want a little time to rest,'
As the primrose spreads so sweetly.

' I wish I had an hour,' she said,
·With a heigh-ho ! and a lily gay,
' To make my will ere I am dead,'
As the primrose spreads so sweetly.

' O what would ye leave to your father dear?'
With a heigh-ho ! and a lily gay.
' The milkwhite steed that brought me here,'
As the primrose spreads so sweetly.

' What would ye give to your mother dear?'
With a heigh-ho ! and a lily gay,
' My wedding-shift which I do wear,'
As the primrose spreads so sweetly.

'But she must wash it very clean,
With a heigh-ho! and a lily gay,
For my heart's blood sticks in every seam,'
As the primrose spreads so sweetly.

'What would ye give to your sister Anne?'
With a heigh-ho! and a lily gay.
'My gay gold ring and my feathered fan,'
As the primrose spreads so sweetly.

'What would ye give to your brother John?'
With a heigh-ho! and a lily gay.
'A rope and a gallows to hang him on!'
As the primrose spreads so sweetly.

'What would ye give to your brother John's
    wife?'
With a heigh-ho! and a lily gay.
'Grief and sorrow to end her life!'
As the primrose spreads so sweetly.

'What would ye give to your own true lover?'
With a heigh-ho! and a lily gay.
'My dying kiss, and my love for ever!'
As the primrose spreads so sweetly.

JELLON GRAME.

(Border Minstrelsy.)

O JELLON GRAME sat in Silverwood,
  He sharp'd his broadsword lang;
And he has call'd his little foot-page
  An errand for to gang.

"Win up, my bonny boy," he says,
  "As quickly as ye may;
For ye maun gang for Lillie Flower
  Before the break of day."—

The boy has buckled his belt about,
  And through the green-wood ran;
And he came to the ladye's bower
  Before the day did dawn.

"O s'eep ye, wake ye, Lillie Flower?
  The red sun's on the rain:
Ye're bidden come to Silverwood,
  But I doubt ye'll never win hame."—

She hadna ridden a mile, a mile,
   A mile but barely three,
Ere she came to a new-made grave,
   Beneath a green aik tree.

O then up started Jellon Grame,
   Out of a bush thereby ;
"Light down, light down, now, Lillie Flower,
   For it's here that ye maun lye."

She lighted aff her milk-white steed,
   And kneel'd upon her knee ;
"O mercy, mercy, Jellon Grame,
   For I'm no prepared to dee !

"Your bairn, that stirs between my sides,
   Maun shortly see the light :
But to see it weltering in my blood,
   Would be a piteous sight."—

"O should I spare your life," he says,
   "Until that bairn were born,
Full weel I ken your auld father
   Would hang me on the morn."-

"O spare my life, now, Jellon Grame !
   My father ye needna dread :
I'll keep my babe in gude green-wood,
   Or wi' it I'll beg my bread."—

He took no pity on Lillie Flower,
  Though she for life did pray;
But pierced her through the fair bodye,
  As at his feet she lay.

He felt nae pity for Lillie Flower,
  Where she was lying dead;
But he felt some for the bonny bairn
  That lay weltering in her bluid.

Up has he ta'en that bonny boy,
  Given him to nurses nine;
Three to sleep, and three to wake,
  And three to go between.

And he bred up that bonny boy,
  Call'd him his sister's son:
And he thought no eye could ever see
  The deed that he had done.

O so it fell upon a day,
  When hunting they might be,
They rested them at Silverwood,
  Beneath that green aik tree.

And many were the green-wood flowers
  Upon that grave that grew,
And marvell'd much that bonny boy
  To see their lovely hue.

11

" What's paler than the prymrose wan ?
   What's redder than the rose ?
What's fairer than the lilye flower
   On this wee knowe that grows ? "—

O out and answer'd Jellon Grame,
   And he spak hastilie—
" Your mother was a fairer flower,
   And lies beneath this tree.

" More pale was she, when she sought my grace,
   Than prymrose pale and wan ;
And redder than rose her ruddy heart's blood,
   That down my broadsword ran."—

Wi' that the boy has bent his bow,
   It was baith stout and lang ;
And thro' and thro' him, Jellon Grame,
   He gar'd an arrow gang.

Says, —" Lie ye there, now, Jellon Grame !
   My malisoun gang you wi' !
The place that my mother lies buried in
   Is far too good for thee."

BROWN ADAM.

(Border Minstrelsy.)

O WHA wad wish the wind to blaw,
   Or the green leaves fa' therewith ?
Or, wha wad wish a lealer love
   Than Brown Adam the Smith ?

But they hae banish'd him, Brown Adam,
   Frae father and frae mother ;
And they hae banish'd him, Brown Adam,
   Frae sister and frae brother.

And they hae banish'd him, Brown Adam,
   The flower o' a' his kin ;
And he's bigged a bower in gude greenwood
   Above his ladye and him.

It fell upon a summer's day,
   Brown Adam he thought lang ;
And, for to hunt some venison,
   To greenwood he wad gang.

He has ta'en his bow his arm o'er,
  His bolts and arrows lang ;
And he is to the gude greenwood
  As fast as he could gang.

O he's shot up, and he's shot down,
  The bird upon the brier ;
And he sent it hame to his ladye,
  Bade her be of gude cheer.

O he's shot up, and he's shot down,
  The bird upon the thorn ;
And sent it hame to his ladye,
  Said he'd be hame the morn.

When he cam' to his lady's bower-door
  He stood a little forbye,
And there he heard a fu' fause knight
  Tempting his gay ladye.

For he's ta'en out a gay goud ring,
  Had cost him many a poun' :
' O grant me love for love, ladye,
  And this sall be thy own.'

' I lo'e Brown Adam weel,' she said ;
  ' I trow sae does he me ;
I wadna gie Brown Adam's love
  For nae fause knight I see.'

Out has he ta'en a purse o' gowd,
   Was a' fou to the string :
' O grant me love for love, ladye,
   And a' this sall be thine.'

' I lo'e Brown Adam weel,' she says ;
   'I wot sae does he me :
I wadna be your light leman,
   For mair than ye could gie.'

Forth he drew his sharp bright brand ;
   His arm was stout and strang :
' Now grant me love for love, ladye,
   Or thro' ye this sall gang ! '
Then, sighing, says that lady fair,
   ' Brown Adam tarries lang ! '

Then in and starts him Brown Adam,
   Says, ' I'm just at your hand.'
He's gar'd him leave his bonny bow,
   He's gar'd him leave his brand,
He's gar'd him leave a dearer pledge—
   Four fingers o' his right hand.

THE LAMENT OF THE BORDER WIDOW.

(Border Minstrelsy.)

My love he built me a bonny bower,
And clad it a' wi' lilye flour,
A brawer bower ye ne'er did see,
Than my true love he built for me.

There came a man, by middle day,
He spied his sport, and went away;
And brought the king that very night,
Who brake my bower, and slew my knight.

He slew my knight, to me sae dear;
He slew my knight, and poin'd his gear;
My servants all for life did flee,
And left me in extremitie.

I sew'd his sheet, making my mane;
I watch'd the corpse, myself alane;
I watch'd his body night and day;
No living creature came that way.

I took his body on my back,
And whiles I gaed, and whiles I sat;
I digg'd a grave, and laid him in,
And happ'd him with the sod sae green.

But think na ye my heart was sair,
When I laid the moul' on his yellow hair?
O think na ye my heart was wae,
When I turn'd about, away to gae?

Nae living man I'll love again,
Since that my lovely knight is slain,
Wi' ae lock of his yellow hair
I'll chain my heart for evermair.

GRÆME AND BEWICK.

(Border Minstrelsy.)

Gude Lord Græme is to Carlisle gane ;
    Sir Robert Bewick there met he ;
And arm in arm to the wine they did go,
    And they drank till they were baith merrie.

Gude Lord Græme has ta'en up the cup,
    "Sir Robert Bewick, and here's to thee !
And here's to our twae sons at hame !
    For they like us best in our ain countrie."—

"O were your son a lad like mine,
    And learn'd some books that he could read,
They might hae been twae brothers bauld,
    And they might hae bragged the Border side.

"But your son's a lad, and he is but bad,
    And billie to my son he canna be ;

" Ye sent him to the schools, and he wadna learn ;
   Ye bought him books, and he wadna read."—
" But my blessing shall he never earn,
   Till I see how his arm can defend his head."—

Gude Lord Græme has a reckoning call'd,
   A reckoning then called he ;
And he paid a crown, and it went roun' ;
   It was all for the gude wine and free.

And he has to the stable gane,
   Where there stude thirty steeds and three :
He's ta'en his ain horse amang them a',
   And hame he rade sae manfullie.

" Welcome, my auld father !" said Christie Græme,
   " But where sae lang frae hame were ye ? "—
" It's I hae been at Carlisle town,
   And a baffled man by thee I be.

" I hae been at Carlisle town,
   Where Sir Robert Bewick he met me ;
He says ye're a lad, and ye are but bad,
   And billie to his son ye canna be.

" I sent ye to the schools, and ye wadna learn ;
   I bought ye books, and ye wadna read ;
Therefore my blessing you shall never earn,
   Till I see with Bewick thou save thy heid."—

" Now, God forbid, my auld father,
  That ever sic a thing suld be !
Billie Bewick was my master, and I was his scholar,
  And aye sae weel as he learned me."—

"O hald thy tongue, thou limmer loon,
  And of thy talking let me be !
If thou does na end me this quarrel soon,
  There is my glove, I'll fight wi' thee."—

Then Christie Græme he stooped low
  Unto the ground, you shall understand ;—
"O father, put on your glove again,
  The wind has blown it from your hand ? "—

" What's that thou says, thou limmer loon ?
  How dares thou stand to speak to me ?
If thou do not end this quarrel soon,
  There's my right hand thou shalt fight with me."—

Then Christie Græme's to his chamber gane,
  To consider weel what then should be ;
Whether he should fight with his auld father,
  Or with his billie Bewick, he.

" If I suld kill my billie dear,
  God's blessing I shall never win ;
But if I strike at my auld father,
  I think 'twald be a mortal sin.

"But if I kill my billie dear,
　　It is God's will, so let it be ;
But I make a vow, ere I gang frae hame,
　　That I shall be the next man's dee."—

Then he's put on's back a gude auld jack,
　　And on his head a cap of steel,
And sword and buckler by his side ;
　　O gin he did not become them weel !

We'll leave off talking of Christie Græme,
　　And talk of him again belive ;
And we will talk of bonny Bewick,
　　Where he was teaching his scholars five.

When he had taught them well to fence,
　　And handle swords without any doubt,
He took his sword under his arm,
　　And he walked his father's close about.

He look'd atween them and the sun,
　　And a' to see what there might be,
Till he spied a man in armour bright,
　　Was riding that way most hastilie.

"O wha is yon, that came this way,
　　Sae hastilie that hither came ?
I think it be my brother dear !
　　I think it be young Christie Græme.—

" Ye're welcome here, my billie dear,
 And thrice ye're welcome unto me ! "—
" But I'm wae to say, I've seen the day,
 When I am come to fight wi 'thee.

" My father's gane to Carlisle town,
 Wi' your father Bewick there met he ;
He says I'm a lad, and I am but bad,
 And a baffled man I trow to be.

" He sent me to schools, and I wadna learn ;
 He gae me books, and I wadna read ;
Sae my father's blessing I'll never earn,
 Till he see how my arm can guard my head."—

" O God forbid, my billie dear,
 That ever such a thing suld be !
We'll take three men on either side,
 And see if we can our fathers agree."—

" O hald thy tongue, now, billie Bewick,
 And of thy talking let me be !
But if thou'rt a man, as I'm sure thou art,
 Come o'er the dyke, and fight wi' me."—

" But I hae nae harness, billie, on my back,
 And weel I see there is on thine."—
" But as little harness as is on thy back,
 As little, billie, shall be on mine."—

Then he's thrown aff his coat of mail,
   His cap of steel away flung he;
He stuck his spear into the ground,
   And he tied his horse unto a tree.

Then Bewick has thrown aff his cloak,
   And's psalter-book frae's hand flung he,
He laid his hand upon the dyke,
   And ower he lap most manfullie.

O they hae fought for twae lang hours;
   When twae lang hours were come and gane,
The sweat drapp'd fast frae aff them baith,
   But a drap of blude could not be seen.

Till Græme gae Bewick an ackward stroke,
   Ane ackward stroke strucken sickerlie;
He has hit him under the left breast,
   And dead-wounded to the ground fell he.

" Rise up, rise up, now, billie dear!
   Arise and speak three words to me!—
Whether thou's gotten thy deadly wound,
   Or if God and good leeching may succour thee!"—

"O horse, O horse, now, billie Græme,
   And get thee far from hence with speed;
And get thee out of this country,
   That none may know who has done the deed."—

"O I have slain thee, billie Bewick,
  If this be true thou tellest to me;
But I made a vow, ere I came frae hame,
  That aye the next man I wad be."

He has pitch'd his sword in a moodie-hill,
  And he has leap'd twenty lang feet and three,
And on his ain sword's point he lap,
  And dead upon the ground fell he.

'Twas then came up Sir Robert Bewick,
  And his brave son alive saw he;
"Rise up, rise up, my son," he said,
  "For I think ye hae gotten the victorie."—

"O hald your tongue, my father dear!
  Of your prideful talking let me be!
Ye might hae drunken your wine in peace,
  And let me and my billie be.

"Gae dig a grave baith wide and deep,
  And a grave to hald baith him and me;
But lay Christie Græme on the sunny side,
  For I'm sure he wan the victorie."—

"Alack! a wae!" auld Bewick cried,
  "Alack! was I not much to blame?
I'm sure I've lost the liveliest lad
  That e'er was born unto my name."—

"Alack ! a wae !" quo' gude Lord Græme—
  "I'm sure I hae lost the deeper lack !
I durst hae ridden the Border through,
  Had Christie Græme been at my back.

" Had I been led through Liddesdale,
  And thirty horsemen guarding me,
And Christie Græme been at my back,
  Sae soon as he had set me free !

" I've lost my hopes, I've lost my joy,
  I've lost the key but and the lock ;
I durst hae ridden the world round,
  Had Christie Græme been at my back."

ERLINTON.

(Border Minstrelsy.)

ERLINTON had a fair daughter,
　　I wat he weird her in a great sin,
For he has built a bigly bower,
　　An' a' to put the lady in.

An' he has warn'd her sisters six,
　　An' sae has he her brethren se'en,
Outher to watch her a' the night,
　　Or else to seek her morn and e'en.

She hadna been i' that bigly bower,
　　Na not a night but barely ane,
Till there was Willie, her ain true love,
　　Chapp'd at the door, cryin', "Peace within!"—

"O whae is this at my bower door,
　　That chaps sae late, or kens the gin?"—
"O it is Willie, your ain true love,
　　I pray you rise and let me in!"—

"But in my bower there is a wake,
    An' at the wake there is a wane;
But I'll come to the green-wood the morn,
    Whar blooms the brier, by mornin' dawn."—

Then she's gane to her bed again,
    Where she has layen till the cock crew thrice,
Then she said to her sisters a',
    "Maidens, 'tis time for us to rise."—

She pat on her back a silken gown,
    An' on her breast a siller pin,
An' she's ta'en a sister in ilka hand,
    And to the green-wood she is gane.

She hadna walk'd in the green-wood,
    Na not a mile but barely ane,
Till there was Willie, her ain true love,
    Wha frae her sisters has her ta'en.

He took her sisters by the hand,
    He kiss'd them baith, and sent them hame,
And he's ta'en his true love him behind,
    And through the green-wood they are gane.

They hadna ridden in the bonnie green-wood,
    Na not a mile but barely ane,
When there came fifteen o' the boldest knights,
    That ever bare flesh, blood, or bane.

The foremost was an aged knight,
  He wore the grey hair on his chin,
Says, "Yield to me thy lady bright,
  An' thou shalt walk the woods within."—

"For me to yield my lady bright
  To such an aged knight as thee,
People wad think I war gane mad,
  Or a' the courage flown frae me."

But up then spak the second knight,
  I wat he spake right boustouslie,
"Yield me thy life, or thy lady bright,
  Or here the tane of us shall die."—

" My lady is my warld's meed:
  My life I winna yield to nane;
But if ye be men of your manhead,
  Ye'll only fight me ane by ane."—

He lighted aff his milk-white steed,
  An' gae his lady him by the head,
Say'n, " See ye dinna change your cheer,
  Until you see my body bleed."—

He set his back unto an aik,
  He set his feet against a stane,
An' he has fought these fifteen men,
  An' killed them a' but barely ane :
For he has left that aged knight,
  An' a' to carry the tidings hame.

When he gaed to his lady fair,
  I wat he kissed her tenderlie :
"Thou art mine ain love, I have thee bought;
  Now we shall walk the green-wood free."

THE GARDENER.

(Allingham.)

THE gard'ner stands in his bower door,
　Wi' a primrose in his hand,
And by there cam' a maiden,
　As jimp as a willow wand.

' O lady can ye fancy me,
　For to be my bride ?
Ye'se get a' the flowers in my garden,
　To be to you a weed.

' The lily white sall be your smock ;
　It becomes your bodie best ;
Your head sall be buskt wi' gilly-flower,
　Wi' the primrose in your breast.

' Your goun sall be the sweet-william ;
　Your coat the camovine ;
Your apron o' the sallads neat,
　That taste baith sweet and fine.

'Your hose sall be the brade kail-blade,
    That is baith brade and lang ;
Narrow, narrow, at the cute,
    And brade, brade at the brawn.

           .

'Your gloves sall be the marigold,
    All glittering to your hand,
Weel spread owre wi' the blue blaewort,
    That grows amang corn-land.'

'O fare ye weil,' young man, she says,
    'Fareweil, and I bid adieu ;
If you can fancy me,' she says,
    'I cannot fancy you.

'Sin ye've provided a weed for me
    Among the simmer flowers,
It's I'se provide anither for you,
    Amang the winter-showers.

'The new fawn snaw to be your smock ;
    It becomes your bodie best ;
Your head sall be wrapt wi' the eastern wind,
    And the cauld rain on your breast.'

LORD RANDAL.

(Border Minstrelsy, vol. ii., p. 263.)

"O WHERE hae ye been, Lord Randal, my son?
() where hae ye been, my handsome young man?"
"I hae been to the wild wood; mother, make my bed
    soon,
For I'm weary wi' hunting, and fain wald lie down."

"Where gat ye your dinner, Lord Randal, my son?
Where gat ye your dinner, my handsome young man?"
"I dined wi' my **true-love**; mother, make my bed soon,
For I'm weary wi' hunting, and fain wald lie down."

"What gat ye to your dinner, Lord Randal, my son?
What gat ye to your dinner, my handsome young man?"
"I gat eels boil'd in broo; mother, make my bed soon,
For I'm weary wi' hunting, and fain wald lie down."

"What became of your bloodhounds, Lord Randal, my
    son?
What became of your bloodhounds, my handsome young
    man?"
"O they swell'd and they died; mother, make my bed
    soon,
For I'm weary wi' hunting, and fain wald lie down."

" O I fear ye are poison'd, Lord Randal, my son !
O I fear ye are poison'd, my handsome young man ! "
"O yes ! I am poison'd ; mother, make my bed soon,
For I'm sick at the heart, and I fain wald lie down."

JOHNIE FAA.

(Pinkerton's *Scottish Ballads*, vol. i., p. 67.)

THE gypsies came to our good lord's gate,
    And wow but they sang sweetly !
Our lady came doun the music to hear,
    They sang sae very completely.

And she came tripping down the stair,
    And a' her maids before her ;
As soon as they saw her weil-fared face,
    They coost the glamour o'er her.

" Gae take frae me this gay mantile,
    And bring to me a plaidie ;
For if kith and kin, and a' had sworn,
    I'll follow the gipsy laddie.

" Yestreen I lay in a weel-made bed,
    And my good lord beside me ;
This night I'll lie in a tenant's barn,
    Whatever sall betide me ! "

"Oh, come to your bed," says Johnie Faa,
　"Oh, come to your bed, my dearie :
For I vow and swear by the hilt of my sword,
　Your lord sall nae mair come near ye."

"I'll go to bed to my Johnie Faa,
　I'll go to bed to my dearie ;
For I vow and swear by what past yestreen,
　My lord sall nae mair come near me."

And when our lord came hame at e'en,
　And speir'd for his fair lady,
The tane she cry'd, and the ither reply'd,
　"She's awa' wi' the gypsy laddie ! "

" Gae saddle to me the black, black steed,
　Gae saddle and mak him ready ;
Before that I either eat or sleep,
　I'll gae and seek my fair lady."

And we were fifteen well-made men,
　Of courage stout and steady ;
And we were a' put down but ane,
　For a fair young wanton lady.

THE TWA CORBIES.

(*Border Minstrelsy*, vol. ii., p. 212.)

As I was walking all alane,
I heard twa corbies making a mane:
The tane unto the t'other say,
" Whar sall we gang and dine the day?"

" In behint yon auld fail dyke,
I wot there lies a new-slain knight;
And naebody kens that he lies there
But his hawk, his hound, and his lady fair.

" His hound is to the hunting gane,
His hawk to fetch the wild-fowl hame,
His lady's ta'en another mate,
So we may make our dinner sweet.

" Ye'll sit on his white hause-bane,
And I'll pike out his bonny blue e'en;
Wi' ae lock o' his gowden hair
We'll theek our nest when it grows bare.

" Mony a one for him makes mane,
But nane sall ken whae he is gane,
O'er his white banes, when they are bare,
The wind sall blaw for evermair."

THE THREE RAVENS.

(Child, Part i., p. 253. *Melismata,* 1611.)

THERE were three ravens sat on a tree,
Downe a downe, hay downe, hay downe;
There were three ravens sat on a tree,
With a downe.
There were three ravens sat on a tree,
They were as blacke as they might be.
With a downe derrie, derrie, derrie, downe,
    downe.

The one of them said to his mate,
"Where shall we our breakefast take?"

"Downe in yonder greene field,
There lies a knight slain under his shield.

"His hounds they lie downe at his feete,
So well they can their master keepe.

"His haukes they flie so eagerly,
There's no fowle dare him come nie."

Downe there comes a fallow doe,
As great with yong as she might goe.

She lift up his bloudy hed,
And kist his wounds that were so red.

She got him up upon her backe,
And carried him to earthen lake.

She buried him before the prime,
She was dead herselfe ere even-song time.

God send every gentleman
Such haukes, such hounds, and such a leman.

SIR HUGH; OR, THE JEW'S DAUGHTER.

(Motherwell, p. 51.)

YESTERDAY was brave Hallowday,
    And, above all days of the year,
The schoolboys all got leave to play,
    And little Sir Hugh was there.

He kicked the ball with his foot,
    And kepped it with his knee,
And even in at the Jew's window
    He gart the bonnie ba' flee.

Out then came the Jew's daughter—
    "Will ye come in and dine?"
"I winna come in, and I canna come in,
    Till I get that ball of mine.

"Throw down that ball to me, maiden,
    Throw down the ball to me."
"I winna throw down your ball, Sir Hugh,
    Till ye come up to me."

She pu'd the apple frae the tree,
 It was baith red and green,
She gave it unto little Sir Hugh,
 With that his heart did win.

She wiled him into ae chamber,
 She wiled him into twa,
She wiled him into the third chamber,
 And that was warst o't a'.

She took out a little penknife,
 Hung low down by her gair,
She twined this young thing o' his life,
 And a word he ne'er spak mair.

And first came out the thick, thick blood,
 And syne came out the thin,
And syne came out the bonnie heart's blood—
 There was nae mair within.

She laid him on a dressing-table,
 She dress'd him like a swine,
Says, "Lie ye there, my bonnie Sir Hugh,
 Wi' ye're apples red and green."

She put him in a case of lead,
 Says, "Lie ye there and sleep;"
She threw him into the deep draw-well
 Was fifty fathom deep.

A schoolboy walking in the garden,
   Did grievously hear him moan,
He ran away to the deep draw-well
   And fell down on his knee.

Says, " Bonnie Sir Hugh, and pretty Sir Hugh,
   I pray you speak to me ;
If you speak to any body in this world,
   I pray you speak to me."

When bells were rung and mass was sung,
   And every body went hame,
Then every lady had her son,
   But Lady Helen had nane.

She rolled her mantle her about,
   And sore, sore did she weep ;
She ran away to the Jew's castle
   When all were fast asleep.

She cries, " Bonnie Sir Hugh, O pretty Sir Hugh,
   I pray you speak to me ;
If you speak to any body in this world,
   I pray you speak to me."

" Lady Helen, if ye want your son,
   I'll tell ye where to seek ;
Lady Helen, if ye want your son,
   He's in the well sae deep."

She ran away to the deep draw-well,
　　And she fell down on her knee,
Saying, "Bonnie Sir Hugh, O pretty Sir Hugh,
　　I pray ye speak to me,
If ye speak to any body in the world,
　　I pray ye speak to me."

"Oh! the lead it is wondrous heavy, mother,
　　The well it is wondrous deep,
The little penknife sticks in my throat,
　　And I downa to ye speak.

"But lift me out o' this deep draw-well,
　　And bury me in yon churchyard;
Put a bible at my head," he says,
　　"And a testament at my feet,
And pen and ink at every side,
　　And I'll lie still and sleep.

"And go to the back of Maitland town,
　　Bring me my winding sheet;
For it's at the back of Maitland town
　　That you and I sall meet."

O the broom, the bonny, bonny broom,
　　The broom that makes full sore;
A woman's mercy is very little,
　　But a man's mercy is more.

MAY COLVEN.

(Child, Part i., p. 56.)

FALSE Sir John a-wooing came
　To a maid of beauty fair;
May Colven was this lady's name,
　Her father's only heir.

He woo'd her butt, he woo'd her ben,
　He woo'd her in the ha',
Until he got this lady's consent
　To mount and ride awa.

He went down to her father's bower,
　Where all the steeds did stand,
And he's taken one of the best steeds
　That was in her father's land.

He's got on, and she's got on,
　As fast as they could flee,
Until they came to a lonesome part,
　A rock by the side of the sea.

"Loup off the steed," says false Sir John,
  "Your bridal bed you see;
For I have drowned seven young ladies,
  The eighth one you shall be.

"Cast off, cast off, my May Colven,
  All and your silken gown,
For it's o'er good and o'er costly
  To rot in the salt sea foam.

"Cast off, cast off, my May Colven,
  All and your embroider'd shoen,
For they're o'er good and o'er costly
  To rot in the salt sea foam."

"O turn you about, O false Sir John,
  And look to the leaf of the tree,
For it never became a gentleman
  A naked woman to see."

He turned himself straight round about,
  To look to the leaf of the tree;
So swift as May Colven was
  To throw him in the sea.

"O help, O help, my May Colven,
  O help, or else I'll drown;
I'll take you home to your father's bower,
  And set you down safe and sound."

"No help, no help, O false Sir John,
    No help, nor pity thee ;
Tho' seven kings' daughters you have drown'd, .
    But the eighth shall not be me."

So she went on her father's steed,
    As swift as she could flee,
And she came home to her father's bower
    Before it was break of day.

Up then and spoke the pretty parrot :
    "May Colven, where have you been ?
What has become of false Sir John,
    That woo'd you so late the streen ?

"He woo'd you butt, he woo'd you ben,
    He woo'd you in the ha',
Until he got your own consent
    For to mount and gang awa."

"O hold your tongue, my pretty parrot,
    Lay not the blame upon me ;
Your cup shall be of the flowered gold,
    Your cage of the root of the tree."

Up then spake the king himself,
    In the bed-chamber where he lay :
"What ails the pretty parrot,
    That prattles so long or day ?"

" There came a cat to my cage door,
  It almost a worried me,
And I was calling on May Colven
  To take the cat from me."

BONNY BARBARA ALLAN.

(Child, Part iv., p. 276.)

IT was in and about the Martinmas time,
  When the green leaves were a falling,
That Sir John Græme in the West Country,
  Fell in love with Barbara Allan.

He sent his men down through the town,
  To the place where she was dwelling :
" O haste and come to my master dear,
  Gin ye be Barbara Allan."

O hooly, hooly rose she up,
  To the place where he was lying,
And when she drew the curtain by,
  "Young man, I think you're dying."

" O it's I'm sick, and very, very sick,
  And 'tis a' for Barbara Allan."
" O the better for me, ye's never be,
  Tho' your heart's-blood were a spilling.

"O dinna ye mind, young man," said she,
  "When ye was in the tavern a drinking,
That ye made the healths gae round and round,
  And slighted Barbara Allan?"

He turn'd his face unto the wall,
  And death was with him dealing:
"Adieu, adieu, my dear friends all,
  And be kind to Barbara Allan."

And slowly, slowly raise she up,
  And slowly, slowly left him;
And sighng said, she could not stay,
  Since death of life had reft him.

She hadna gane a mile but twa,
  When she heard the dead-bell knelling,
And every jow that the dead-bell geid,
  It cried, "Woe to Barbara Allan!"

"O mother, mother, make my bed!
  O make it saft and narrow!
Since my love died for me to-day,
  I'll die for him to-morrow."

EDWARD, EDWARD.

(From Percy's *Reliques*. The spelling is modernised.)

" WHY does your brand sae drop wi' blude,
   Edward, Edward ?
Why does your brand sae drop wi' blude
  And why sae sad gang ye, O ? "
"O I hae killed my hawk sae gude,
   Mither, mither ;
O I hae killed my hawk sae gude,
  And I hae nae mair but he, O."

" Your hawk's blude was never sae red,
   Edward, Edward ;
Your hawk's blude was never sae red,
  My dear son, I tell thee, O,"
"O I hae killed my red-roan steed,
   Mither, mither ;
O I hae killed my red-roan steed,
  That was sae fair and free, O."

" Your steed was auld, and ye've plenty mair,
   Edward, Edward ;
Your steed was auld, and ye've plenty mair ;
  Same ither dule ye dree, O."

"O I hae killed my father dear,
    Mither, mither;
O I hae killed my father dear,
    Alas, and wae is me, O!"

"And whatten penance will ye dree for that,
    Edward, Edward?
Whatten penance will ye dree for that?
    My dear son, now tell me, O."
"I'll set my feet in yonder boat,
    Mither, mither;
I'll set my feet in yonder boat,
    And I'll fare over the sea, O."

"And what will ye do wi' your tow'rs and your ha',
    Edward, Edward?
And what will ye do wi' your tow'rs and your ha',
    That were sae fair to see, O?"
"Ill let them stand till they doun fa',
    Mither, mither;
I'll let them stand till they doun fa',
    For here never mair maun I be, O."

"And what will ye leave to your bairns and your wife,
    Edward, Edward?
And what will ye leave to your bairns and your wife,
    When ye gang ower the sea, O?"
"The warld's room: let them beg through life,
    Mither, mither;
The warld's room: let them beg through life;
    For them never mair will I see, O."

" And what will ye leave to your ain mither dear,
　　　Edward, Edward ?
And what will ye leave to your ain mither dear,
　　My dear son, now tell me, O ? "
" The curse of hell frae me sall ye bear,
　　　Mither, mither ;
The curse of hell frae me sall ye bear :
　　Sic counsels ye gave to me, O ! "

ANNAN WATER.

(Border Minstrelsy, vol. iii., p. 75.)

" ANNAN water's wading deep,　　.
　　And my love Annie's wondrous bonny;
And I am laith she suld weet her feet,
　　Because I love her best of ony.

" Gar saddle me the bonny black;
　　Gar saddle sune, and make him ready:
For I will down the Gatehope-slack,
　　And all to see my bonny ladye."

He has loupen on the bonny black,
　　He stirr'd him wi' the spur right sairly;
But, or he wan the Gatehope-slack,
　　I think the steed was wae and weary.

He has loupen on the bonny gray,
　　He rade the right gate and the ready;
I trow he would neither stint nor stay,
　　For he was seeking his bonny ladye.

O he has ridden ower field and fell,
   Through muir and moss, and mony a mire;
His spurs o' steel were sair to bide,
   And frae her fore-feet flew the fire.

"Now, bonny gray, now play your part!
   Gin ye be the steed that wins my deary,
Wi' corn and hay ye'se be fed for aye,
   And never spur sall make you wearie."

The gray was a mare, and a right good mare;
   But when she wan the Annan water,
She could na hae ridden a furlong mair,
   Had a thousand merks been wadded* at her.

"O boatman, boatman, put off your boat!
   Put off your boat for gowden monie!
I cross the drumly stream the night,
   Or never mair I see my honey."

"O I was sworn sae late yestreen,
   And not by ae aith, but by many;
And for a' the gowd in fair Scotland,
   I dare na take ye through to Annie."

The side was stey, and the bottom deep,
   Frae bank to brae the water pouring;
And the bonny gray mare did sweat for fear,
   For she heard the water kelpy roaring,

       * Wagered.

O he has pou'd aff his dapperpy coat,
  The silver buttons glancèd bonny;
The waistcoat bursted aff his breast,
  He was sae full of melancholy.

He has ta'en the ford at that stream tail;
  I wot he swam both strong and steady;
But the stream was broad, and his strength did fail,
  And he never saw his bonny ladye.

" O wae betide the frush* saugh wand !
  And wae betide the bush of briar !
It brake into my true love's hand,
  When his strength did fail, and his limbs did tire.

" And wae betide ye, Annan water,
  This night that ye are a drumlie river !
For over thee I'll build a bridge,
  That ye never more true love may sever."

* *Frush*—brittle.

LORD LOVEL.

(Child, Part iii., p. 211.)

LORD LOVEL he stood at his castle gate,
  Combing his milk-white steed
When up came Lady Nancy Belle,
  To wish her lover good spced, speed,
  To wish her lover good speed.

" Where are you going, Lord Lovel? " she said,
  " O where are you going ? " said she ;
" I'm going, my Lady Nancy Belle,
  Strange countries for to see."

" When will you be back, Lord Lovel ? " she said,
  " O when will you come back ? " said she :
" In a year or two, or three, at the most,
  I'll return to my fair Nancy."

But he had not been gone a year and a day,
  Strange countries for to see,
When languishing thoughts came into his head,
  Lady Nancy Belle he would go see.

So he rode, and he rode, on his milk-white steed,
  Till he came to London town,
And there he heard St. Pancras' bells,
  And the people all mourning round.

"O what is the matter?" Lord Lovel he said,
  "O what is the matter?" said he;
"A lord's lady is dead," a woman replied,
  "And some call her Lady Nancy."

So he ordered the grave to be opened wide,
  And the shroud he turnèd down,
And there he kissed her clay-cold lips,
  Till the tears came trickling down.

Lady Nancy she died, as it might be, to-day,
  Lord Lovel he died as to-morrow,
Lady Nancy she died out of pure, pure grief,
  Lord Lovel he died out of sorrow.

Lady Nancy was laid in St. Pancras church,
  Lord Lovel was laid in the choir;
And out of her bosom there grew a red rose,
  And out of her lover's a briar.

They grew, and they grew, to the church steeple too,
  And then they could grow no higher;
So there they entwined in a true lover's knot,
  For all lovers true to admire.

THE HEIR OF LYNNE.

(Bishop Percy's Folio MS.   Hales and Furnival.)

OF all the lords in faire Scotland
  A song I will begin :
Amongst them all dwelled a lord
  Which was the unthrifty Lord of Lynne.

His father and mother were dead him froe,
  And so was the head of all his kinne ;
He did neither cease nor blinne
  To the cards and dice that he did run.

To drinke the wine that was so cleere ;
  With every man he would make merry.
And then bespake him John of the Scales,
  Unto the heire of Lynne say'd hee,

Sayes " how dost thou, Lord of Lynne,
  Doest either want gold or fee ?
Wilt thou not sell thy land so brode
  To such a good fellow as me ?

"For . . I . . " he said,
  " My land, take it unto thee ;
I draw you to record, my lords all ; "
  With that he cast him a Gods pennie.

He told him the gold upon the bord,
  It wanted never a bare penny.
" That gold is thine, the land is mine,
  The heire of Lynne I will bee."

" Heeres gold enough," saithe the heire of Lynne,
  " Both for me and my company."
He drunke the wine that was so cleere,
  And with every man he made merry.

Within three quarters of a yeare
  His gold and fee it waxed thinne,
His merry men were from him gone,
  And left himselfe all alone.

He had never a penny left in his purse,
  Never a penny but three,
And one was brasse and another was lead
  And another was white mony.

" Now well-a-day ! " said the heire of Lynne
  " Now well-a-day, and woe is mee !
For when I was the Lord of Lynne,
  I neither wanted gold nor fee ;

" For I have sold my lands so broad,
　And have not left me one penny !
I must go now and take some read
　Unto Edenborrow and beg my bread."

He had not beene in Edenborrow
　Not three quarters of a yeare,
But some did give him and some said nay,
　And some bid "to the deele gang yee !

"For if we should hang some land selfeer,
　The first we would begin with thee."
" Now-well-a-day !" said the heire of Lynne
　"Now well-a-day, and woe is mee !

" For now I have sold my lands so broad
　That merry man is irke with mee ;
But when that I was the Lord of Lynne
　Then on my land I lived merrily ;

" And now I have sold my land so broade
　That I have not left me one pennye !
God be with my father ! " he said,
　" On his land he lived merrily."

Still in a study there as he stood,
　He unbethought him of a bill,
He unbethought him of a bill
　Which his father had left with him.

14

Bade him he should never on it looke
　Till he was in extreame neede,
"Then by my faith," said the heire of Lynne,
　"Then now I had never more neede."

He tooke the bill and looked it on,
　Good comfort that he found there;
It told him of a castle wall
　Where there stood three chests in feare:

Two were full of the beaten gold,
　The third was full of white money.
He turned then downe his bags of bread
　And filled them full of gold so red.

Then he did never cease nor blinne
Till John of the Scales house he did winne
When that he came John of the Scales,
Up at the speere he looked then;
There sate three lords upon a rowe,
And John o' the Scales sate at the bord's head,
And John o' the Scales sate at the bord's head
Because he was the lord of Lynne.

And then bespake the heire of Lynne
　To John o' the Scales wife thus sayd hee
Sayd " Dame, wilt thou not trust me one shott
　That I may sit downe in this company ? "

"Now Christ's curse on my head," she said,
  "If I do trust thee one pennye,"
Then bespake a good fellowe,
  Which sate by John o' the Scales his knee,

Said " have thou here, thou heire of Lynne,
  Forty-pence I will lend thee,—
Some time a good fellow thou hast beene
  And other forty if it need bee."

They drunken wine that was so cleere,
  And every man they made merry,
And then bespake him John o' the Scales,
  Unto the Lord of Lynne said hee ;

Said "how doest thou heire of Lynne,
  Since I did buy thy lands of thee ?
I will sell it to thee twenty better cheepe
  Nor ever did I buy it of thee."

" I draw you to recorde, lords all : "
  With that he cast him god's penny ;
Then he tooke to his bags of bread,
  And they were full of the gold so red.

He told him the gold then over the borde
  It wanted never a broad pennye ;
" That gold is thine, the land is mine,
  And the heire of Lynne again I will bee."

"Now well-a-day!" said John o' the Scales' wife,
  "Well-a-day, and woe is me!
Yesterday I was the lady of Lynne,
  And now I am but John o' the Scales' wife!"

Says "have thou here, thou good fellow,
Forty pence thou did lend me;
Forty pence thou did lend me,
And forty I will give thee,
I'll make thee keeper of my forrest,
Both of the wild deere and the tame."

But then bespake the heire of Lynne,
  These were the words, and thus spake hee,
"Christ's curse light upon my crowne
  If ere my land stand in any jeopardye!"

Border, or Riding Ballads.

BORDER, OR RIDING BALLADS.

------◆------

JAMIE TELFER.

(*Border Minstrelsy*, vol. i., p. 144.)

It fell about the Martinmas tyde,
  When our Border steeds get corn and hay,
The captain of Bewcastle hath bound him to ryde
  And he's ower to Tividale to drive a prey.

The first ae guide that they met wi',
  It was high up Hardhaughswire ;
The second guide that we met wi',
  It was laigh down in Borthwick water.

"What tidings, what tidings, my trusty guide ? "
  " Nae tidings, nae tidings, I hae to thee ;
But, gin ye'll gae to the fair Dodhead,
  Mony a cow's cauf I'll let thee see."

And whan they cam to the fair Dodhead,
  Right hastily they clam the peel ;
They loosed the kye out, ane and a',
  And ranshackled the house right weel.

Now Jamie Telfer's heart was sair,
　　The tear aye rowing in his e'e ;
He pled wi' the captain to hae his gear,
　　Or else revenged he wad be.

The captain turned him round and leugh ;
　　Said—" Man, there's naething in thy house,
But ae auld sword without a sheath,
　　That hardly now wad fell a mouse ! "

The sun was na up, but the moon was down,
　　It was the gryming o' a new fa'n snaw,
Jamie Telfer has run three myles a-foot,
　　Between the Dodhead and the Stobs's Ha'.

And whan he cam to the fair tower yate,
　　He shouted loud, and cried weel hie,
Till out bespak auld Gibby Elliot—
　　" Wha's this that brings the fraye to me ? "

" It's I, Jamie Telfer o' the fair Dodhead,
　　And a harried man I think I be !
There's naething left at the fair Dodhead,
　　But a waefu' wife and bairnies three."

"Gae seek your succour at Branksome Ha',
　　For succour ye'se get nane frae me !
Gae seek your succour where ye paid black-mail,
　　For, man ! ye ne'er paid money to me."

Jamie has turned him round about,
   I wat the tear blinded his e'e—
" I'll ne'er pay mail to Elliot again,
   And the fair Dodhead I'll never see !

" My hounds may a' rin masterless,
   My hawks may fly frae tree to tree ;
My lord may grip my vassal lands,
   For there again maun I never be."

He has turned him to the Tiviot side,
   E'en as fast as he could drie,
Till he cam to the Coultart Cleugh,
   And there he shouted baith loud and hie.

Then up bespak him auld Jock Grieve—
   "Wha's this that brings the fray to me ?"
" It's I, Jamie Telfer o' the fair Dodhead,
   A harried man I trow I be.

" There's naething left in the fair Dodhead
   But a greeting wife and bairnies three,
And sax poor ca's stand in the sta',
   A' routing loud for their minnie."

" Alack a wae !" quo' auld Jock Grieve,
   " Alack ! my heart is sair for thee !
For I was married on the elder sister,
   And you on the youngest of a' the three."

Then he has ta'en out a bonny black,
    Was right weel fed wi' corn and hay,
And he's set Jamie Telfer on his back,
    To the Catslockhill to tak' the fray.

And whan he cam to the Catslockhill,
    He shouted loud and weel cried he,
Till out and spak him William's Wat—
    "O wha's this brings the fraye to me?"

"It's I, Jamie Telfer o' the fair Dodhead,
    A harried man I think I be!
The captain of Bewcastle has driven my gear;
    For God's sake rise, and succour me!"

"Alas for wae!" quo' William's Wat,
    "Alack, for thee my heart is sair!
I never cam by the fair Dodhead,
    That ever I fand thy basket bare."

He's set his twa sons on coal-black steeds,
    Himsel' upon a freckled gray,
And they are on wi' Jamie Telfer,
    To Branksome Ha' to tak the fray.

And whan they came to Branksome Ha',
    They shouted a' baith loud and hie,
Till up and spak him auld Buccleugh,
    Said—"Wha's this brings the fray to me?"

" It's I, Jamie Telfer o' the fair Dodhead,
   And a harried man I think I be !
There's nought left in the fair Dodhead,
   But a greeting wife and bairnies three."

" Alack for wae ! " quoth the gude auld lord,
   " And ever my heart is wae for thee !
But fye gar cry on Willie, my son,
   And see that he come to me speedilie !

" Gar warn the water, braid and wide,
   Gar warn it soon and hastily !
They that winna ride for Telfer's kye,
   Let them never look in the face o' me !

" Warn Wat o' Harden, and his sons,
   Wi' them will Borthwick water ride ;
Warn Gaudilands, and Allanhaugh,
   And Gilmanscleugh, and Commonside.

" Ride by the gate at Priesthaughswire,
   And warn the Currors o' the Lee ;
As ye come down the Hermitage Slack,
   Warn doughty Willie o' Gorrinberry."

The Scots they rade, the Scots they ran,
   Sae starkly and sae steadilie !
And aye the ower-word o' the thrang,
   Was—" Rise for Branksome readilie ! "

The gear was driven the Frostylee up,
  Frae the Frostylee unto the plain,
Whan Willie has looked his men before,
  And saw the kye right fast driving.

"Wha drives thir kye?" 'gan Willie say,
  "To mak an outspeckle* o' me?"
"It's I, the captain o' Bewcastle, Willie;
  I winna laynet my name for thee."

"O will ye let Telfer's kye gae back,
  Or will ye do aught for regard o' me?
Or, by the faith o' my body," quo' Willie Scott,
  "I'se ware my dame's cauf's skin on thee!"

"I winna let the kye gae back,
  Neither for thy love, nor yet thy fear,
But I will drive Jamie Telfer's kye,
  In spite of every Scot that's here."

"Set on them, lads!" quo' Willie than,
  "Fye, lads, set on them cruellie!
For ere they win to the Ritterford,
  Mony a toom saddle there sall be!"

But Willie was stricken ower the head,
  And through the knapscap the sword has gane;
And Harden grat for very rage,
  Whan Willie on the ground lay slain.

          * Laughing-stock.   † Hide.

But he's ta'en aff his gude steel-cap,
   And thrice he's waved it in the air—
The Dinlay snaw was ne'er mair white,
   Nor the lyart locks of Harden's hair.

"Revenge! revenge!" auld Wat 'gan cry;
   "Fye, lads, lay on them cruellie!
We'll ne'er see Tiviotside again,
   Or Willie's death revenged shall be."

O mony a horse ran masterless,
   The splintered lances flew on hie;
But or they wan to the Kershope ford
   The Scots had gotten the victory.

John o' Brigham there was slain,
   And John o' Barlow, as I hear say;
And thirty mae o' the captain's men,
   Lay bleeding on the grund that day.

The captain was run thro' the thick of the thigh—
   And broken was his right leg bane;
If he had lived this hundred year,
   He had never been loved by woman again.

"Hae back thy kye!" the captain said;
   "Dear kye, I trow, to some they be!
For gin I suld live a hundred years,
   There will ne'er fair lady smile on me."

Then word is gane to the captain's bride,
    Even in the bower where that she lay,
That her lord was prisoner in enemy's land,
    Since into Tividale he had led the way.

"I wad lourd* have had a winding-sheet,
    And helped to put it ower his head,
Ere he had been disgraced by the Border Scot,
    When he ower Liddel his men did lead!"

There was a wild gallant amang us a',
    His name was Watty wi' the Wudspurs,
Cried—"On for his house in Stanegirthside,
    If ony man will ride with us!"

When they cam to the Stanegirthside,
    They dang wi' trees, and burst the door;
They loosed out a' the captain's kye,
    And set them forth our lads before.

There was an auld wife ayont the fire,
    A wee bit o' the captain's kin—
"Wha daur loose out the captain's kye,
    Or answer to him and his men?"

"It's I, Watty Wudspurs, loose the kye!
    I winna layne my name frae thee!
And I will loose out the captain's kye,
    In scorn of a' his men and he."

          * *Lourd*—rather.

When they cam to the fair Dodhead,
    They were a wellcum sight to see !
For instead of his ain ten milk-kye,
    Jamie Telfer has gotten thirty and three.

And he has paid the rescue shot,
    Baith wi' goud, and white monie :
And at the burial o' Willie Scott,
    I wot was mony a weeping e'e.

KINMONT WILLIE.

(*Border Minstrelsy*, vol. i., p. 193.)

O HAVE ye na heard o' the fause Sakelde?
  O have ye na heard o' the keen Lord Scroope?
How they hae ta'en bauld Kinmont Willie,
  On Hairibee to hang him up?

Had Willie had but twenty men,
  But twenty men as stout as he,
Fause Sakelde had never the Kinmont ta'en,
  Wi' eight score in his cumpanie.

They band his legs beneath the steed,
  They tied his hands behind his back;
They guarded him, fivesome on each side,
  And they brought him ower the Liddel-rack.

They led him thro' the Liddel-rack,
  And also thro' the Carlisle sands; ·
They brought him on to Carlisle castle,
  To be at my Lord Scroope's commands.

'My hands are tied, but my tongue is free,
　And wha will dare this deed avow?
Or answer by the Border law?
　Or answer to the bauld Buccleuch?'

'Now haud thy tongue, thou rank reiver!
　There's never a Scot shall set ye free:
Before ye cross my castle yate,
　I trow ye shall take farewell o' me.'

'Fear na ye that, my lord,' quo' Willie:
　'By the faith o' my body, Lord Scroope,' he said,
'I never yet lodged in a hostelrie,
　But I paid my lawing before I gaed.'

Now word is gane to the bauld Keeper,
　In Branksome Ha' where that he lay,
That Lord Scroope has ta'en the Kinmont Willie,
　Between the hours of night and day.

He has ta'en the table wi' his hand,
　He garr'd the red wine spring on hie—
'Now Christ's curse on my head,' he said,
　'But avengèd of Lord Scroope I'll be!

'O is my basnet a widow's curch?
　Or my lance a wand of the willow-tree?
Or my arm a lady's lilye hand,
　That an English lord should lightly me!

15

‘And have they ta’en him, Kinmont Willie,
 Against the truce of Border tide?
And forgotten that the bauld Buccleuch
 Is Keeper here on the Scottish side?

‘And have they e’en ta’en him, Kinmont Willie,
 Withouten either dread or fear?
And forgotten that the bauld Buccleuch
 Can back a steed, or shake a spear?

‘O were there war between the lands,
 As well I wot that there is none,
I would slight Carlisle castell high,
 Tho’ it were builded of marble stone.

‘I would set that castell in a low
 And sloken it with English blood!
There’s nevir a man in Cumberland
 Should ken where Carlisle castell stood.

‘But since nae war’s between the lands,
 And there is peace, and peace should be;
I’ll neither harm English lad or lass,
 And yet the Kinmont freed shall be!’

He has call’d him forty marchmen bauld,
 I trow they were of his ain name,
Except Sir Gilbert Elliot, call’d
 The laird of Stobs, I mean the same.

He has call'd him forty marchmen bauld,
  Were kinsmen to the bauld Buccleuch ;
With spur on heel, and splent on spauld,
  And gleuves of green, and feathers blue.

There were five and five before them a',
  Wi' hunting-horns and bugles bright ;
And five and five came wi' Buccleuch,
  Like warden's men, arrayed for fight.

And five and five, like a mason gang,
  That carried the ladders lang and hie ;
And five and five, like broken men ;
  And so they reached the Woodhouselee.

And as we cross'd the Bateable Land,
  When to the English side we held,
The first o' men that we met wi',
  Whae sould it be but fause Sakelde ?

' Where be ye gaun, ye hunters keen ?
  Quo' fause Salkelde, ' come tell me true ! '
' We go to hunt an English stag,
  Has trespass'd on the Scots countrie.'

' Where be ye gaun, ye marshal men ? '
  Quo' fause Sakelde ; ' come tell me true ! '
' We go to catch a rank reiver,
  Has broken faith wi' the bauld Buccleuch.'

' Where are ye gaun, ye mason lads,
  Wi' a' your ladders lang and hie ? '
' We gang to herry a corbie's nest,
  That wons not far frae Woodhouselee.'

' Where be ye gaun, ye broken men ? '
  Quo' fause Sakelde ; ' come tell to me ! '
Now Dickie of Dryhope led that band,
  And the never a word o' lear had he.

' Why trespass ye on the English side ?
  Row-footed outlaws, stand ! ' quo' he ;
The nevir a word had Dickie to say,
  Sae he thrust the lance through his fause bodie.

Then on we held for Carlisle toun,
  And at Staneshaw-bank the Eden we cross'd ;
The water was great and meikle of spait,
  But the never a horse nor man we lost.

And when we reach'd the Staneshaw-bank,
  The wind was rising loud and hie ;
And there the laird garr'd leave our steeds,
  For fear that they should stamp and nie.

And when we left the Staneshaw-bank,
  The wind began full loud to blaw ;
But 'twas wind and weet, and fire and sleet,
  When we came beneath the castle wa'.

We crept on knees, and held our breath,
    Till we placed the ladders against the wa' ;
And sae ready was Buccleuch himsell
    To mount the first, before us a'.

He has ta'en the watchman by the throat,
    He flung him down upon the lead—
'Had there not been peace between our lands,
    Upon the other side thou hadst gaed !

'Now sound out, trumpets !' quo' Buccleuch ;
    'Let's waken Lord Scroope right merrilie !'
Then loud the warden's trumpet blew—
    " O wha dare meddle wi' me ? "

Then speedilie to work we gaed,
    And raised the slogan ane and a',
And cut a hole thro' a sheet of lead,
    And so we wan to the castle ha'.

They thought King James and a' his men
    Had won the house wi' bow and spear ;
It was but twenty Scots and ten,
    That put a thousand in sic a stear !

Wi' coulters, and wi' fore-hammers,
    We garr'd the bars bang merrilie
Until we cam' to the inner prison,
    Where Willie o' Kinmont he did lie.

And when we cam' to the lower prison,
  Where Willie o' Kinmont he did lie—
'O sleep ye, wake ye, Kinmont Willie,
  Upon the morn that thou's to die?'

'O I sleep saft, and I wake aft;
  It's lang since sleeping was fley'd frae me;
Gie my service back to my wife and bairns,
  And a' gude fellows that spier for me.'

Then Red Rowan has hente him up,
  The starkest man in Teviotdale—
'Abide, abide now, Red Rowan,
  Till of my Lord Scroope I take farewell.

'Farewell, farewell, my gude Lord Scroope!
  My gude Lord Scroope, farewell!' he cried—
'I'll pay you for my lodging maill,
  When first we meet on the Border side.'

Then shoulder high, with shout and cry,
  We bore him down the ladder lang;
At every stride Red Rowan made,
  I wot the Kinmont's airns play'd clang!

'O mony a time,' quo' Kinmont Willie,
  'I have ridden horse baith wild and wood;
But a rougher beast than Red Rowan,
  I ween my legs have ne'er bestrode.

'And mony a time,' quo' Kinmont Willie,
   'I've pricked a horse out oure the furs;
But since the day I backed a steed,
   I never wore sic cumbrous spurs!'

We scarce had won the Staneshaw-bank,
   When a' the Carlisle bells were rung,
And a thousand men, in horse and foot,
   Cam' wi' the keen Lord Scroope along.

Buccleuch has turned to Eden water,
   Even where it flow'd frae bank to brim,
And he has plunged in wi' a' his band,
   And safely swam them thro' the stream.

He turned him on the other side,
   And at Lord Scroope his glove flung he—
'If ye like na my visit in merry England,
   In fair Scotland come visit me!'

All sore astonished stood Lord Scroope,
   He stood as still as rock of stane;
He scarcely dared to trew his eyes,
   When thro' the water they had gane.

'He is either himsell a devil frae hell,
   Or else his mother a witch maun be;
I wadna have ridden that wan water
   For a' the gowd in Christentie.'

JOHNIE ARMSTRANG.

(*Border Minstrelsy*, vol. i., p. 120.)

SUM speikis of lords, sum speikis of lairds,
  And sic lyke men of hie degrie;
Of a gentleman I sing a sang,
  Sum tyme called laird of Gilnockie.

The king he wrytes a luving letter,
  With his ain hand sae tenderly,
And he hath sent it to Johnie Armstrang,
  To cum and speik with him speedily.

The Eliots and Armstrangs did convene;
  They were a gallant cumpanie—
" We'll ride and meit our lawful king,
  And bring him safe to Gilnockie.

"Make kinnen and capon ready then,
  And venison in great plentie;
We'll wellcum here our royal king;
  I hope he'll dine at Gilnockie!"

They ran their horse on the Langhome howm,
  And brak their speirs wi' mickle main ;
The ladies lukit frae their loft windows—
  "God bring our men weel back agen!"

When Johnie cam before the king,
  Wi' a' his men sae brave to see,
The king he movit his bonnet to him ;
  He ween'd he was a king as well as he.

"May I find grace, my sovereign liege,
  Grace for my loyal men and me?
For my name it is Johnie Armstrang,
  And subject of yours, my liege," said he.

"Away, away, thou traitor strang !
  Out o' my sight soon may'st thou be !
I grantit nevir a traitor's life,
  And now I'll not begin wi' thee."

"Grant me my life, my liege, my king !
  And a bonny gift I'll gie to thee—
Full four and twenty milk-white steids,
  Were a' foaled in ae year to me.

"I'll gie thee a' these milk-white steids,
  That prance and nicker at a speir ;
And as mickle gude English goud,
  As four o' their braid backs dow* bear."

  * *Dow*—able to.

" Away, away, thou traitor strang !
   Out o' my sight soon may'st thou be !
I grantit never a traitor's life,
   And now I'll not begin wi' thee."

" Grant me my life, my liege, my king !
   And a bonny gift I'll gie to thee—
Gude four and twenty ganging mills,
   That gang thro' a' the yeir to me.

" These four and twenty mills complete
   Sall gang for thee thro' a' the yeir ;
And as mickle of gude red wheit,
   As a' their happers dow to bear."

" Away, away, thou traitor strang !
   Out o' my sight soon may'st thou be!
I grantit nevir a traitor's life,
   And now I'll not begin wi' thee."

" Grant me my life, my liege, my king!
   And a great gift I'll gie to thee—
Bauld four-and-twenty sisters' sons,
   Sall for thee fecht, tho' a' should flee ! "

" Away, away, thou traitor strang !
   Out o' my sight soon may'st thou be !
I grantit nevir a traitor's life,
   And now I'll not begin wi' thee."

"Grant me my life, my liege, my king!
   And a brave gift I'll gie to thee—
All between here and Newcastle town
   Sall pay their yeirly rent to thee."

"Away, away, thou traitor strang!
   Out o' my sight soon may'st thou be!
I grantit nevir a traitor's life,
   And now I'll not begin wi' thee."

"Ye lied, ye lied, now, king," he says,
   "Altho' a king and prince ye be!
For I've luved naething in my life,
   I weel dare say it, but honesty—

"Save a fast horse, and a fair woman,
   Twa bonny dogs to kill a deir;
But England suld have found me meal and mault,
   Gif I had lived this hundred yeir!

"Sche suld have found me meal and mault,
   And beef and mutton in a' plentie;
But nevir a Scot's wyfe could have said,
   That e'er I skaithed her a pure flee.

"To seek het water beneith cauld ice,
   Surely it is a great folie—
I have asked grace at a graceless face,
   But there is nane for my men and me!

" But had I kenn'd ere I cam frae hame,
    How thou unkind wadst been to me !
I wad have keepit the border side,
    In spite of all thy force and thee.

" Wist England's king that I was ta'en,
    O gin a blythe man he wad be !
For anes I slew his sister's son,
    And on his breist bane brak a trie."

John wore a girdle about his middle,
    Imbroidered ower wi' burning gold,
Bespangled wi' the same metal ;
    Maist beautiful was to behold.

There hang nine targats* at Johnie's hat,
    And ilk ane worth three hundred pound—
" What wants that knave that a king suld have,
    But the sword of honour and the crown ?

" O whair got thou these targats, Johnie,
    That blink sae brawly abune thy brie ? "
" I gat them in the field fechting,
    Where, cruel king, thou durst not be.

" Had I my horse, and harness gude,
    And riding as I wont to be,
It suld have been told this hundred ycir,
    The meeting of my king and me !

* *Targets*—tassels.

"God be with thee, Kirsty, my brother !
　Lang live thou laird of Mangertoun !
Lang may'st thou live on the border syde,
　Ere thou see thy brother ride up and down !

"And God be with thee, Kirsty, my son,
　Where thou sits on thy nurse's knee !
But and thou live this hundred yeir,
　Thy father's better thou'lt nevir be.

"Farewell ! my bonny Gilnock hall,
　Where on Esk side thou standest stout !
Gif I had lived but seven years mair,
　I wad hae gilt thee round about."

John murdered was at Carlinrigg,
　And all his gallant cumpanie ;
But Scotland's heart was ne'er sae wae,
　To see sae mony brave men die—

Because they saved their countrey deir,
　Frae Englishmen !　Nane were sae bauld
While Johnie lived on the border syde,
　Nane of them durst curn neir his hauld.

GORDON OF BRACKLEY.

(Mackay's Edition of Motherwell.)

Down Deeside cam Inveraye,
 Whistlin' and playing,
An' called loud at Brackley gate
 Ere the day dawning—
"Come, Gordon of Brackley,
 Proud Gordon, come down,
There's a sword at your threshold
 Mair sharp than your own."

"Arise now, gay Gordon,"
 His lady 'gan cry,
"Look, here is bold Inveraye
 Driving your kye."
"How can I go, lady,
 An' win them again,
When I have but ae sword,
 And Inveraye ten?"

"Arise up, my maidens,
 Wi' roke and wi' fan,
How blest had I been
 Had I married a man!

Arise up, my maidens,
  Tak' spear and tak' sword,
Go milk the ewes, Gordon,
  An' I will be lord."

The Gordon sprung up
  Wi' his helm on his head,
Laid his hand on his sword,
  An' his thigh on his steed,
An he stooped low, and said,
  As he kissed the young dame,
"There's a Gordon rides out
  That will never ride hame."

There rode with fierce Inveraye
  Thirty and three,
But wi' Brackley were nane
  But his brother and he;
Twa gallanter Gordons
  Did never blade draw,
But against three-and-thirty
  Wae's me! what are twa?

Wi' sword and wi' dagger
  They rushed on him rude;
The twa gallant Gordons
  Lie bathed in their blude.

Frae the springs o' the Dee
To the mouth o' the Tay,
The Gordons mourn for him,
And curse Inveraye.

"O were ye at Brackley?
An' what saw ye there?
Was his young widow weeping
An' tearing her hair?"
"I looked in at Brackley,
I looked in, and oh!
There was mirth, there was feasting,
But naething o' woe.

"As a rose bloomed the lady,
An' blithe as a bride,
As a bridegroom bold Inveraye
Smiled by her side.
Oh! she feasted him there
As she ne'er feasted lord,
While the blood of her husband
Was moist on his sword.

"In her chamber she kept him
Till morning grew gray,
Thro' the dark woods of Brackley
She shewed him the way.
'Yon wild hill,' she said,
'Where the sun's shining on,
Is the hill of Glentanner,—
One kiss, and begone!'"

There's grief in the cottage,
  There's grief in the ha',
For the gude, gallant Gordon
  That's dead an' awa'.
To the bush comes the bud,
  An' the flower to the plain,
But the gude and the brave
  They come never again.

HOBBIE NOBLE.

(*Border Minstrelsy*, vol. i., p. 243.)

FOUL fa' the breast first treason bred in !
   That Liddesdale may safely say :
For in it there was baith meat and drink,
   And corn unto our geldings gay.

And we were a' stout-hearted men,
   As England she might often say ;
But now we may turn our backs and flee,
   Since brave Noble is sold away.

Now Hobbie was an English man,
   And born into Bewcastle dale ;
But his misdeeds they were sae great,
   They banish'd him to Liddesdale.

At Kershope foot the tryst was set,
   Kershope of the lilye lee ;
And there was traitor Sim o' the Mains,
   And with him a private companie.

Then Hobbie has graithed his body fair
   Baith wi' the iron and wi' the steil ;
And he has ta'en out his fringed grey,
   And there, brave Hobbie, he rade him weel.

Then Hobbie is down the water gane,
   E'en as fast as he could hie ;
Tho' a' should hae bursten and broken their hearts,
   Frae that riding tryst he wad na be.

" Weel be ye met, my feres five !
   And now, what is your will wi' me ? "
Then they cried a' wi' ae consent,
   " Thou'rt welcome here, brave Noble, to me.

" Wilt thou with us into England ride,
   And thy safe warrant we will be ?
If we get a horse worth a hundred pound,
   Upon his back thou sune sall't be."

" I dare not by day into England ride ;
   The land-sergeant has me at feid :
And I know not what evil may betide,
   For Peter of Whitfield, his brother, is dead.

" And Anton Shiel he loves not me,
   For I gat twa drifts o' his sheep ;
The great Earl of Whitfield loves me not,
   For nae gear frae me he e'er could keep.

" But will ye stay till the day gae down,
    Untill the night come o'er the grund,
And I'll be a guide worth ony twa,
    That may in Liddesdale be found?

" Tho' the night be black as pitch and tar,
    I'll guide ye o'er yon hill sae hie;
And bring ye a' in safety back,
    If ye'll be true, and follow me."

He has guided them o'er moss and muir,
    O'er hill and hope, and mony a down;
Until they came to the Foulbogshiel,
    And there, brave Noble, he lighted down.

But word is gane to the land-serjeant,
    In Askerton where that he lay—
"The deer that ye hae hunted sae lang,
    Is seen into the Waste this day."

"Then Hobbie Noble is that deer!
    I wat he carries the style fu' hie;
Aft has he driven our bluidhounds back,
    And set ourselves at little lee.

"Gar warn the bows of Hartlie-burn;
    See they sharp their arrows on the wa';
Warn Willeva and Speir Edom,
    And see the morn they meet me a'.

"Gar meet me on the Rodric-haugh,
    And see it be by break o' day;
And we will on to Conscouthart-green,
    For there, I think, we'll get our prey."

Then Hobbie Noble has dreimit a dreim,
    In the Foulbogshiel, where that he lay;
He dreimit his horse was aneath him shot,
    And he himself got hard away.

The cocks could craw, the day could daw,
    And I wot sae even fell down the rain;
Had Hobbie na wakened at that time,
    In the Foulbogshiel he had been ta'en or slain.

"Awake, awake, my feres five!
    I trow here makes a fu' ill day;
Yet the worst cloak o' this company,
    I hope, sall cross the Waste this day."

Now Hobbie thought the gates were clear;
    But, ever alas! it was na sae:
They were beset by cruel men and keen,
    That away brave Hobbie might na gae.

"Yet follow me, my feres five,
    And see ye keep of me guid ray;
And the worst cloak o' this company
    Even yet may cross the Waste this day."

But the land-sergeant's men came Hobbie before,
　The traitor Sim came Hobbie behin',
So had Noble been wight as Wallace was,
　Away, alas! he might na win.

Then Hobbie had but a laddie's sword;
　But he did mair than a laddie's deed;
For that sword had cleared Conscouthart-green,
　Had it not broke o'er Jerswigham's head.

Then they hae ta'en brave Hobbie Noble,
　Wi's ain bowstring they band him sae;
But his gentle heart was ne'er sae sair,
　As when his ain five bound him on the brae.

They hae ta'en him on for West Carlisle;
　They asked him if he kend the way;
Tho' much he thought, yet little he said;
　He knew the gate as weel as they.

They hae ta'en him up the Ricker-gate;*
　The wives they cast their windows wide;
And every wife to another 'gan say,
　" That's the man loosed Jock o' the Side !"

" Fy on ye, women ! why ca' ye me man?
　For it's nae man that I'm used like;
I am but like a forfoughen† hound,
　Has been fighting in a dirty syke."

　　　* A street in Carlisle.　　　† Exhausted.

They hae had him up thro' Carlisle town,
    And set him by the chimney fire ;
They gave brave Noble a loaf to eat,
    And that was little his desire.

They gave him a wheaten loaf to eat,
    And after that a can of beer ;
And they a' cried, with one consent,
    "Eat, brave Noble, and make gude cheir !

"Confess my lord's horse, Hobbie," they said,
    "And to-morrow in Carlisle thou's na die."
"How can I confess them," Hobbie says,
    "When I never saw them with my e'e ? "

Then Hobbie has sworn a fu' great aith,
    By the day that he was gotten and born,
He never had ony thing o' my lord's,
    That either eat the grass or corn.

"Now fare thee weel, sweet Mangerton !
    For I think again I'll ne'er thee see :
I wad hae betrayed nae lad alive,
    For a' the gowd o' Christentie.

"And fare thee weel, sweet Liddesdale!
  Baith the hie land and the law ;
Keep ye weel frae the traitor Mains !
  For gowd and gear he'll sell ye a'.

"Yet wad I rather be ca'd Hobbie Noble,
  In Carlisle where he suffers for his faut,
Than I'd be ca'd the traitor Mains,
  That eats and drinks o' the meal and maut."

JOCK O' THE SIDE.

(Border Minstrelsy.)

Now Liddesdale has ridden a raid,
  But I wat they had better hae staid at hame ;
For Michael o' Winfield he is dead,
  And Jock o' the Side is prisoner ta'en.

For Mangerton house Lady Downie has gane,
  Her coats she has kilted up to her knee :
And down the water wi' speed she rins,
  While tears in spaits fa' fast frae her ee.

Then up and spoke her gude auld lord—
  " What news, what news, sister Downie, to me ! "
" Bad news, bad news, my lord Mangerton ;
  Michael is killed, and they hae ta'en my son
      Johnie."

" Ne'er fear, sister Downie," quo' Mangerton ;
  " I have yokes of ousen, eighty and three ;
My barns, my byres, and my faulds, a' weil fill'd,
  I'll part wi' them a' ere Johnie shall die.

"Three men I'll send to set him free,
   A' harneist wi' the best o' steil;
The English louns may hear, and drie
   The weight o' their braid-swords to feel.

"The laird's Jock ane, the laird's Wat twa,
   O Hobbie Noble, thou ane maun be!
Thy coat is blue, thou hast been true,
   Since England banished thee to me."—

Now Hobbie was an Englishman,
   In Bewcastle-dale was bred and born;
But his misdeeds they were sae great,
   They banished him ne'er to return.

Lord Mangerton then orders gave,
   "Your horses they wrang way maun be shod,
Like gentleman ye mauna seem,
   But look like corn-caugers ga'en the road.

"Your armour gude ye mauna shaw,
   Nor yet appear like men o' weir;
As country lads be a' array'd,
   Wi' branks and brecham on each mare."—

Sae now their horses are the wrang way shod,
   And Hobbie has mounted his gray sac fine;
Jock his lively bay, Wat's on his white horse behind,
   And on they rode for the water of Tyne.

At the Cholerford they a' light down,
   And there, wi' the help of the light o' the moon,
A tree they cut, wi' fifteen nogs on each side,
   To climb up the wa' of Newcastle toun.

But when they cam to Newcastle toun,
   And were alighted at the wa',
They fand thair tree three ells ower laigh,
   They fand their stick baith short and sma'.

Then up spake the laird's ain Jock ;
   "There's naething for't ; the gates we maun force."—
But when they cam the gate until,
   A proud porter withstood baith men and horse.

His neck in twa the Armstrangs wrang ;
   Wi' fute or hand he ne'er play'd pa !
His life and his keys at anes they hae ta'en,
   And cast his body ahint the wa'.

Now sune they reached Newcastle jail,
   And to the prisoner thus they call ;
"Sleeps thou, wakes thou, Jock o' the Side,
   Or art thou weary of thy thrall ? "

Jock answers thus, wi' dolefu' tone ;
   " Aft, aft I wake—I seldom sleep ;
But whae's this kens my name sae weel,
   And thus to mese my waes does seek ? "

Then out and spak the gude laird's Jock,
    "Now fear ye na, my billie," quo' he;
"For here are the laird's Jock, the laird's Wat,
    And Hobbie Noble, come to set thee free."—

"Now haud thy tongue, my gude laird's Jock,
    For ever, alas! this canna be;
For if a' Liddesdale were here the night,
    The morn's the day that I maun die.

"Full fifteen stane o' Spanish iron,
    They hae laid a' right sair on me;
Wi' locks and keys I am fast bound
    Into this dungeon dark and dreirie."—

"Fear ye na that," quo' the laird's Jock;
    "A faint heart ne'er wan a fair ladie;
Work thou within, we'll work without,
    And I'll be sworn we'll set thee free."—

The first strong door that they cam at,
    They loosed it without a key;
The next chain'd door that they cam at,
    They garr'd it a' to flinders flee.

The prisoner now upon his back
    The laird's Jock has gotten up fu' hie:
And down the stairs, him, airns and a',
    Wi' nae sma' speed and joy brings he.

"Now, Jock, my man," quo' Hobbie Noble,
   "Some o' his weight ye may lay on me."—
"I wat weel no !" quo' the laird's ain Jock,
   "I count him lighter than a flee."—

Sae out at the gates they a' are gane,
   The prisoner's set on horseback hie ;
And now wi' speed they've ta'en the gate,
   While ilk ane jokes fu' wantonlie :

"O Jock ! sae winsomely ye ride,
   Wi' baith your feet upon ae side ;
Sae weel ye're harneist, and sae trig,
   In troth ye sit like ony bride ! "

The night, tho' wat, they did na mind,
   But hied them on fu' merrilie,
Until they cam to Cholerford brae,
   Where the water ran like mountains hie.

But when they cam to Cholerford,
   There they met with with an auld man ;
Says—"Honest man, will the water ride ?
   Tell us in haste, if that ye can."—

"I wat weel no," quo' the gude auld man ;
   "I hae lived here thretty years and three,
And I ne'er saw the Tyne sae big,
   Nor running anes sae like the sea."—

Then out and spake the laird's saft Wat,
 The greatest coward in the cumpanie,
"Now halt, now halt! we need na try't,
 The day is come wee a' maun die!"—

"Puir faint-hearted thief!" cried the laird's ain Jock,
 "There'll nae man die but him that's fie;
I'll guide ye a' right safely thro';
 Lift ye the pris'ner on ahint me."—

Wi' that the water they hae ta'en,
 By ane's and twa's they a' swam thro';
"Here are we a' safe," quo' the Laird's Jock,
 "And, puir faint Wat, what think ye now?"—

They scarce the other brae had won,
 When twenty men they saw pursue;
Frae Newcastle toun they had been sent,
 A' English lads baith stout and true.

But when the land-sergeant the water saw,
 "It winna ride, my lads," says he;
Then cried aloud—"The prisoner take,
 But leave the fetters, I pray, to me."—

"I wat weel no," quo' the laird's ain Jock,
 "I'll keep them a'; shoon to my mare they'll be:
My gude bay mare—for I am sure,
 She has bought them a' right dear frae thee."—

Sae now they are on to Liddesdale,
　E'en as fast as they could them hie ;
The prisoner is brought to's ain fireside,
　And there o's airns they mak him free.

"Now, Jock, my billie," quo' a' the three,
　"The day is comed thou was to dee ;
But thou's as weel at thy ain ingle-side,
　Now sitting, I think, 'twixt thee and me."

DICK O' THE COW.

(Border Minstrelsy.)

Now Liddesdale has layen lang in,
   There is na ryding there at a';
The horses are a' grown sae lither fat,
   They downa stir out o' the sta'.

Fair Johnie Armstrong to Willie did say—
   " Billie, a riding we will gae;
England and us have been lang at feid;
   Ablins we'll light on some bootie."—

Then they are come on to Hutton Ha';
   They rade that proper place about,
But the laird he was the wiser man,
   For he had left nae gear without.

For he had left nae gear to steal,
   Except sax sheep upon a lea:
Quo' Johnie—" I'd rather in England dee,
   Ere thir sax sheep gae to Liddesdale wi' me.

"But how ca' they the man we last met,
    Billie, as we cam owre the knowe?"—
"That same he is an innocent fule,
    And men they call him Dick o' the Cow.—

"That fule has three as good kye o' his ain,
    As there are in a' Cumberland, billie," quo' he :
"Betide me life, betide me death,
    These kye shall go to Liddesdale wi' me."—

Then they have come to the pure fule's house,
    And they hae broken his wa's sae wide ;
They have loosed out Dick o' the Cow's three kye
    And ta'en three co'erlets frae his wife's bed.

Then on the morn when the day was light,
    The shouts and cries raise loud and hie :
"O haud thy tongue, my wife," he says,
    "And o' thy crying let me be !

"O haud thy tongue, my wife," he says,
    "And o' thy crying let me be ;
And aye where thou hast lost ae cow,
    In guid suith I shall bring thee three."—

Now Dickie's gane to the gude lord Scroope,
    And I wat a dreirie fule was he ;
"Now haud thy tongue, my fule," he says,
    "For I may not stand to jest wi' thee."—

17

"Shame fa' your jesting, my lord!" quo' Dickie,
  "For nae sic jesting 'grees wi' me;
Liddesdale's been in my house last night,
  And they hae awa my three kye frae me.

"But I may nae longer in Cumberland dwell,
  To be your puir fule and your leal,
Unless you gie me leave, my lord,
  To gae to Liddesdale and steal."—

"I gie thee leave, my fule!" he says;
  "Thou speakest against my honour and me,
Unless thou gie me thy trowth and thy hand,
  Thou'lt steal frae nane but whae sta' frae thee."—

"There is my trowth, and my right hand!
  My head shall hang on Hairibee;
I'll ne'er cross Carlisle sands again,
  If I steal frae a man but whae sta' frae me."

"Dickie's ta'en leave o' lord and master;
  I wat a merry fule was he!
He's bought a bridle and a pair o' new spurs,
  And packed them up in his breek thie.

Then Dickie's come on to Pudding-burn house,
  E'en as fast as he might dree;
Then Dickie's come on to Pudding-burn,
  Where there were thirty Armstrangs and three.

"O what's this come o' me now?" quo' Dickie;
 "What mickle wae is this?" quo' he;
"For here is but ae innocent fule,
 And there are thirty Armstrangs and three!"

Yet he has come up to the fair ha' board,
 Sae weil he's become his courtesie!
"Weil may ye be, my gude laird's Jock!
 But the deil bless a' your cumpanie.

"I'm come to 'plain o' your man, fair Johnie Armstrang,
 And syne o' his billie Willie," quo' he;
"How they've been in my house last nicht,
 And they ha' ta'en my three kye frae me."—

"Ha!" quo' fair Johnie Armstrang, "we will him hang."
 —"Na," quo' Willie, "we'll him slae."—
Then up and spak another young Armstrang,
 "We'll gae him his batts, and let him gae."—

But up and spak the gude laird's Jock,
 The best falla in a' the cumpanie,
"Sit down thy ways a little while, Dickie,
 And a piece o' thy ain cow's hough I'll gie ye."—

But Dickie's heart it grew sae grit,
 That the ne'er a bit o' the dought to eat—
Then he was aware of an auld peat-house,
 Where a' the night he thought for to sleep.

Then Dickie was aware of an auld peat-house,
    Where a' the night he thought for to lye—
And a' the prayers the puir fule pray'd,
    Were, " I wish I had amends for my three gude kye."

It was then the use of Pudding-burn house,
    And the house of Mangerton, all hail,
Them that cam na at the first ca',
    Gat nae mair meat till the neist meal.

The lads, that hungry and weary were,
    Abune the door-head they threw the key;
Dickie he took gude notice o' that,
    Says—"There will be a bootie for me."

Then Dickie has into the stable gane,
    Where there stood thirty horses and three;
He has tied them a' wi' St. Mary's knot,
    A' these horses but barely three.

He has tied them a' wi' St. Mary's knot,
    A' these horses but barely three;
He's loupen on ane, ta'en another in hand,
    And away as fast as he can hie.

But on the morn, when the day grew light,
    The shouts and cries raise loud and hie—
" Ah ! whae has done this ?" quo' the gude laird's Jock,
    " Tell me the truth and the verity !"—

"Whae has done this deed?" quo' the gude laird's Jock,
  "See that to me ye dinna lie!"—
"Dickie has been in the stable last nicht,
  And has ta'en my brother's horses and mine frae me."—

"Ye wad ne'er be tauld," quo' the gude laird's Jock;
  "Have ye not found my tales fu' leil?
Ye ne'er wad out o' England bide,
  Till crooked, and blind, and a' would steal."—

"But lend me thy bay," fair Johnie 'gan say;
  "There's nae horse loose in the stable save he;
And I'll either fetch Dick o' the Cow again,
  Or the day is come that he shall die."—

"To lend thee my bay!" the laird's Jock 'gan say;
  "He's baith worth gowd and gude monie:
Dick o' the Cow has awa' twa horse:
  I wish na thou may make him three."—

He has ta'en the laird's jack on his back,
  A twa-handed sword to hang by his thie;
He has ta'en a steel cap on his head,
  And galloped on to follow Dickie.

Dickie was na a mile frae aff the town,
  I wat a mile but barely three,
When he was o'erta'en by fair Johnie Armstrong,
  Hand for hand, on Cannobie lee.

"Abide, abide, thou traitour thief!
    The day is come that thou maun die."—
Then Dickie look't ower his left shouther,
    Said—"Johnie, hast thou nae mae in companie?

"There is a preacher in our chapell,
    And a' the live-lang day teaches he:
When day is gane and night is come,
    There's ne'er a word I mark but three.

"The first and second is—Faith and Conscience;
    The third—Ne'er let a traitour free:
But, Johnie, what faith and conscience was thine,
    When thou took awa my three kye frae me?

"And when thou had ta'en awa my three kye,
    Thou thought in thy heart thou wast not weil sped,
Till thou sent thy billie Willie ower the knowe,
    To tak three coverlets off my wife's bed!"—

Then Johnie let a spear fa' laigh by his thie,
    Thought weel to hae slain the innocent, I trow;
But the powers above were mair than he,
    For he ran but the puir fule's jerkin through.

Together they ran, or ever they blan:
    This was Dickie the fule and he!
Dickie could na win at him wi' the blade o' the sword,
    But fell'd him wi' the plummet under the ee.

Thus Dickie has fell'd fair Johnie Armstrang,
　　The prettiest man in the south country—
"Gramercy!" then 'gan Dickie say,
　　"I had but twa horse, thou hast made me three!"—

He's ta'en the steil jack aff Johnie's back,
　　The twa-handed sword that hung low by his thie;
He's ta'en the steil cap aff his head—
　　"Johnie, I'll tell my master I met wi' thee."

When Johnie wakened out o' his dream,
　　I wat a dreirie man was he:
"And is thou gane? Now, Dickie, than
　　The shame and dule is left wi' me.

"And is thou gane? Now, Dickie, than
　　The deil gae in thy companie!
For if I should live these hundred years,
　　I ne'er shall fight wi' a fule after thee."—

Then Dickie's come hame to the gude lord Scroope,
　　E'en as fast as he might hie;
"Now, Dickie, I'll neither eat nor drink,
　　Till hie hanged thou shalt be."—

"The shame speed the liars, my lord!" quo' Dickie:
　　"This was na the promise ye made to me!
For I'd ne'er gang to Liddesdale to steal,
　　Had I not got my leave frae thee."—

" But what garr'd ye steal the laird's Jock's horse?
   And, limmer, what garr'd ye steal him ? " quo he ;
"For lang thou mightst in Cumberland dwelt,
   Ere the laird's Jock had stown frae thee."—

" Indeed I wat ye lied, my lord !
   And e'en sae loud as I hear ye lie !
I wan the horse frae fair Johnnie Armstrang,
   Hand to hand, on Cannobie lee.

" There is the jack was on his back ;
   This twa-handed sword hung laigh by his thie ;
And there's the steil cap was on his head ;
   I brought a' these tokens to let thee see."—

"If that be true thou to me tells
   (And I think thou dares na tell a lie),
I'll gie thee fifteen punds for the horse,
   Weil tauld on thy cloak lap shall be.

" I'll gie the ane o' my best milk kye,
   To maintain thy wife and children three ;
And that may be as gude, I think,
   As ony twa o' thine would be."—

" The shame speed the liars, my lord ! " quo' Dickie ;
   " Trow ye aye to mak a fule o' me ?
I'll either hae twenty punds for the gude horse,
   Or he's gae to Morton fair wi' me."—

He's gi'en him twenty punds for the gude horse,
   A' in goud and gude monie ;
He's gi'en him ane o' his best milk kye,
   To maintain his wife and children three.

Then Dickie's come down thro' Carlisle toun,
   E'en as fast as he could drie ;
The first o' men that he met wi',
   Was my lord's brother, bailiff Glozenburrie.

" Well be ye met, my gude Ralph Scroope ! "
   " Welcome, my brother fule ! " quo' he :
" Where didst thou get fair Johnie Armstrang's horse ? "
   —" Where did I get him, but steal him," quo' he.

" But wilt thou sell me the bonny horse ?
   And, billie, wilt thou sell him to me ? " quo' he :—
" Ay ; if thou'lt tell me the monie on my cloak lap :
   For there's never ae penny I'll trust thee."—

" I'll gie thee ten punds for the gude horse,
   Well tauld on thy cloak lap they shall be ;
And I'll gie thee ane o' the best milk kye,
   To maintain thy wife and children three."—

" The shame speed the liars, my lord ! " quo' Dickie ;
   " Trow ye aye to make a fule o' me !
I'll either hae twenty punds for the gude horse,
   Or he's gae to Morton fair wi' me."—

Then up and spak him mettled John Hall,
　(The luve of Tiviotdale aye was he),
"An I had eleven men to mysell,
　It's aye the twalt man I wad be."—

Then up bespak him coarse Ca'field
　(I wot and little gude worth was he),
"Thirty men is few anew,
　And a' to ride in our companie."—

There was horsing, horsing in haste,
　And there was marching on the lee;
Until they came to Murraywhate,
　And they lighted there right speedilie.

"A smith! a smith!" Dickie he cries,
　"A smith, a smith, right speedilie,
To turn back the caukers of our horses' shoon!
　For it's unkensome we wad be."—

"There lives a smith on the water-side,
　Will shoe my little black mare for me;
And I've a croun in my pocket,
　And every groat of it I wad gie."—

"The night is mirk, and its very mirk,
　And by candle-light I canna weel see;
The night is mirk, and its very pit mirk,
　And there will never a nail ca' right for me."—

"Shame fa' you and your trade baith,
    Canna beet a good fellow by your mystery;
But leeze me on thee, my little black mare,
    Thou's worth thy weight in gold to me."—

There was horsing, horsing in haste,
    And there was marching upon the lee;
Until they cam to Dumfries port,
    And they lighted there right speedilie.

"There's five of us will hold the horse,
    And other five will watchmen be:
But wha's the man among ye a',
    Will gae to the Tolbooth door wi' me?"

O up then spak him mettled John Hall,
    (Frae the Laigh Teviotdale was he),
"If it should cost my life this very night,
    I'll gae to the Talbooth door wi' thee."

"Be of gude cheir, now, Archie, lad!
    Be of gude cheir, now, dear billie!
Work thou within, and we without,
    And the morn thou'se dine at Ca'field wi' me."—

O Jockie Hall stepp'd to the door,
    And he bended low back his knee,
And he made the bolts, the door hang on,
    Loup frae the wa' right wantonlie.

He took the prisoner on his back,
   And down the Tolbooth stair cam he ;
The black mare stood ready at the door,
   I wot a foot ne'er stirred she.

They laid the links out owre her neck,
   And that was her gold twist to be ;
And they cam doun thro' Dumfries toun,
   And wow but they cam speedilie.

The live-lang night these twelve men rade,
   And aye till they were right wearie,
Until they cam to the Murraywhate,
   And they lighted there right speedilie.

"A smith ! a smith !" then Dickie he cries,
   " A smith, a smith, right speedilie.
To file the irons frae my dear brither !
   For forward, forward we wad be."—

They hadna filed a shackle of iron,
   A shackle of iron but barely thrie,
When out and spak young Simon brave,
   "O dinna you see what I do see ?

"Lo ! yonder comes lieutenant Gordon,
   Wi' a hundred men in his companie ;
This night will be our lyke-wake night,
   The morn the day we a' maun die."—

O there was mounting, mounting in haste,
   And there was marching upon the lee ;
Until they cam to Annan water,
   And it was flowing like the sea.

" My mare is young and very skeigh,
   And in o' the weil she will drown me ;
But ye'll tak mine, and I'll tak thine,
   And sune through the water we sall be."—

Then up and spak him coarse Ca'field,
   (I wot and little gude worth was he),
" We had better lose ane than lose a' the lave ;
   We'll lose the prisoner, we'll gae free."—

"Shame fa' you and your lands baith !
   Wad ye e'en your lands to your born billy ?
But hey ! bear up, my bonnie black mare,
   And yet thro' the water we sall be."—

Now they did swim the wan water,
   And wow but they swam bonnilie !
Until they cam to the other side,
   And they rung their cloathes right drunkily.

" Come thro', come thro', lieutenant Gordon !
   Come thro' and drink some wine w' me !
For there is an ale-house here hard by,
   And it shall not cost thee ae penny."—

"Throw me my irons," quo' lieutenant Gordon;
  "I wot they cost me dear eneugh."—
"The shame a ma," quo' mettled John Ha',
  "They'll be gude shackles to my pleugh."—

"Come thro', come thro', lieutenant Gordon!
  Come thro' and drink some wine wi' me!
Yestreen I was your prisoner,
  But now this morning am I free."

THE RAID OF THE REIDSWIRE.

(Border Minstrelsy.)

THE seventh of July, the suith to say,
　At the Reidswire the tryst was set;
Our wardens they affixed the day,
　And, as they promised, so they met.
Alas! that day I'll ne'er forgett!
Was sure sae feard, and then sae faine—
　They cam theare justice for to gett,
Will never green to come again.

Carmichael was our warden then,
　He caused the country to conveen;
And the Laird's Wat, that worthie man,
　Brought in that sirname weil beseen;
　The Armestranges, that aye hae been
A hardy house, but not a hail,
　The Elliots honours to maintaine,
Brought down the lave o' Liddesdale.

Then Tividale came to wi' spied;
　The Sheriffe brought the Douglas down,
Wi' Cranstane, Gladstain, good at need,
　Baith Rewle water, and Hawick town.

18

Beanjeddart bauldy made him boun,
  Wi' a' the Trumbills, stronge and stout ;
The Rutherfords, with grit renown,
  Convoyed the town of Jedbrugh out.

Of other clans I cannot tell,
  Because our warning was not wide—
Be this our folks hae ta'en the fell,
  And planted down palliones, there to bide,
  We looked down the other side,
And saw come breasting ower the brae,
  Wi' sir John Forster for their guyde,
Full fifteen hundred men and mae.

It grieved him sair that day, I trow,
  Wi' sir George Hearoune of Schipsydehouse ;
Because we were not men enow,
  They counted us not worth a louse.
  Sir George was gentle, meek, and douse,
But he was hail and het as fire ;
  And yet, for all his cracking crouse,
He rewd the raid o' the Reidswire.

To deal with pryud men is but pain;
  For either must ye fight or flee,
Or else no answer make again,
  But play the beast, and let them be.
  It was nae wonder he was hie,
Had Tindaill, Reedsdail, at his hand,
  Wi' Cukdaill, Gladsdaill on the lee,
And Hebsrime, and Northumberland.

Yett was our meeting meek eneuch,
  Begun wi' merriment and mowes,
And at the brae, aboon the heugh,
  The clark sat down to call the rowes.
  And some for kyne, and some for ewes,
Call'd in of Dandrie, Hob, and Jock—
  We saw come marching ower the knowes,
Five hundred Fennicks in a flock,—

With jack and speir, and bows all bent,
  And warlike weapons at their will:
Although we were na weel content,
  Yet, by my trouth, we fear'd no ill.
  Some gaed to drink, and some stude still,
And some to cards and dice them sped;
  Till on ane Farnstein they fyled a bill,
And he was fugitive and fled.

Carmichaell bade them speik out plainlie,
  And cloke no cause for ill nor good;
The other, answering him as vainlie,
  Began to reckon kin and blood:
  He raise, and raxed him where he stood,
And bade him match him with his marrows;
  Then Tindaill heard them reasun rude,
And they loot off a flight of arrows.

Then was there nought but bow and speir,
  And every man pull'd out a brand;
"A Schafton and a Fenwick" thare:
  Gude Symington was slain frae hand.

The Scotsmen cried on other to stand,
Frac time they saw John Robson slain—
   What should they cry? the King's command
Could cause no cowards turn again.

Up rose the laird to red the cumber,
   Which would not be for all his boast;—
What could we doe with sic a number—
   Fyve thousand men into a host?
   Then Henry Purdie proved his cost,
And very narrowlie had mischief'd him,
   And there we had our warden lost,
Wert not the grit God he relieved him.

Another throw the breiks him bair,
   Whill flatlies to the ground he fell:
Than thought I weel we had lost him there,
   Into my stomack it struck a knell!
   Yet up he raise, the treuth to tell ye,
And laid about him dints full dour;
   His horsemen they raid sturdily,
And stude about him in the stoure.

Then raise the slogan with ane shout—
   " Fy, Tindaill, to it! Jedburgh's here!"
I trow he was not half sae stout,
   But anis his stomach was asteir.
   With gun and genzie, bow and speir,
Men might see many a cracked crown!
   But up amang the merchant geir,
They were as busy as we were down.

The swallow taill frae tackles flew,
　Five hundredth flain into a flight.
But we had pestelets enew,
　And shot amang them as we might,
　With help of God the game gaed right,
Fra time the foremost of them fell;
　Then ower the knowe, without goodnight,
They ran with mony a shout and yell.

But after they had turned backs,
　Yet Tindaill men they turn'd again,
And had not been the merchant packs,
　There had been mae of Scotland slain.
　But, Jesu! if the folks were fain
To put the bussing on their thies;
　And so they fled, wi' a' their main,
Down ower the brae, like clogged bees.

Sir Francis Russell ta'en was there,
　And hurt, as we hear men rehearse;
Proud Wallinton was wounded sair,
　Albeit he be a Fennick fierce.
　But if ye wald a souldier search,
Among them a' were ta'en that night,
　Was nane sae wordie to put in verse,
As Collingwood, that courteous knight.

Young Henry Schafton, he is hurt;
　A souldier shot him wi' a bow;
Scotland has cause to mak great sturt,
　For laiming of the Laird of Mowe.

The Laird's Wat did weel indeed;
His friends stood stoutlie by himsell,
  With little Gladstain, gude in need,
For Gretein kend na gude be ill.

The Sheriffe wanted not gude will,
    Howbeit he might not fight so fast;
Beanjeddart, Hundlie, and Hunthill,
    Three, on they laid weel at the last.
    Except the horsemen of the guard,
If I could put men to availe,
    None stoutlier stood out for their laird,
Nor did the lads of Liddisdail.

But little harness had we there;
    But auld Badrule had on a jack,
And did right weel, I you declare,
    With all his Trumbills at his back.
    Gude Edderstane was not to lack,
Nor Kirktoun, Newton, noble men!
    Thir's all the specials I of speake,
By others that I could not ken.

Who did invent that day of play,
    We need not fear to find him soon;
For Sir John Forster, I dare well say,
    Made us this noisome afternoon.
    Not that I speak preceislie out,
That he supposed it would be perril;
    But pride, and breaking out of feuid,
Garr'd Tindaill lads begin the quarrel.

ROOKHOPE RYDE.

(Border Minstrelsy.)

Rookhope stands in a pleasant place,
　　If the false thieves wad let it be,
But away they steal our goods apace,
　　And ever an ill death may they dee !

And so is the men of Thirlwall and Willie-haver,
　　And all their companies thereabout,
That is minded to do mischief,
　　And at their stealing stands not out.

But yet we will not slander them all,
　　For there is of them good enow ;
It is a sore consumed tree
　　That on it bears not one fresh bough.

Lord God ! is not this a pitiful case,
　　That men dare not drive their goods to the fell,
But limmer thieves drives them away,
　　That fears neither heaven nor hell ?

Lord, send us peace into the realm,
　　That every man may live on his own !
I trust to God, if it be his will,
　　That Weardale men may never be overthrown.

For great troubles they've had in hand,
　　With Borderers pricking hither and thither,
But the greatest fray that e'er they had,
　　Was with the men of Thirlwall and Willie-haver.

They gather'd together so royally,
　　The stoutest men and the best in gear ;
And he that rade not on a horse,
　　I wat he rade on a weel-fed mear.

So in the morning before they came out,
　　So weel I wot they broke their fast ;
In the forenoon they came into a bye fell,
　　Where some of them did eat their last.

When they had eaten aye and done,
　　They say'd some captains here needs must be :
Then they choosed forth Harry Corbyl,
　　And "Symon Fell," and Martin Ridley.

Then o'er the moss, where as they came,
　　With many a brank and whew,
One of them could to another say,
　　"I think this day we are men enew.

"For Weardale men have a journey ta'en,
  They are so far out o'er yon fell,
That some of them's with the two earls,
  And others fast in Bernard castell.

"There we shall get gear enough;
  For there is nane but women at hame;
The sorrowful fend that they can make,
  Is loudly cries as they were slain."

Then in at the Rookhope-head they came,
  And there they thought tul a' had their prey,
But they were spy'd coming over the Dry-rig,
  Soon upon St. Nicolas' day.

Then in at Rookhope-head they came,
  They ran the forest but a mile;
They gather'd together in four hours
  Six hundred sheep within a while.

And horses I trow they gat,
  But either ane or twa,
And they gat them all but ane
  That belang'd to great Rowley.

That Rowley was the first man that did them spy,
  With that he raised a mighty cry;
They cry it came down Rookhope burn,
  And spread through Weardale hasteyly.

Then word came to the bailiff's house
  At the East-gate, where he did dwell;
He was walk'd out to the Smale-burns,
  Which stands above the Hanging-well.

His wife was wae when she heard tell,
  So weel she wist her husband wanted gear!
She gar'd saddle him his horse in haste,
  And neither forget sword, jack, nor spear.

The bailiff got wit before his gear came,
  That such news was in the land,
He was sore troubled in his heart,
  That on no earth that he could stand.

His brother was hurt three days before,
  With limmer thieves that did him prick
Nineteen bloody wounds lay him upon,
  What ferly was't that he lay sick?

But yet the bailiff shrinked nought,
  But fast after them he did hye,
And so did all his neighbours near,
  That went to bear him company.

But when the bailiff was gathered,
  And all his company,
They were numbered to never a man
  But forty under fifty.

The thieves were numbered a hundred men,
    I wat they were not of the worst ;
That could be choosed out of Thirlwall and Willie-haver,
    "I trow they were the very first."

But all that was in Rookhope-head,
    And all that was i' Nuketon-cleugh,
Where Weardale-men o'ertook the thieves,
    And there they gave them fighting eneugh.

So sore they made them fain to flee,
    As many was a' out of hand,
And, for tul have been at home again,
    They would have been in iron bands.

And for the space of long seven years
    As sore they mighten a' had their lives,
But there was never one of them
    That ever thought to have seen their wives.

About the time the fray began,
    I trow it lasted but an hour,
Till many a man lay weaponless,
    And was sore wounded in that stour.

Also before that hour was done,
    Four of the thieves were slain,
Besides all those that wounded were,
    And eleven prisoners there was ta'en.

George Carrick, and his brother Edie,
   Them two, I wot they were both slain ;
Harry Corbyl, and Lennie Carrick,
   Bore them company in their pain.

One of our Weardale-men was slain,
   Rowland Emerson his name hight ;
I trust to God his soul is well,
   Because he fought unto the right.

But thus they say'd, " We'll not depart
   While we have one :—Speed back again !"—
And when they came amongst the dead men,
   There they found George Carrick slain.

And when they found George Carrick slain,
   I wot it went well near their heart :
Lord, let them never make a better end,
   That comes to play them sicken a part.

I trust to God, no more they shall,
   Except it be one for a great chance ;
For God will punish all those
   With a great heavy pestilence.

Thir limmer thieves, they have good hearts,
   They nevir think to be o'erthrown ;
Three banners against Weardale-men they bare,
   As if the world had been all their own.

Thir Weardale-men, they have good hearts,
    They are as stiff as any tree ;
For, if they'd every one been slain,
    Never a foot back man would flee.

And such a storm amongst them fell,
    As I think you never heard the like ;
For he that bears his head so high,
    He oft-tymes falls into the dyke.

And now I do entreat you all,
    As many as are present here,
To pray for the singer of this song,
    For he sings to make blythe your cheer.

" As I came down by Merriemass,
　　And down among the scroggs,
The bonniest childe that ever I saw
　　Lay sleeping amang his dogs.

" The shirt that was upon his back
　　Was o' the Holland fine ;
The doublet which was over that
　　Was o' the lincome twine.

" The buttons that were on his sleeve
　　Were o' the goud sae gude :
The gude graie hounds he lay amang,
　　Their mouths were dyed wi' blude."—

Then out and spak the First Forester,
　　The heid man ower them a'—
"If this be Johnie o' Breadislee,
　　Nae nearer will we draw."—

But up and spak the Sixth Forester,
　　(His sister's son was he,)
"If this be Johnie o' Breadislee,
　　We soon shall gar him dee !"

The first flight of arrows the Foresters shot,
　　They wounded him on the knee ;
And out and spak the Seventh Forester,
　　" The next will gar him dee."

Johnie's set his back against an aik,
　　His fute against a stane ;
And he has slain the Seven Foresters,
　　He has slain them a' but ane.

He has broke three ribs in that ane's side
　　But and his collar bane ;
He's laid him twa-fald ower his steed,
　　Bade him carry the tidings hame.

" O is there nae a bonnie bird,
　　Can sing as I can say ;
Could flee away to my mother's bower,
　　And tell to fetch Johnie away ? "—

The starling flew to his mother's window stane
　　It whistled and it sang ;
And aye the ower word o' the tune
　　Was—" Johnie tarries lang."

They made a rod o' the hazel bush,
　　Another o' the slae-thorn tree,
And mony mony were the men
　　At the fetching o'er Johnie.

Then out and spak his auld mither,
　　And fast her tears did fa'—
" Ye wad nae be warn'd, my son Johnie,
　　Frae the hunting to bide awa'.

"Aft hae I brought to Breadislee,
　The less gear and the mair,
But I ne'er brought to Breadislee,
　What grieved my heart sae sair.

"But wae betyde that silly auld carle !
　An ill death shall he dee !
For the highest tree in Merriemas
　Shall be his morning's fee."

Now Johnie's gude bend bow is broke,
　And his gude graie dogs are slain ;
And his bodie lies dead in Durrisdeer,
　And his hunting it is dune.

KATHARINE JANFARIE.

(*Border Minstrelsy.*)

THERE was a may, and a weel-far'd may,
   Lived high up in yon glen ;
Her name was Katharine Janfarie,
   She was courted by mony men.

Up then came lord Lauderdale,
   Up frae the Lawland Border ;
And he has come to court this may,
   A' mounted in good order.

He told na her father, he told na her mother,
   And he told na ane o' her kin ;
But he whisper'd the bonnie lassie hersell,
   And has her favour won.

But out then cam lord Lochinvar,
   Out frae the English Border,
All for to court this bonny may,
   Weel mounted, and in good order.

He told her father, he told her mother,
　　And a' the lave o' her kin ;
But he told na the bonny may hersell,
　　Till on her wedding e'en.

She sent to the lord o' Lauderdale,
　　Gin he wad come and see ;
And he has sent word back again,
　　Weel answer'd she suld be.

And he has sent a messenger
　　Right quickly through the land,
And raised mony an armed man
　　To be at his command.

The bride looked out at a high window,
　　Behold baith dale and down,
And she was aware of her first true love,
　　With riders mony a one.

She scoffed him, and scorned him,
　　Upon her wedding day ;
And said—" It was the fairy court
　　To see him in array !

" O come ye here to fight, young lord,
　　Or come ye here to play ?
Or come ye here to drink good wine
　　Upon the wedding day ? "

"I come na here to fight," he said,
　I come na here to play ;
I'll but lead a dance wi' the bonny bride,
　And mount, and go my way."

It is a glass of the blood-red wine
　Was filled up them between,
And aye she drank to Lauderdale,
　Wha her true love had been.

He's ta'en her by the milk-white hand,
　And by the grass-green sleeve ;
He's mounted her hie behind himsell,
　At her kinsmen spiered na leave.

" Now take your bride, lord Lochinvar !
　Now take her if you may !
But if you take your bride again,
　We'll call it but foul play."

There were four-and-twenty bonnie boys,
　A' clad in the Johnstone grey ;
They said they would take the bride again,
　By the strong hand, if they may.

Some o' them were right willing men,
　But they were na willing a' ;
And four-and-twenty Leader lads
　Bid them mount and ride awa'.

Then whingers flew frae gentles' sides,
  And swords flew frae the shea's,
And red and rosy was the blood
  Ran down the lily braes.

The blood ran down by Caddon bank,
  And down by Caddon brae ;
And, sighing, said the bonnie bride—
  "O wae's me for foul play !"

My blessing on your heart, sweet thing !
  Wae to your wilfu' will !
There's mony a gallant gentleman
  Whae's bluid ye have garr'd to spill.

Now a' you lords of fair England,
  And that dwell by the English Border,
Come never here to seek a wife,
  For fear of sic disorder.

They'll haik ye up, and settle ye bye,
  Till on your wedding day ;
Then gie ye frogs instead of fish,
  And play ye foul foul play.

Historical.

THE BONNY HOUSE OF AIRLY.

(Kinloch's *Ancient Scottish Ballads*, p. 104.)

O GLEY'D Argyll has written to Montrose,
    To see gin the fields they war fairly·;
And to see whether he shou'd stay at hame,
    Or come to plunder bonny Airly.

The great Montrose has written to Argyll,
    And that the fields they were fairly,
And no to keep his men at hame,
    But come and plunder bonny Airly.

The lady was looking owre the castle wa',
    She was carrying her courage sae rarely,
And there she spied him, gley'd Argyll,
    Coming for to plunder bonny Airly.

"Wae be to ye, gley'd Argyll,
    And are ye there sae rarely?
Ye micht hae kept your men at hame,
    And no come to plunder bonny Airly."

" And wae be to ye, Lady Ogilvie,
    And are ye there sae rarely?
Gin ye had bow'd whan first I bade,
    I never wad hae plunder'd bonny Airly."

"O gin my guid Lord had been at hame,
    As he is wi' Prince Charlie,
There durst na a rebel on a' Scottish grund
    Set a foot on the bonny green o' Airly.

" But ye'll tak me by the milk-white hand,
    And ye'll lift me up sae rarely;
And ye'll throw me out owre my ain castle wa',
    Let me never see the burning o' Airly."

He has ta'en her by the milk-white hand,
    And he has lifted her up sae rarely,
He has thrown her out owre her ain castle wa',
    And she never saw the plundering o' Airly.

Now gley'd Argyll he has gane hame,
    Awa frae the plundering o' Airly,
And there he has met wi' Captain Ogilvie,
    Coming over the mountains sae rarely.

"O wae be to ye, gley'd Argyll,
    And are ye there sae rarely?
Ye micht hae kept your men at hame,
    And na gane to plunder bonny Airly."

"O wae be to ye, Captain Ogilvie,
　　And are ye there sae rarely?
Gin ye had bow'd whan first I bade,
　　I never wad hae plunder'd bonny Airly."

"But gin I had my lady gay,
　　Bot and my sister Mary,
Ae fig I wadna gie for ye a',
　　Nor yet for the plundering o' Airly."

THE FIRE OF FRENDRAUGHT.

(Motherwell's *Minstrelsy*, p. 167.)

THE eighteenth of October,
  A dismal tale to hear,
How good Lord John and Rothiemay
  Was both burnt in the fire.

When steeds were saddled, and well bridled,
  And ready for to ride,
Then out it came her, false Frendraught,
  Inviting them to bide.

Said—" Stay this night untill we sup,
  The morn untill we dine ;
'Twill be a token of good 'greement
  'Twixt your good Lord and mine."

" We'll turn again," said good Lord John—
  " But no," said Rothiemay—
" My steed's trapan'd, my bridle's broken,
  I fear the day I'm fey."

When mass was sung, and bells was rung,
   And all men bound for bed,
Then good Lord John and Rothiemay
   In one chamber was laid.

They had not long cast off their cloaths,
   And were but now asleep—
When the weary smoke began to rise,
   Likewise the scorching heat.

" O waken, waken, Rothiemay,
   O waken, brother dear,
And turn you to our Saviour ;
   There is strong treason here."

When they were dressed in their cloaths,
   And ready for to boun,
The doors and windows was all secur'd,
   The roof tree burning down.

He did him to the wire-window,
   As fast as he could gang—
Says—" Wae to the hands put in the stancheons,
   For out we'll never win."

When he stood at the wire-window,
   Most doleful to be seen,
He did espy her, Lady Frendraught,
   Who stood upon the green,

Cried—" Mercy, mercy, Lady Frendraught,
    Will ye not sink with sin?
For first your husband killed my father,
    And now you burn his son."

O then out spoke her, Lady Frendraught,
    And loudly did she cry—
" It were great pity for good Lord John,
    But none for Rothiemay.
But the keys are casten in the deep draw-well,
    Ye cannot get away."

While he stood in this dreadful plight,
    Most piteous to be seen,
There called out his servant Gordon,
    As he had frantic been.

" O loup, O loup, my dear master,
    O loup and come to me;
I'll catch you in my arms two,
    One foot I will not flee.

" O loup, O loup, my dear master,
    O loup and come away,
I'll catch you in my arms two,
    But Rothiemay may lie."

" The fish sall never swim in the flood,
  Nor corn grow through the clay,
Nor the fiercest fire that ever was kindled
  Twin me and Rothiemay.

" But I cannot loup, I cannot come,
  I cannot win to thee ;
My head's fast in the wire-window,
  My feet burning from me.

" My eyes are seething in my head,
  My flesh roasting also,
My bowels are boiling with my blood,
  Is not that a woeful woe ?

" Take here the rings from my white fingers,
  That are so long and small,
And give them to my Lady fair,
  Where she sits in her hall.

" So I cannot loup, I cannot come,
  I cannot loup to thee—
My earthly part is all consumed,
  My spirit but speaks to thee."

Wringing her hands, tearing her hair,
  His Lady she was seen,
And thus addressed his servant Gordon,
  Where he stood on the green.

"O wae be to you, George Gordon,
 An ill death may you die,
So safe and sound as you stand there,
 And my Lord bereaved from me."

"I bad him loup, I bad him come,
 I bad him loup to me,
I'd catch him in my arms two,
 A foot I should not flee.

"He threw me the rings from his white fingers,
 Which were so long and small,
To give to you, his Lady fair,
 Where you sat in your hall."

Sophia Hay, Sophia Hay,
 O bonny Sophia was her name—
Her waiting maid put on her cloaths,
 But I wat she tore them off again.

And aft she cried, "Ohon ! alas, alas,
 A sair heart's ill to win ;
I wan a sair heart when I married him,
 And the day it's well returned again."

WILLIE WALLACE.

(Motherwell's *Minstrelsy*, p. 364.)

WALLACE in the high highlan's,
  Neither meat nor drink got he ;
Said, " Fa' me life, or fa' me death,
  Now to some town I maun be."

He's put on his short claiding,
  And on his short claiding put he,
Says, " Fa' me life, or fa' me death,
  Now to Perth-town I maun be."

He stepped o'er the river Tay,
  I wat ne stepped on dry land ;
He wasna aware of a well-faured maid
  Was washing there her lilie hands.

" What news, what news, ye well-faured maid ?
  What news hae ye this day to me ; "
" No news, no news, ye gentle knight,
  No news hae I this day to thee,
But fifteen lords in the hostage house,
  Waiting Wallace for to see."

" If I had but in my pocket
　　The worth of one single pennie,
I would go to the hostage house,
　　And there the gentlemen to see."

She put her hand in her pocket,
　　And she has pull'd out half-a-crown.
Says, " Take' ye that, ye belted knight,
　　'Twill pay your way till ye come down."

As he went from the well-faured maid,
　　A beggar bold I wat met he,
Was covered wi' a clouted cloak,
　　And in his hand a trusty tree.

" What news, what news, ye silly auld man,
　　What news hae ye this day to gie? "
" No news, no news, ye belted knight,
　　No news hae I this day to thee,
But fifteen lords in the hostage house
　　Waiting Wallace for to see."

" Ye'll lend me your clouted cloak
　　That covers you frae head to shie,
And I'll go to the hostage house,
　　Asking there for some supplie."

Now he's gone to the West-muir wood,
    And there he pull'd a trusty tree,
And then he's on to the hostage gone,
    Asking there for charitie.

Down the stair the captain comes,
    Aye the poor man for to see :
" If ye be a captain as good as ye look,
    Ye'll give a poor man some supplie ;
If ye be a captain as good as ye look,
    A guinea, this day, ye'll gie to me."

" Where were ye born, ye crooked carle ?
    Where were ye born, in what countrie ? "
" In fair Scotland I was born,
    Crooked carle that I be."

" I would give you fifty pounds,
    Of gold and white monie ;
I would give you fifty pounds
    If the traitor Wallace ye'd let me see."

" Tell down your money," said Willie Wallace,
    " Tell down your money if it be good,
I'm sure I have it in my power,
    And never had a better bode.

" Tell down your money if it be good,
  And let me see if it be fine,
I'm sure I have it in my power
  To bring the traitor Wallace in."

The money was told on the table,
  Silver bright of pounds fiftie ;
"Now, here I stand," said Willie Wallace,
  "And what hae ye to say to me ?"

He slew the captain where he stood,
  The rest they did quack an' roar ;
He slew the rest around the room,
  And ask'd if there were any more.

"Come cover the table," said Willie Wallace,
  "Come cover the table now, make haste,
For it will soon be three lang days
  Sin I a bit o' meat did taste."

The table was not well covered,
  Nor yet had he sat down to dine,
Till fifteen more of the English lords
  Surrounded the house where he was in.

The guidwife she ran butt the floor,
  And aye the guidman he ran ben ;
From eight o'clock till four at noon,
  He has kill'd full thirty men.

He put the house in sic a swither,
   That five o' them he sticket dead ;
Five o' them he drown'd in the river,
   And five hung in the West-muir wood.

Now he is on to the North-Inch gone,
   Where the maid was washing tenderlie;
"Now by my sooth," said Willie Wallace,
   "It's been a sair day's wark to me."

He's put his hand in his pocket,
   And he has pull'd out twenty pounds,
Says "Tak' ye that, ye weel-faured maid,
   For the gude luck of your half-crown."

SIR PATRICK SPENS.

(Border Minstrelsy, vol. i., p. 7.)

THE king sits in Dunfermline town,
　Drinking the blude-red wine :
'O whare will I get a skeely skipper
　To sail this new ship of mine ? '

O up and spake an eldern-knight,
　Sat at the king's right knee—
'Sir Patrick Spens is the best sailor
　That ever sail'd the sea.'

Our king has written a braid letter,
　And sealed it with his hand,
And sent it to Sir Patrick Spens,
　Was walking on the strand.

'To Noroway, to Noroway,
　To Noroway o'er the faem ;
The king's daughter of Noroway,
　'Tis thou maun bring her hame.

The first word that Sir Patrick read,
   Sac loud, loud laughed he ;
The neist word that Sir Patrick read,
   The tear blinded his e'e.

'O wha is this has done this deed,
   And tauld the king o' me,
To send us out, at this time of the year,
   To sail upon the sea?'

' Be it wind, be it weet, be it hail, be it sleet,
   Our ship must sail the faem ;
The king's daughter of Noroway,
   'Tis we must fetch her hame.'

They hoysed their sails on Monenday morn,
   Wi' a' the haste they may ;
And they hae landed in Noroway
   Upon a Wodensday.

They hadna been a week, a week,
   In Noroway but twae,
When that the lords o' Noroway
   Began aloud to say—

'Ye Scottishmen spend a' our king's goud,
   And a' our queenis fee.'
'Ye lie, ye lie, ye liars loud !
   Fu' loud I hear ye lie !

'For I brought as much white monie
  As gane my men and me,
And I brought a half-fou' o' gude red goud,
  Out o'er the sea wi' me.

'Make ready, make ready, my merry-men a'!
  Our gude ship sails the morn.'
'Now ever alake, my master dear,
  I fear a deadly storm!

'I saw the new moon, late yestreen,
  Wi' the auld moon in her arm;
And if we gang to sea, master,
  I fear we'll come to harm.'

They hadna sail'd a league, a league,
  A league but barely three,
When the lift grew dark, and the wind blew loud,
  And gurly grew the sea.

The ankers brak, and the top-masts lap,
  It was sic a deadly storm;
And the waves cam o'er the broken ship,
  Till a' her sides were torn.

'O where will I get a gude sailor,
  To take my helm in hand,
Till I get up to the tall top-mast,
  To see if I can spy land?'

'O here am I a sailor gude,
　To take the helm in hand,
Till ye get up to the tall top-mast;
　But I fear you'll ne'er spy land.'

He hadna gane a step, a step,
　A step but barely ane,
When a bolt flew out of our goodly ship,
　And the salt sea it came in.

'Gae, fetch a web o' the silken claith,
　Another o' the twine,
And wap them into our ship's side,
　And let na the sea come in.'

They fetch'd a web o' the silken claith,
　Another o' the twine,
And they wapped them round that gude ship's side,
　But still the sea came in.

O laith, laith, were our gude Scots lords
　To weet their cork-heel'd shoon!
But lang ere a' the play was play'd
　They wat their hats aboon.

And mony was the feather-bed
　That fluttered on the faem,
And mony was the gude lord's son
　That never mair cam hame.

The ladyes wrang their fingers white,
  The maidens tore their hair,
A' for the sake of their true loves,
  For them they'll see na mair.

O lang, lang may the ladyes sit,
  Wi' their fans into their hand,
Before they see Sir Patrick Spens
  Come sailing to the strand !

And lang, lang may the maidens sit,
  Wi' the goud kaims in their hair,
A' waiting for their ain dear loves !
  For them they'll see na mair.

O forty miles off Aberdour,
  'Tis fifty fathoms deep,
And there lies gude Sir Patrick Spens,
  Wi' the Scots lords at his feet.

EDOM O' GORDON.

(Aytoun, vol. i., p. 20.)

IT fell about the Martinmas,
    When the wind blew shrill and cauld,
Said Edom o' Gordon to his men,
    ' We maun draw to a hauld.

' And whatna hauld sall we draw to,
    My merry men and me ?
We will gae to the house o' the Rodes,
    To see that fair ladye.'

The ladye stood on her castle wa',
    Beheld baith dale and down ;
There she was ware of a host of men
    Were riding towards the town.

' O see ye not, my merry men a',
    O see ye not what I see ?
Methinks I see a host of men ;
    I marvel who they be.'

She ween'd it had been her lovely lord,
   As he cam' riding hame ;
It was the traitor, Edom o' Gordon,
   Wha reck'd nor sin nor shame.

She had nae sooner buskit hersell,
   And putten on her gown,
Till Edom o' Gordon an' his men
   Were round about the town.

They had nae sooner supper set,
   Nae sooner said the grace,
But Edom o' Gordon an' his men
   Were lighted about the place.

The lady ran up to her tower-head,
   As fast as she could hie,
To see if by her fair speeches
   She could wi' him agree.

'Come doun to me, ye lady gay,
   Come doun, come doun to me ;
This night sall ye lie within mine arms,
   The morn my bride sall be.'

'I winna come down, ye fause Gordon,
   I winna come down to thee ;
I winna forsake my ain dear lord,—
   That is sae far fra me.'

'Gie owre your house, ye lady fair,
  Gie owre your house to me ;
Or I sall burn yoursell therein,
  But and your babies three.'

'I winna gie owre, ye fause Gordon,
  To nae sic traitor as thee ;
And if ye burn my ain dear babes,
  My lord sall mak' ye dree.

'Now reach my pistol, Glaud, my man,
  And charge ye weel my gun ;
For, but an I pierce that bluidy butcher,
  My babes, we be undone !'

She stood upon the castle wa',
  And let twa bullets flee :
She miss'd that bluidy butcher's heart,
  And only razed his knee.

'Set fire to the house !' quo' the fause Gordon,
  All wude wi' dule and ire :
'Fause ladye, ye sall rue that shot
  As ye burn in the fire !'

'Wae worth, wae worth ye, Jock, my man !
  I paid ye weel your fee ;
Why pu' ye out the grund-wa' stane,
  Lets in the reek to me ?

'And e'en wae worth ye, Jock, my man !
 I paid ye weel your hire ;
Why pu' out the grund-wa' stane,
 To me lets in the fire ? '

'Ye paid me weel my hire, ladye,
 Ye paid me weel my fee :
But now I'm Edom o' Gordon's man,—
 Maun either do or die.'

O then bespake her youngest son,
 Sat on the nourice' knee :
Says, 'O mither dear, gie owre this house,
 For the reek it smothers me.'

'I wad gie a' my goud, my bairn,
 Sae wad I a' my fee,
For ae blast o' the western wind,
 To blaw the reek frae thee ! '

O then bespake her daughter dear,—
 She was baith jimp and sma' :
'O row me in a pair o' sheets,
 An' tow me owre the wa'.'

They row'd her in a pair o' sheets,
 And tow'd her owre the wa' ;
But on the point o' Gordon's spear
 She gat a deadly fa'.

O bonnie, bonnie was her mouth,
　　And cherry were her cheeks,
And clear, clear was her yellow hair,
　　Whereon the red blood dreeps.

Then wi' his spear he turn'd her owre ;
　　O gin her face was wan !
He said, 'Ye are the first that e'er
　　I wish'd alive again.'

He turned her owre and owre again,
　　O gin her skin was white !
' I might hae spared that bonnie face
　　To hae been some man's delight.

'Busk and boun, my merry men a',
　　For ill dooms I do guess ;—
I cannot look on that bonnie face
　　As it lies on the grass.'

' Wha looks to freits, my master dear,
　　Its freits will follow them ;
Let it ne'er be said that Edom o' Gordon
　　Was daunted by a dame.'

But when the ladye saw the fire
　　Come flaming owre her head,
She wept, and kissed her children twain,
　　Says, ' Bairns, we been but dead.'

The Gordon then his bugle blew,
   And said, 'Awa', awa' !
This house o' the Rodes is a' in a flame ;
   I hold it time to ga'.'

O then bespied her ain dear lord,
   As he came owre the lea ;
He saw his castle a' in a lowe,
   Sae far as he could see.

'Put on, put on, my wighty men,
   As fast as ye can dri'e !
For he that's hindmost o' the thrang
   Sall ne'er get gude o' me !'

Then some they rade, and some they ran,
   Fu' fast out-owre the bent ;
But ere the foremost could win up,
   Baith lady and babes were brent.

And after the Gordon he is gane,
   Sae fast as he might dri'e ;
And soon i' the Gordon's foul heart's blude
   He's wroken his fair ladye.

THE QUEEN'S MARIE.

(*Border Minstrelsy*, vol. iii., p. 91.)

MARIE HAMILTON'S to the kirk gane,
   Wi' ribbons on her hair ;
The king thought mair o' Marie Hamilton
   Than ony that were there.

Marie Hamilton's to the kirk gane,
   Wi' ribbons on her breast ;
The king thought mair o' Marie Hamilton
   Than he listen'd to the priest.

Marie Hamilton's to the kirk gane,
   Wi' gluves upon her hands ;
The king thought mair o' Marie Hamilton
   Than the queen and a' her lands.

She hadna been about the king's court
   A month, but barely one,
Till she was beloved by a' the king's court,
   And the king the only man.

She hadna been about the king's court
 A month, but barely three,
Till frae the king's court Marie Hamilton,
 Marie Hamilton durst na be.

The king is to the Abbey gane,
 To pu' the Abbey tree,
To scale the babe from Marie's heart;
 But the thing it wadna be.

O she has row'd it in her apron,
 And set it on the sea,—
"Gae sink ye, or swim ye, bonny babe,
 Ye's get na mair o' me."

Word is to the kitchen gane,
 And word is to the ha',
And word is to the noble room,
 Amang the ladyes a',
That Marie Hamilton's brought to bed,
 And the bonny babe's mist and awa'.

Scarcely had she lain down again,
 And scarcely fa'n asleep,
When up then started our gude queen,
 Just at her bed-feet;
Saying "Marie Hamilton, where's your babe?
 For I'm sure I heard it greet."

"O no, O no, my noble queen !
    Think no such thing to be ;
'Twas but a stitch into my side,
    And sair it troubles me."

"Get up, get up, Marie Hamilton,
    Get up and follow me ; .
For I am going to Edinburgh town,
    A rich wedding for to see."

O slowly, slowly raise she up,
    And slowly put she on ;
And slowly rode she out the way
    Wi' mony a weary groan.

The queen was clad in scarlet,
    Her merry maids all in green ;
And every town that they cam to,
    They took Marie for the queen.

" Ride hooly, hooly, gentlemen,
    Ride hooly now wi' me !
For never, I am sure, a wearier burd
    Rade in your cumpanie."

But little wist Marie Hamilton,
    When she rade on the brown,
That she was ga'en to Edinburgh town,
    And a' to be put down.

" Why weep ye so, ye burgess wives,
　Why look ye so on me ?
O, I am going to Edinburgh town,
　A rich wedding for to see."

When she gaed up the tolbooth stairs,
　The corks frae her heels did flee ;
And lang or e'er she cam down again,
　She was condemned to die.

When she cam to the Netherbow port,
　She laughed loud laughters three ;
But when she cam to the gallows foot,
　The tears blinded her e'e.

" Yestreen the queen had four Maries,
　The night she'll hae but three ;
There was Marie Seaton, and Marie Beaton,
　And Marie Carmichael, and me.

" O, often have I dress'd my queen,
　And put gold upon her hair ;
But now I've gotten for my reward
　The gallows to be my share ;

" Often have I dress'd my queen,
　And often made her bed ;
But now I've gotten for my reward
　The gallows tree to tread.

"O a' ye mariners far and near,
   When ye sail ower the faem,
Let neither my father nor mother get wit,
   But that I'm coming hame.

"O a' ye mariners far and near,
   That sail upon the sea,
Let neither my father nor mother get wit,
   This dog's death I'm to die.

"For if my father and mother got wit,
   And my bold brethren three,
O mickle wad be the gude red blude,
   This day wad be spilt for me !

"O little did my mother ken,
   The day she cradled me,
The lands I was to travel in,
   Or the death I was to die !"

BATTLE OF OTTERBOURNE.

(*Border Minstrelsy*, vol. i., p. 64.)

It fell about the Lammas tide,
   When the muir-men win their hay,
The doughty earl of Douglas rode
   Into England, to catch a prey.

He chose the Gordons and the Graemes,
   With them the Lindesays, light and gay ;
But the Jardines wald not with him ride,
   And they rue it to this day.

And he has burn'd the dales of Tyne,
   And part of Bambrough shire :
And three good towers on Roxburgh fells,
   He left them all on fire.

And he march'd up to Newcastle,
   And rode it round about ;
" O wha's the lord of this castle,
   Or wha's the lady o't ? "

But up spake proud Lord Percy, then,
 And O but he spake hie !
" I am the lord of this castle,
 My wife's the lady gay ? "

"If thou'rt the lord of this castle,
 Sae weel it pleases me !
For, ere I cross the border fells,
 The tane of us sall die."

He took a lang spear in his hand,
 Shod with the metal free,
And for to meet the Douglas there,
 He rode right furiouslie.

But O how pale his lady look'd,
 Frae aff the castle wa',
When down, before the Scottish spear,
 She saw proud Percy fa'.

" Had we twa been upon the green,
 And never an eye to see,
I wad hae had you, flesh and fell ;
 But your sword sall gae wi' me."

" But gae ye up to Otterbourne,
 And wait there dayis three ;
And, if I come not ere three dayis end,
 A fause knight ca' ye me."

" The Otterbourne's a bonnie burn ;
 'Tis pleasant there to be ;
But there is nought at Otterbourne,
 To feed my men and me.

" The deer rins wild on hill and dale,
 The birds fly wild from tree to tree ;
But there is neither bread nor kale,
 To fend* my men and me.

" Yet I will stay at Otterbourne,
 Where you sall welcome be ;
And, if ye come not at three dayis end,
 A fause lord I'll ca' thee."

" Thither will I come," proud Percy said,
 " By the might of Our Ladye ! "—
" There will I bide thee," said the Douglas,
 " My trowth I plight to thee."

They lighted high on Otterbourne,
 Upon the bent sae brown ;
They lighted high on Otterbourne,
 And threw their pallions down.

   * *Fend*—support.

And he that had a bonnie boy,
　Sent out his horse to grass ;
And he that had not a bonnie boy,
　His ain servant he was.

But up then spake a little page,
　Before the peep of dawn—
"O waken ye, waken ye, my good lord,
　For Percy's hard at hand."

" Ye lie, ye lie, ye liar loud !
　Sae loud I hear ye lie ;
For Percy had not men yestreen,
　To dight my men and me.

" But I hae dream'd a dreary dream,
　Beyond the Isle of Sky ;
I saw a dead man win a fight,
　And I think that man was I."

He belted on his good braid sword,
　And to the field he ran ;
But he forgot the helmet good,
　That should have kept his brain.

When Percy wi' the Douglas met,
　I wat he was fu' fain !
They swakked their swords, till sair they swat,
　And the blood ran down like rain.

But Percy with his good braid sword,
   That could so sharply wound,
Has wounded Douglas on the brow,
   Till he fell to the ground.

Then he called on his little foot-page,
   And said—"Run speedilie,
And fetch my ain dear sister's son,
   Sir Hugh Montgomery.

"My nephew good," the Douglas said,
   "What recks the death of ane !
Last night I dream'd a dreary dream,
   And I ken the day's thy ain.

"My wound is deep; I fain would sleep;
   Take thou the vanguard of the three,
And hide me by the braken bush,
   That grows on yonder lilye lee.

"O bury me by the braken bush,
   Beneath the blooming briar;
Let never living mortal ken,
   That ere a kindly Scot lies here."

He lifted up that noble lord,
   Wi' the saut tear in his e'e;
He hid him in the braken bush,
   That his merrie men might not see.

The moon was clear, the day drew near,
  The spears in flinders flew,
But mony a gallant Englishman
  Ere day the Scotsmen slew.

The Gordons good, in English blood,
  They steeped their·hose and shoon ;
The Lindesays flew like fire about,
  Till all the fray was done.

The Percy and Montgomery met,
  That either of other were fain ;
They swapped swords, and they twa swat,
  And àye the blude ran down between.

"Yield thee, O yield thee, Percy !" he said,
  " Or else I vow I'll lay thee low ! "
"Whom to sall I yield," said Earl Percy,
  " Now that I see it must be so ? "

" Thou sall't not yield to lord nor loun,
  Nor yet sall't thou yield to me ;
But yield thee to the braken bush,
  That grows upon yon lilye lee ! "

" I will not yield to a braken bush,
  Nor yet will I yield to a briar ;
But I would yield to Earl Douglas,
  Or Sir Hugh the Montgomery, if he were here."

As soon as he knew it was Montgomery,
  He stuck his sword's point in the grounde;
And the Montgomery was a courteous knight,
  And quickly took him by the hande.

This deed was done at Otterbourne,
  About the breaking of the day;
Earl Douglas was buried at the braken bush,
  And the Percy led captive away.

.   .   .   .   .

THE BATTLE OF PHILIPHAUGH.

(Border Minstrelsy.)

On Philiphaugh a fray began,
 At Hairhead-wood it ended ;
The Scots out o'er the Græmes they ran,
 Sae merrily they bended.

Sir David frae the Border came,
 Wi' heart an' hand came he ;
Wi' him three thousand bonny Scots,
 To bear him company.

Wi' him three thousand valiant men,
 A noble sight to see !
A cloud o' mist them weel conceal'd,
 As close as e'er might be.

When they came to the Shaw burn,
 Said he, " Sae weel we frame,
I think it is convenient
 That we should sing a psalm."—

When they came to the Lingly burn,
 As daylight did appear,
They spy'd an aged father,
 And he did draw them near.

"Come hither, aged father !"
 Sir David he did cry,
" And tell me where Montrose lies,
 With all his great army."—-

"But, first, you must come tell to me,
 If friends or foes you be ;
I fear you are Montrose's men,
 Come frae the north country."

"No, we are nane o' Montrose's men,
 Nor e'er intend to be ;
I am Sir David Lesly,
 That's speaking unto thee."

" If you're Sir David Lesly,
 As I think weel you be,
I am sorry ye hae brought so few
 Into your company.

" There's fifteen thousand armed men,
 Encamped on yon lee ;
Ye'll never be a bite to them,
 For aught that I can see.

" But halve your men in equal parts,
    Your purpose to fulfill ;
Let ae half keep the water side,
    The rest gae round the hill.

" Your nether party fire must,
    Then beat a flying drum ;
And then they'll think the day's their ain,
    And frae the trench they'll come ;

" Then, those that are behind them, maun
    Gie shot, baith grit and sma' ;
And so, between your armies twa,
    Ye may make them to fa'."—

" O were ye ever a soldier ? "—
    Sir David Lesly said ;
" O yes ; I was at Solway Flow,
    Where we were all betray'd.

" Again I was at curst Dunbar,
    And was a pris'ner ta'en :
And many weary night and day,
    In prison I hae lien."—

" If ye will lead these men aright,
    Rewarded sall ye be ;
But, if that ye a traitor prove,
    I'll hang thee on a tree."—

"Sir, I will not a traitor prove,
   Montrose has plunder'd me;
I'll do my best to banish him
   Away frae this country."—

He halved his men in equal parts,
   His purpose to fulfil;
The one part kept the water side,
   The other gaed round the hill.

The nether party fired brisk,
   Then turn'd and seem'd to rin;
And then they a' came frae the trench,
   And cry'd, "The day's our ain!"—

The rest then ran into the trench,
   And loosed their cannons a':
And thus, between his armies twa,
   He made them fast to fa'.

Now, let us a' for Lesly pray,
   And his brave company!
For they hae vanquish'd great Montrose,
   Our cruel enemy.

THE GALLANT GRAHAMS.

(*Border Minstrelsy.*)

Now, fáre thee well, sweet Ennerdale !
  Baith kith and countrie I bid adieu ;
For I maun away, and I may not stay,
  To some uncouth land which I never knew.

To wear the blue I think it best,
  Of all the colours that I see ;
And I'll wear it for the gallant Grahams,
  That are banished frae their countrie.

I have no gold, I have no land,
  I have no pearl nor precious stane ;
But I wald sell my silken snood,
  To see the gallant Grahams come hame.

In Wallace days, when they began,
  Sir John the Graham did bear the gree
Through all the lands of Scotland wide :
  He was a lord of the south countrie.

And so was seen full many a time :
   For the summer flowers did never spring,
But every Graham, in armour bright,
   Would then appear before the king.

They were all drest in armour sheen,
   Upon the pleasant banks of Tay ;
Before a king they might be seen,
   These gallant Grahams in their array.

At the Goukhead our camp we set,
   Our leaguer down there for to lay ;
And, in the bonny summer light,
   We rode our white horse and our gray.

Our false commander sold our king
   Unto his deadly enemie,
Who was the traitor, Cromwell, then ;
   So I care not what they do with me.

They have betray'd our noble prince,
   And banish'd him from his royal crown ;
But the gallant Grahams have ta'en in hand
   For to command those traitors down.

In Glen-Prosen we rendezvous'd,
   March'd to Glenshee by night and day,
And took the town of Aberdeen,
   And met the Campbells in their array.

Five thousand men, in armour strong,
  Did meet the gallant Grahams that day
At Inverlochie, where war began,
  And scarce two thousand men were they.

Gallant Montrose, that chieftain bold,
  Courageous in the best degree,
Did for the king fight well that day ;—
  The Lord preserve his majestie !

Nathaniel Gordon, stout and bold,
  Did for King Charles wear the blue ;
But the cavaliers they all were sold,
  And brave Harthill, a cavalier too.

And Newton Gordon, burd alone,
  And Dalgatie, both stout and keen,
And gallant Veitch upon the field,
  A braver face was never seen.

Now, fare ye weel, Sweet Ennerdale !
  Countrie and kin I quit ye free ;
Cheer up your hearts, brave cavaliers,
  For the Grahams have gone to High Germany.

Now brave Montrose he went to France,
  And to Germany, to gather fame ;
And bold Aboyne is to the sea,
  Young Huntly is his noble name.

Montrose again, that chieftain bold,
　　Back into Scotland fair he came,
For to redeem fair Scotland's land,
　　The pleasant, gallant, worthy Graham !

At the water of Carron he did begin,
　　And fought the battle to the end ;
Where there were kill'd, for our noble king,
　　Two thousand of our Danish men.

Gilbert Menzies, of high degree,
　　By whom the king's banner was borne ;
For a brave cavalier was he,
　　But now to glory he gone.

Then woe to Strachan, and Hacket baith !
　　And Leslie, ill death may thou die !
For ye have betray'd the gallant Grahams,
　　Who aye were true to majestie.

And the Laird of Assint has seized Montrose,
　　And had him into Edinburgh town ;
And frae his body taken the head,
　　And quarter'd him upon a trone.

And Huntly's gone the self-same way,
　　And our noble king is also gone ;
He suffer'd death for our nation,
　　Our mourning tears can ne'er be done.

But our brave young king is now come home,
   King Charles the Second in degree ;
The Lord send peace into his time,
   And God preserve his majestie !

THE BATTLE OF PENTLAND HILLS.

THIS BALLAD IS COPIED VERBATIM FROM THE OLD WOMAN'S
RECITATION.

THE gallant Grahams cam from the west,
Wi' their horses black as ony craw;
The Lothian lads they marched fast,
To be at the Rhyns o' Gallowa.

Betwixt Dumfries town and Argyle,
The lads they marched mony a mile;
Souters and tailors unto them drew,
Their covenants for to renew.

The Whigs, they, wi' their merry cracks,
Gar'd the poor pedlars lay down their packs;
But aye sinsyne they do repent
The renewing o' their Covenant.

At the Mauchline muir, where they were review'd,
Ten thousand men in armour show'd;
But, ere they came to the Brockie's burn,
The half of them did back return.

General Dalyell, as I hear tell,
Was our lieutenant-general;
And Captain Welsh, wi' his wit and skill,
Was to guide them on to the Pentland hill.

General Dalyell held to the hill,
Asking at them what was their will;
And who gave them this protestation,
To rise in arms against the nation?

"Although we all in armour be,
It's not against his majesty;
Nor yet to spill our neighbour's bluid,
But wi' the country we'll conclude."—

"Lay down your arms, in the king's name,
And ye shall a' gae safely hame;"—
But they a' cried out with ae consent,
"We'll fight for a broken Covenant."—

"O well," says he, "since it is so,
A wilfu' man never wanted woe."—
He gave a sign unto his lads,
And they drew up in their brigades.

The trumpets blew, and the colours flew,
And every man to his armour drew;
The Whigs were never so much aghast,
As to see their saddles toom sae fast.

The cleverest men stood in the van,
The Whigs they took their heels and ran ;
But such a raking was never seen, .
As the raking o' the Rullion Green.

THE BATTLE OF LOUDON HILL.

(Border Minstrelsy.)

YOU'LL marvel when I tell ye o'
    Our noble Burly, and his train ;
When last he march'd up through the land,
    Wi' sax-and-twenty Westland men.

Than they I ne'er o' braver heard,
    For they had a' baith wit and skill ;
They proved right well, as I heard tell,
    As they cam up o'er Loudon HilL

Weel prosper'd a' the gospel lads,
    That are into the west countrie ;
Aye wicked Claver'se to demean,
    And aye an ill deid may he die !

For he's drawn up i' the battle rank,
    An' that baith soon an' hastilie ;
But they wha live till simmer come,
    Some bludie days for this will see.

But up spak cruel Claver'se, then,
  Wi' hastie wit, an' wicked skill;
"Gae fire on yon Weslan' men;
  I think it is my sov'reign's will."—

But up bespake his cornet then,
  "It's be wi' nae consent o' me!
I ken I'll ne'er come back again,
  An' mony mae as weel as me.

"There is not ane of a' yon men,
  But wha is worthy other three;
There is na ane amang them a',
  That in his cause will stan' to die.

"An' as for Burly, him I knaw;
  He's a man of honour, birth, and fame;
Gie him a sword into his hand,
  He'll fight thysell an' other ten."—

But up spake wicked Claver'se, then,
  I wat his heart it raise fu' hie!
And he has cried that a' might hear,
  "Man, ye hae sair deceived me.

"I never ken'd the like afore,
  Na, never since I came frae hame.
That you sae cowardly here suld prove,
  An' yet come of a noble Græme."—

But up bespake his cornet, then,
    "Since that it is your honour's will,
Mysell shall be the foremost man,
    That shall gie fire on Loudon Hill—

" At your command I'll lead them on,
    But yet wi' nae consent o' me ;
For weel I ken I'll ne'er return,
    And mony mae as weel as me."—

Then up he drew his battle rank ;
    I wat he had a bonny train !
But the first time that bullets flew,
    Aye he lost twenty o' his men.

Then back he came the way he gaed,
    I wat right soon and suddenly !
He gave command amang his men,
    And sent them back, and bade them flee.

Then up came Burly, bauld an' stout,
    Wi's little train o' Westland men,
Wha mair than either aince or twice
    In Edinburgh confined had been.

They hae been up to London sent,
    An' yet they're a' come safely down ;
Sax troop o' horsemen they hae beat,
    And chased them into Glasgow town.

THE BATTLE OF BOTHWELL BRIG.

(*Border Minstrelsy.*)

"O, BILLIE, billie, bonny billie,
   Will ye go to the wood wi' me ?
We'll ca' our horse hame masterless,
   And gar them trow slain men are we."—

"O no, O no!" says Earlstoun,
   "For that's the thing that mauna be ;
For I am sworn to Bothwell Hill,
   Where I maun either gae or dee."—

So Earlstoun rose in the morning,
   An' mounted by the break o' day ;
An' he has joined our Scottish lads,
   As they were marching out the way.

"Now, farewell, father, and farewell, mother,
   And fare ye weel, my sisters three ;
An' fare ye weel, my Earlstoun,
   For thee again I'll never see !"—

So they're awa' to Bothwell Hill,
 An' waly they rode bonnily !
When the duke o' Monmouth saw them comin',
 He went to view their company.

" Ye're welcome, lads," the Monmouth said,
 " Ye're welcome, brave Scots lads, to me ;
And sae are you, brave Earlstoun,
 The foremost o' your company !

" But yield your weapons ane an' a' ;
 O yield your weapons, lads, to me ;
For gin ye'll yield your weapons up,
 Ye'se a' gae hame to your country."—

Out then spak a Lennox lad,
 And waly but he spoke bonnily !
" I winna yield my weapons up,
 To you nor nae man that I see."—

Then he set up the flag o' red,
 A' set about wi' bonny blue ;
" Since ye'll no cease, and be at peace,
 See that ye stand by ither true."—

They stell'd their cannons on the height,
 And shower'd their shot down in the howe ;
An' beat our Scots lads even down,
 Thick they lay slain on every knowe.

As e'er you saw the rain down fa',
  Or yet the arrow frae the bow—
Sae our Scottish lads fell even down,
  An' they lay slain on every knowe.

"O hold your hand," then Monmouth cry'd,
  "Gie quarters to yon men for me!"—
But wicked Claver'se swore an oath,
  His cornet's death revenged sud be.

"O hold your hand," then Monmouth cry'd,
  "If onything you'll do for me;
Hold up your hand, you curs'd Græme,
  Else a rebel to our king ye'll be."—

Then wicked Claver'se turn'd about
  I wot an angry man was he;
And he has lifted up his hat,
  And cry'd, "God bless his majesty!"

Then he's awa' to London town,
  Aye e'en as fast as he can dree;
Fause witnesses he has wi' him ta'en,
  And ta'en Monmouth's head frae his body.

Alang the brae, beyond the brig,
  Mony a brave man lies cauld and still;
But lang we'll mind, and sair we'll rue,
  The bloody battle of Bothwell Hill.

MARY AMBREE.

(*Reliques of Ancient English Poetry*, vol. ii., p. 230.)

WHEN captaines couragious, whom death cold not daunte,
Did march to the siege of the citty of Gaunt,
They mustred their souldiers by two and by three,
And the formost in battle was Mary Ambree.

When [the] brave sergeant-major was slaine in her sight,
Who was her true lover, her joy, and delight,
Because he was slaine most treacherouslie
Then vow'd to revenge him Mary Ambree.

She clothed herselfe from the top to the toe
In buffe of the bravest, most seemelye to showe;
A faire shirt of male then slipped on shee:
Was not this a brave bonny lasse, Mary Ambree?

A helmett of proofe shee strait did provide,
A stronge arminge-sword she girt by her side,
On her hand a goodly faire gauntlett putt shee;
Was not this a brave bonny lasse, Mary Ambree?

Then tooke shee her sworde and her targett in hand,
Bidding all such, as wold, [to] bee of her band;
To wayte on her person came thousand and three:
Was not this a brave bonny lasse, Mary Ambree?

"My soldiers," she saith, "soe valliant and bold,
Nowe followe your captaine, whom you doe beholde;
Still formost in battell myselfe will I bee:"
Was not this a brave bonny lasse, Mary Ambree?

Then cryed out her souldiers, and loude they did say,
"Soe well thou becomest this gallant array,
Thy harte and thy weapons so well do agree,
Noe mayden was ever like Mary Ambree."

She cheared her souldiers, that foughten for life,
With ancyent and standard, with drum and with fife;
With brave clanging trumpetts, that sounded so free;
Was not this a brave bonny lasse, Mary Ambree?

"Before I will see the worst of you all
To come into danger of death or of thrall,
This hand and this life I will venture so free:"
Was not this a brave bonny lasse, Mary Ambree?

Shee ledd upp her souldiers in battaile array,
Gainst three times theyr number by breake of the daye;
Seven howers in skirmish continued shee:
Was not this a brave bonny lasse, Mary Ambree?

She filled the skyes with the smoke of her shott,
And her enemyes bodyes with bulletts so hott;
For one of her own men a score killed shee:
Was not this a brave bonny lasse, Mary Ambree?

And when her false gunner, to spoyle her intent,
Away all her pellets and powder had sent,
Straight with her keen weapon she slasht him in three:
Was not this a brave bonny lasse, Mary Ambree?

Being falselye betrayed for lucre of hyre,
At length she was forced to make a retyre;
Then her souldiers into a strong castle drew shee:
Was not this a brave bonny lasse, Mary Ambree?

Her foes they besett her on everye side,
As thinking close siege shee cold never abide;
To beate down the walles they all did decree:
But stoutlye deffyd them brave Mary Ambree.

Then tooke shee her sword and her targett in hand,
And mounting the walls all undaunted did stand,
There daring their captaines to match any three:
O what a brave captaine was Mary Ambree!

"Now saye, English captaine, what woldest thou give
To ransome thy selfe, which else must not live?
Come yield thy selfe quicklye, or slaine thou must bee:"
Then smiled sweetlye brave Mary Ambree.

"Ye captaines couragious, of valour so bold,
Whom thinke you before you now you doe behold?"
"A knight, sir, of England, and captaine soe free,
Who shortlye with us a prisoner must be."

"No captaine of England; behold in your sight
Two brests in my bosome, and therefore no knight:
Noe knight, sirs, of England, nor captaine you see,
But a poor simple mayden called Mary Ambree."

"But art thou a woman, as thou dost declare,
Whose valor hath proved so undaunted in warre?
If England doth yield such brave maydens as thee,
Full well may they conquer, fair Mary Ambree."

The Prince of Great Parma heard of her renowne,
Who long had advanced for England's fair crowne;
Hee wooed her and sued her his mistress to bee,
And offered rich presents to Mary Ambree.

But this virtuous mayden despised them all:
"'Ile nere sell my honour for purple nor pall;
A mayden of England, sir, never will bee
The wench of a monarcke," quoth Mary Ambree.

Then to her owne country shee backe did returne,
Still holding the foes of faire England in scorne;
Therfore English captaines of every degree
Sing forth the brave valours of Mary Ambree.

Ballads of Robin Hood.

" Lytil John and Robyn Hude
Waithmen ware commendyd gude,
In Yngilwode and Barnys-dale
Thai oysyd all this time thare travale."

Weyntoun's " Scottish Chronicle,"
about 1420.

ROBIN HOOD RESCUING THE WIDOW'S THREE SONS.

(Allingham, p. 110.)

THERE are twelve months in all the year,
   As I hear many say,
But the merriest month in all the year
   Is the merry month of May.

Now Robin Hood is to Nottingham gone,
   With a link a down, and a day,
And there he met a silly old woman,
   Was weeping on the way.

'What news? what news? thou silly old woman,
   What news hast thou for me?'
Said she, 'There's my three sons in Nottingham town
   To-day condemned to die.'

'O, have they parishes burnt?' he said,
   'Or have they ministers slain?
Or have they robbed any virgin?
   Or other men's wives have ta'en?'

'They have no parishes burnt, good sir,
    Nor yet have ministers slain,
Nor have they robbed any virgin,
    Nor other men's wives have ta'en.'

'O, what have they done?' said Robin Hood,
    'I pray thee tell to me.'
'It's for slaying of the king's fallow deer,
    Bearing their long bows with thee.'

'Dost thou not mind, old woman,' he said,
    'How thou madest me sup and dine?
By the truth of my body,' quo bold Robin Hood,
    'You could not tell it in better time.'

Now Robin Hood is to Nottingham gone,
    With a link and a down, and a day,
And there he met with a silly old palmer
    Was walking along the highway.

'What news? what news? thou silly old man,
    What news, I do thee pray?'
Said he, 'Three squires in Nottingham town
    Are condemn'd to die this day.'

'Come change thy apparel with me, old man,
    Come change thy apparel for mine;
Here is ten shillings in good silvèr,
    Go drink it in beer or wine.'

'O, thine apparel is good,' he said,
    'And mine is ragged and torn ;
Wherever you go, wherever you ride,
    Laugh not an old man to scorn.'

'Come change thy apparel with me, old churl,
    Come change thy apparel with mine ;
Here is a piece of good broad gold,
    Go feast thy brethren with wine.'

Then he put on the old man's hat,
    It stood full high on the crown :
'The first bold bargain that I come at,
    It shall make thee come down.'

Then he put on the old man's cloak,
    Was patch'd black, blue, and red ;
He thought it no shame, all the day long,
    To wear the bags of bread.

Then he put on the old man's breeks,
    Was patch'd from leg to side :
'By the truth of my body,' bold Robin can say,
    'This man loved little pride.'

Then he put on the old man's hose,
    Were patch'd from knee to wrist :
'By the truth of my body,' said bold Robin Hood,
    'I'd laugh if I had any list.'

Then he put on the old man's shoes,
　　Were patch'd both beneath and aboon;
Then Robin Hood swore a solemn oath,
　　'It's good habit that makes a man.'

Now Robin Hood is to Nottingham gone,
　　With a link a down and a down,
And there he met with the proud sheriff,
　　Was walking along the town.

'Save you, save you, sheriff!' he said;
　　'Now heaven you save and see!
And what will you give to a silly old man
　　To-day will your hangman be?'

'Some suits, some suits,' the sheriff he said,
　　'Some suits I'll give to thee;
Some suits, some suits, and pence thirteen,
　　To-day's a hangman's fee.'

Then Robin he turns him round about,
　　And jumps from stock to stone:
'By the truth of my body,' the sheriff he said,
　　'That's well jumpt, thou nimble old man.'

'I was ne'er a hangman in all my life,
　　Nor yet intends to trade;
But curst be he,' said bold Robin,
　　'That first a hangman was made!

' I've a bag for meal, and a bag for malt,
  And a bag for barley and corn ;
A bag for bread, and a bag for beef,
  And a bag for my little small horn. '

' I have a horn in my pockèt,
  I got it from Robin Hood,
And still when I set it to my mouth,
  For thee it blows little good.'

' O, wind thy horn, thou proud fellòw !
  Of thee I have no doubt.
I wish that thou give such a blast,
  Till both thy eyes fall out.'

The first loud blast that he did blow,
  He blew both loud and shrill ;
A hundred and fifty of Robin Hood's men
  Came riding over the hill.

The next loud blast that he did give,
  He blew both loud and amain,
And quickly sixty of Robin Hood's men
  Came shining over the plain.

' O, who are those,' the sheriff he said,
  ' Come tripping over the lee ? '
' They're my attendants,' brave Robin did say ;
  ' They'll pay a visit to thee.'

They took the gallows from the slack,
　　They set it in the glen,
They hanged the proud sheriff on that,
　　Released their own three men.

A LYTELL GESTE OF ROBYN HODE.

The Firste Fytte.

[*How Robin lent a poor Knight four hundred pounds.*]

(Allingham, p. 159.)

LITHE and lysten, gentylmen,
   That be of frebore blode;
I shall you tell of a good yemàn,
   His name was Robyn Hode.

Robyn was a proude outlawe,
   Whyles he walked on grounde,
So curteyse an outlawe as he was one
   Was never none yfounde.

Robyn stode in Barnysdale,
   And lened hym to a tree,
And by hym stode Lytell Johan,
   A good yeman was he;

And also dyd good Scathelock,
   And Much the miller's sone;
There was no ynche of his body,
   But it was worthe a grome.

Then bespake him Lytell Johan
   All unto Robin Hode,
'Mayster, yf ye wolde dyne betyme,
   It wolde do you moch good.'

Then bespake good Robyn,
   'To dyne I have no lust,
Tyll I have some bolde baròn,
   Or some unketh guest,

'[Or els some byshop or abbot]
   That may paye for the best;
Or some knyght or some squyere
   That dwelleth here by west.'

A good maner than had Robyn,
   In londe where that he were:
Every daye or he woulde dyne
   Thre messes wolde he here.

Robyn loved Our Dere Lady;
   For doute of dedely synne
Wolde he never do company harme
   That ony woman was ynne.

'Mayster,' than sayd Lytell Johan,
   'And we our borde shall sprede,
Tell us whither we shall gone,
   And what lyfe we shall lede;

' Where we shall take, where we shall leve,
    Where we shall abide behynde,
Where we shall robbe, where we shall reve,
    Where we shall bete and bynde.'

' Thereof no fors,' sayd Robyn,
    ' We shall do well enow ;
But loke ye do no housbonde harme
    That tylleth with his plough ;

' No more ye shall no good yemàn,
    That walketh by grene wode shawe,
Ne no knyght, ne no squyèr,
    That wolde be a good felawe.

' These yalhoppes, and thyse archebysshoppes,
    Ye shall them bete and bynde ;
The hye sheryfe of Notynghame,
    Hym holde in your mynde.'

' This worde shall be holde,' sayd Lytyll Johan,
    ' And this lesson shall we lere ;
It is ferre dayes, god sende us a guest,
    That we were at our dynere.'

' Take thy good bowe in thy hande,' said Robyn,
    ' Let Moche wende with the,
And so shall Wyllyam Scathelocke,
    And no man abyde with me :

'And walke up to the Sayles,
　And so to Watlynge-strete,
And wayte after some unketh guest,
　Up-chaunce ye mowe them mete.

'Be he erle or ony baròn,
　Abbot or ony knyght,
Brynge hym to lodge to me,
　Hys dyner shall be dyght.'

They wente unto the Sayles,
　These yemen all thre,
They loked est, they loked west,
　They myght no man see.

But as they loked in Barnysdale,
　By a derne strete
Then came there a knyght rydynge,
　Full sone they gan hym mete.

All dreri then was his semblaunte,
　And lytell was hys pryde,
Hys one fote in the sterope stode,
　That other waved besyde.

Hys hode hangynge over hys eyen two,
　He rode in symple aray ;
A soryer man than he was one
　Rode never in somers-day.

Lytell Johan was curteyse,
  And set hym on his kne:
'Welcome be ye, gentyll knyght,
  Welcome are you to me;

' Welcome be thou to grene wood,
  Hende knyght and fre ;
My mayster hath abyden you fastynge,
  Syr, all these oures thre.'

'Who is your mayster?' sayd the knyght,
  Johan sayd, ' Robyn Hode.'
' He is a good yeman,' sayd the knyght,
  'Of hym I have herde moch good.

' I graunte,' he sayd, 'with you to wende,
  My brethren all in-fere ;
My purpose was to have deyned to day
  At Blythe or Dankastere.'

Forthe than went this gentyll knyght,
  With a carefull chere,
The teres out of his eyen ran,
  And fell downe by his lere.

They brought hym unto the lodge dore ;
  When Robyn gan hym se,
Full curteysly dyd of his hode,
  And set hym on his kne.

'Welcome, syr knyght,' then said Robyn,
  'Welcome thou art to me;
I haue abyde you fastynge, syr,
  All these houres thre.'

Then answered the gentyll knyght,
  With wordes fayre and fre,
'God the save, good Robyn,
  And all thy fayre meynè!'

They washed togyder and wyped bothe,
  And set tyll theyr dynere;
Brede and wyne they had ynough,
  And nombles of the dere;

Swannes and fesauntes they had full good,
  And foules of the rivere;
There fayled never so lytell a byrde,
  That ever was bred on brere.

'Do gladly, syr knyght,' said Robyn.
  'Gramercy, syr,' sayd he,
'Suche a dyner had I not
  Of all these wekes thre:

'If I come agayne, Robyn,
  Here by this countrè,
As good a dyner I shall thee make,
  As thou hast made to me.'

'Gramercy, knyght,' sayd Robyn,
   'My dyner whan I have,
I was never so gredy [I swear to thee],
    My dyner for to crave.

'But pay or ye wende,' sayd Robyn,
   'Me thynketh it is good ryght ;
It was never the maner, by my troth,
   A yeman to pay for a knyght.'

'I have nought in my cofers,' said the knyght,
   'That I may profer for shame.'
'Lytell Johan, go loke,' sayd Robyn,
   'Ne let not for no blame.

'Tell me trouth,' sayd Robyn,
   'So god have parte of thee,'
'I have no more but ten shillings,' sayd the knyght,
   'So god have parte of me.'

'Yf thou have no more,' sayd Robyn,
   'I will not one peny ;
And yf thou have nede of ony more,
   More shall I len thee.

'Go now forth, Lytell Johan,
   The trouthe tell thou me :
Yf there be no more but ten shillings,
   Not one peny that I se.'

24

Lytell Johan spred downe his mantèll
  Full fayre upon the grounde,
And there he founde in the knyghtes cofer
  But even halfe a pounde.

Lytyll Johan let it lye full styll,
  And went to his mayster full lowe.
'What tydynge, Johan?' sayd Robyn.
  'Syr, the knyght is trewe inough.'

'Fyll of the best wyne,' sayd Robyn,
  'The knyght shall begynne;
Moch wonder thynketh me
  Thy clothynge is so thynne.

'Tell me one worde,' sayd Robyn,
  'And counsell shall it be;
I trowe thou were made a knyght of forse,
  Or elles of yemanry;

'Or elles thou hast ben a sory housband,
  And leved in stroke and stryfe;
An okerer, or elles a lechoure,' sayd Robyn,
  'With wronge hast thou lede thy lyfe.'

'I am none of them,' sayd the knyght,
  'By [him] that made me:
An hondreth wynter here before,
  Myne aunsetters knyghtes have be.

'But ofte it hath befal, Robyn,
   A man hath be dysgrate;
But [he] that syteth in heven above
   May amend his state.

'Within two or thre yere, Robyn,' he sayd,
   'My neyghbores well it kende,
Foure hondreth pounde of good money
   Full wel than myght I spende.

'Now have I no good,' sayd the knyght,
   'But my chyldren and my wyfe;
God hath shapen such an ende,
   Tyll it may amende my lyfe.'

'In what maner,' sayd Robyn,
   'Hast thou lore thy richès?'
'For my grete foly,' he sayd,
   'And for my kindenesse.

'I had a sone, for soth, Robyn,
   That sholde have ben my eyre,
When he was twenty wynter olde,
   In felde wolde juste full feyre;

'He slewe a knyght of Lancastshyre,
   And a squyre bold;
For to save hym in his ryght
   My goodes beth sette and solde;

'My londes beth set to wedde, Robyn,
  Untyll a certayne daye,
To a ryche abbot here besyde,
  Of Saynt Mary abbay.'

'What is the somme?' sayd Robyn,
  'Trouthe than tell thou me.'
'Syr,' he sayd, 'foure hondred pounde,
  The abbot tolde it to me.'

'Now, and thou lese thy londe,' sayd Robyn,
  'What shall fall of thee?'
'Hastely I wyll me buske,' sayd the knyght,
  'Over the salte see,

'And se where Cryst was quycke and deed,
  On the mounte of Calvarè,
Fare well, frende, and have good daye,
  It may noo better be—'

Teeres fell out of his eyen two,
  He wolde haue gone his waye—
'Farewell, frendes, and have good day;
  I ne have more to say.'

'Where be thy frendes?' sayd Robyn.
  'Syr, never one wyll me know;
Whyle I was ryche inow at home,
  Grete bost then wolde they blowe,

'And now they renne awaye fro me,
　As bestes on a rawe ;
They take no more heed of me
　Then they me never sawe.'

For ruthe then wept Lytell Johan,
　Scathelocke, and Much in fere.
'Fyll of the best wyne,' sayd Robyn,
　'For here is a symple chere.

'Has thou ony frendes,' said Robyn,
　'Thy borowes that wyll be ? '
'[None other] but Our Dere Lady ;
　She [never hath] fayled me.'

'Now by my hand,' said Robyn,
　'To serche all Englond thorowe,
Yet founde I never to my pay,
　A moch better borowe.

'Come now forthe, Lytell Johan,
　And goo to my tresourè,
And brynge me foure hondred pounde,
　And loke that it well tolde be.'

Forthe then wente Lytell Johan,
　And Scathelocke went before,
He tolde out foure hondred pounde,
　By two and twenty score.

' Is this well tolde?' sayd lytell Much.
　　Johan sayd, 'What greveth thee?
It is almes to helpe a gentyll knyght
　　That is fall in povertè.'

' Mayster,' then sayd Lytell Johan,
　' His clothynge is full thynne;
Ye must gyve the knyght a lyveray,
　　To lappe his body ther in.

' For ye have scarlet and grene, mayster,
　　And many a ryche aray;
There is no marchaunt in mery Englònde
　　So ryche, I dare well saye.'

' Take hym thre yerdes of every coloure,
　　And loke that well mete it be.'
Lytell Johan toke none other mesure
　　But his bowe tre,

And of every handfull that he met
　　He lept over fotes thre.
'What devilkyns draper,' sayd litell Much,
　　'Thynkyst thou to be?'

Scathelocke stoode full styll and lough,
　　[And swore it was but right];
Johan may give hym the better mesure
　　It costeth him but lyght.

'Mayster,' sayd Lytell Johan,
   All unto Robyn Hode,
'Ye must gyve that knight an hors,
   To lede home.al this good.'

'Take hym a gray courser,' sayd Robyn,
   'And a sadell newe ;
He is our ladyes messengere,
   [I hope] that he be true.'

'And a good palfraye,' sayd lytell Much,
   'To mayntayne hym in his ryght.'
'And a payre of botes,' sayd Scathelocke,
   'For he is a gentyll knyght.'

'What shalt thou gyve hym, Lytel Johan ?' sayd Robyn.
   'Syr, a payre of gylte spurres clene,
To pray. for all this company—
   God brynge hym out of tene !'

'Whan shall my day be,' sayd the knyght,
   'Syr, and your wyll be ?'
'This daye twelve moneth,' sayd Robyn,
   'Under this grene wode tre.

'It were grete shame,' sayd Robyn,
   'A knyght alone to ryde,
Without squyer, yeman, or page,
   To walke by hys syde.

'I shall thee lene Lytyll Johan my man,
For he shall be thy knave;
In a yemen's steed he may thee stonde,
Yf thou grete nede have.'

ROBIN HOOD'S DEATH AND BURIAL.

(Allingham, p. 280.)

WHEN Robin Hood and Little John,
  Down a down, a down, a down,
Went o'er yon bank of broom,
Said Robin Hood to Little John,
  'We have shot for many a pound :
  Hey down, a down, a down.

' But I am not able to shoot one shot more,
  My arrows will not flee ;
But I have a cousin lives down below,
  Please God, she will bleed me.'

Now Robin is to fair Kirkley gone,
  As fast as he can win ;
But before he came there, as we do hear,
  He was taken very ill.

And when that he came to fair Kirkley-hall,
  He knock'd all at the ring,
But none was so ready as his cousin herself
  For to let bold Robin in.

'Will you please to sit down, cousin Robin,' she said,
  'And drink some beer with me?'
'No, I will neither eat nor drink
  Till I am blooded by thee.'

'Well, I have a room, cousin Robin,' she said,
  'Which you did never see,
And if you please to walk therein,
  You blooded by me shall be.'

She took him by the lily-white hand,
  And led him to a private room,
And there she blooded bold Robin Hood,
  Whilst one drop of blood would run.

She blooded him in the vein of the arm,
  And locked him up in the room;
There did he bleed all the live-long day,
  Until the next day at noon.

He then bethought him of a casement door,
  Thinking for to be gone;
He was so weak he could not leap,
  Nor he could not get down.

He then bethought him of his bugle-horn,
  Which hung low down to his knee;
He set his horn unto his mouth,
  And blew out weak blasts three.

Then Little John, when hearing him,
   As he sat under the tree,
' I fear my master is near dead,
   He blows so wearily.'

Then Little John to fair Kirkley is gone,
   As fast as he can dri'e ;
But when he came to Kirkley-hall,
   He broke locks two or three:

Until he came bold Robin to,
   Then he fell on his knee ;
' A boon, a boon,' cries Little John,
   ' Master, I beg of thee.'

' What is that boon,' quoth Robin Hood,
   ' Little John, thou begs of me ? '
' It is to burn fair Kirkley-hall,
   And all their nunnery.'

'Now nay, now nay,' quoth Robin Hood,
   ' That boon I'll not grant thee ;
I never hurt woman in all my life,
   Nor man in woman's company.

' I never hurt fair maid in all my time,
   Nor at my end shall it be ;
But give me my bent bow in my hand,
   And a broad arrow I'll let flee ;

And where this arrow is taken up,
   There shall my grave digg'd be.

' Lay me a green sod under my head,
   And another at my feet ;
And lay my bent bow by my side,
   Which was my music sweet ;
And make my grave of gravel and green,
   Which is most right and meet.

' Let me have length and breadth enough,
   With a green sod under my head ;
That they may say, when I am dead,
   Here lies bold Robin Hood.'

These words they readily promis'd him,
   Which did bold Robin please ;
And there they buried bold Robin Hood,
   Near to the fair Kirklèys.

Comic, or Humorous.

———◆———

GET UP AND BAR THE DOOR.

(Pinkerton's *Scottish Ballads*, vol. ii., p. 150.)

IT fell about the Martinmas time,
 And a gay time it was than,
That our gudewife had puddings to mak,
 And she boil'd them in the pan.

The wind blew cauld frae east and north,
 And blew into the floor;
Quoth our gudeman to our gudewife,
 "Get up and bar the door."

"My hand is in my hussyskep,
 Goodman, as ye may see;
An it should na be barred this hunder year,
 It's ne'er be barr'd by me."

They made a paction 'tween them twa,
 They made it firm and sure,
That the first word whoever spak,
 Should rise and bar the door.

Than by there come twa gentlemen
  At twelve o'clock at night,
Whan they can see na ither house ;
  And at the door they light.

"Now whether is this a rich man's house,
  Or whether is it a poor?"
But ne'er a word would ane o' them speak
  For barring of the door.

And first they ate the white puddings,
  And syne they ate the black :
Muckle thought the gudewife to hersell,
  Yet ne'er a word she spak.

Then ane unto the ither said,
  "Here, man, tak ye my knife,
Do ye tak aff the auld man's beard ;
  And I'll kiss the gudewife."

"But there's na water in the house,
  And what shall we do than?"
"What ails ye at the pudding-bree
  That boils into the pan?"

O up then started our gudeman,
  An angry man was he ;
"Will ye kiss my wife before my een,
  And scald me wi' pudding-bree?"

O up then started our gudewife,
   Gied three skips on the floor;
"Gudeman you have spak the first word,
   Get up and bar the door."

THE GRAY COCK.

(Pinkerton's *Scottish Ballads*, vol. ii., p. 153.)

"O SAW ye my father, or saw ye my mither,
    Or saw ye my true-love John?"
"I saw nae your father, I saw nae your mither,
    But I saw your true-love John."

"It's now ten at night, and the stars gie na light,
    And the bells they ring, ding, dang;
He's met wi' some delay, that causes him to stay,
    But he will be here ere lang."

The surly auld carl did naithing but snarl,
    And Johny's face it grew red;
Yet tho' he often sigh'd, he ne'er a word replied,
    Till a' were asleep in bed.

Then up Johny rose, and to the door he goes,
    And gently tirled the pin;
The lassie taking tent, unto the door she went,
    And she opened and lat him in.

" And are ye come at last, and do I hold ye fast ?
   And is my Johny true ? "
" I have nae time to tell ; but sae lang's I like mysel',
   Sae lang sall I like you."

" Flee, flee up, my bonny gray cock,
   And craw whan it is day ;
And your neck sall be like the bonny beaten gold,
   And your wings of the silver gray ! "

The cock prov'd false, and untrue he was,
   For he crew an hour owre soon ;
The lassie thought it day when she sent her love away,
   And it was but a blink of the moon.

BELL, MY WIFFE.

(Bishop Percy's Folio MS.   Hales and Furnivall.)

THIS winter's weather it waxeth cold,
And frost it freezeth on every hill,
And Boreas blowes his blasts soe bold
That all our cattle are like to spill.
Bell my wiffe, she loves noe strife,
She said unto me quietlye,
" Rise up, and save Cow Crumbocke's liffe !
Man ! put thine old cloake about thee ! "

" O Bell, my wiffe ! why dost thou flyte ?
Thou kens my cloake is very thin ;
It is soe sore over-worne,
A cricke thereon cannot run :
I'll goe find the court within,
I'll noe longer lend nor borrow ;
I'll goe find the court within,
For I'll have a new cloake about me."

"Cow Crumbocke is a very good cow,
She has always been good to the pail,
She has helped us to butter and cheese, I trow,
And other things she will not fail ;

For I would be loth to see her pine ;
Therefore, good husband, follow my counsel now,
Forsake the court and follow the plough ;
Man ! take thine old cloake about thee ! "

" My cloake it was a very good cloake,
It hath beene always good to the weare,
It hath cost me many a groat,
I have had it this forty-four yeare ;
Sometime it was of the cloth in graine,
It is now but a sigh* clout, as you may see :
It will neither hold out winde nor raine ;
And I'll have a new cloake about me."

" It is forty-four years agoe
Since the one of us the other did ken,
And we have had betwixt us both,
Children either nine or ten ;
We have brought them up to women and men,
In the feare of God I trow they be ;
And why wilt thou thy selfe misken?
Man ! take thine old cloake about thee ! "

" O Bell, my wiffe ! why dost thou flyte ?
Now is now, and then was then ;
Seek all the world now throughout,
Thou kens not clowns from gentlemen ;
They are clad in black, green, yellow, and blue,
So far above their own degree ;
Once in my liffe I'll take a vew,
For I'll have a new cloake about me."

* Sigh—sorry.

"King Harry was a verry good king;
I trow his hose cost but a crowne;
He thought them twelve-pence over too deare,
Therefore he called the taylor clowne.
He was king and wore the crowne,
And thoust but of a low degree;
It's pride that puts this countrye downe;
Man! put thine old cloake about thee!"

"O Bell, my wiffe! why dost thou flyte?
Now is now, and then was then;
We will live now obedient liffe,
Thou the woman, and I the man.
It's not for a man with a woman to threape,
Unlesse he first give over the play;
We will live now as we began,
And I'll have mine old cloake about me."

OUR GUDEMAN.

(Aytoun, vol. i., p. 125.)

Our gudeman cam' hame at e'en,
　And hame cam' he ;
And there he saw a saddle horse.
　Whare nae horse should be.
"O how cam' this horse here ?
　How can this be ?
How cam this horse here,
　Without the leave o' me ?"
　　"A horse !" quo' she :
　　"Ay, a horse !" quo' he.
"Ye auld blind doited carle,
　Blind mat ye be !
'Tis naething but a bonny milk cow
　My minnie sent to me."
　　"A bonny milk cow !" quo' he ;
　　"Ay, a milk cow," quo' she.
"Far hae I ridden,
　And meikle hae I seen,
But a saddle on a cow's back
　Saw I never nane !"

Our gudeman cam' hame at e'en,
　And hame cam' he ;
He spy'd a pair o' jack-boots
　Whare nae boots should be.

" What's this now, gudewife ?
 What's this I see ?
How cam these boots here,
 Without the leave o' me ? "
  " Boots ! " quo' she ;
  " Ay, boots," quo' he.
" Shame fa' your cuckold face,
 And ill mat ye see ;
It's but a pair o' water-stoups
 The cooper sent to me."
  "Water-stoups ! " quo' he ;
  " Ay, water-stoups," quo' she.
"Far hae I ridden,
 And far'er hae I gane,
But siller spurs on water-stoups
 Saw I never nane ! "

Our gudeman cam' hame at e'en,
 And hame cam' he :
And there he saw a sword
 Where a sword should nae be.
" What's this now, gudewife ?
 " What's this I see ?
O how cam' this sword here,
 Without the leave o' me ?
  " A sword ! " quo' she ;
  " Ay, a sword," quo' he.
" Shame fa' your cuckold face,
 And ill mat ye see ;
It's but a parritch spurtle
 My minnie sent to me."
  " A spurtle ! " quo' he,
  " Ay, a spurtle," quo' she.

" Weel—far hae I ridden,
  And meikle hae I seen,
But siller-handled spurtles
  Saw I never nane !"

Our gudeman cam' hame at e'en,
  And hame cam' he ;
There he spy'd a pouther'd wig
  Whare nae wig should be.
" What's this now, gudewife ?
  What's this I see ?
How cam' this wig here,
  Without the leave o' me ?"
    " A wig !" quo' she ;
    " Ay, a wig," quo' he.
" Shame fa' your cuckold face,
  And ill mat ye see ;
'Tis naething but a clocken hen
  My minnie sent to me."
    " Clocken hen !" quo' he :
    " Ay, clocken hen," quo' she.
" Far hae I ridden,
  And meikle hae I seen,
But pouther on a clocken hen
  Saw I never nane !"

Our gudeman cam' hame at e'en,
  And hame cam' he ;
And there he saw a riding coat,
  Where nae coat should be.

"O how cam' this coat here?
   How can this be?
How cam' this coat here,
   Without the leave o' me?"
      "A coat!" quo' she;
      "Ay, a coat," quo' he
"Ye auld blind doited carle,
   Blind mat ye be;
It's but a pair o' blankets
   My minnie sent to me."
      "Blankets!" quo' he;
      "Ay, blankets," quo' she.
"Far hae I ridden,
   And meikle hae I seen,
But buttons upon blankets
   Saw I never nane!"

Ben went our gudeman,
   And ben went he;
And there he spy'd a sturdy man,
   Whare nae man should be.
"How cam' this man here?
   How can this be?
How cam' this man here,
   Without the leave o' me?"
      "A man!" quo' she;
      "Ay, a man," quo' he.
"Puir blind body,
   And blinder mat ye be:
It's a new milking maid
   My mither sent to me."
      "A maid!" quo' he:
      "Ay, a maid," quo' she.

" Far hae I ridden,
    And meikle hae I seen,
But lang-bearded maidens
    Saw I never nane ! "

THE LOCHMABEN HARPER.

(Border Minstrelsy.)

O HEARD ye na o' the silly blind Harper,
   How long he lived in Lochmaben toun?
And how he wad gang to fair England,
   To steal the lord Warden's Wanton Broun?

But first he gaed to his gude wyfe,
   Wi' a' the haste that he could thole—
"This wark," quo' he, "will ne'er gae weel,
   Without a mare that has a foal."—

Quo' she, "Thou hast a gude grey mare,
   That can baith lance o'er laigh and hie;
Sae set thee on the gray mare's back,
   And leave the foal at hame wi' me."—

So he is up to England gane,
   And even as fast as he may drie;
And when he cam to Carlisle gate,
   O whae was there but the Warden hie?

"Come into my hall, thou silly blind Harper,
  And of thy harping let me hear ! "—
"O, by my sooth," quo' the silly blind Harper,
  "I wad rather hae stabling for my mare."—

The Warden look'd ower his left shoulder,
  And said unto his stable groom—
"Gae take the silly blind Harper's mare,
  And tie her beside my Wanton Brown."

Then aye he harped, and aye he carped,
  Till a' the lordlings footed the floor ;
But an the music was sae sweet,
  The groom had nae mind o' the stable door.

And aye he harped, and aye he carped,
  Till a' the nobles were fast asleep ;
Then quickly he took aff his shoon,
  And saftly down the stair did creep.

Syne to the stable door he hied,
  Wi' tread as light as light could be ;
And when he open'd and gaed in,
  There he fand thirty steeds and three.

He took a cowt halter frae his hose,
  And o' his purpose he didna fail ;
He slipt it ower the Wanton's nose,
  And tied it to his gray mare's tail.

He turn'd them loose at the castle gate,
　　Ower muir and moss and ilka dale ;
And she ne'er let the Wanton bait,
　　But kept him a-galloping hame to her foal.

The mare she was right swift o' foot,
　　She didna fail to find the way ;
For she was at Lochmaben gate
　　A lang three hours before the day.

When she cam to the Harper's door,
　　There she gave mony a nicher and a sneer*--
" Rise up," quo' the wife, "thou lazy lass ;
　　Let in thy master and his mare."—

Then up she rose, put on her clothes,
　　And keekit through at the lock-hole—
" O ! by my sooth," then cried the lass,
　　" Our mare has gotten a braw brown foal ! "—

" Come, haud thy tongue, thou silly wench !
　　The morn's but glancing in your ee."—
" I'll wad my hail fee againt a groat,
　　He's bigger than e'er our foal will be."—

Now all this while in merry Carlisle
　　The Harper harped to hie and law ;
And fiend thing dought they do but listen him to,
　　Until that day began to daw.

　　　　* Nicher and sneer—Neigh and snort.

But on the morn at fair daylight,
   When they had ended a' their cheer,
Behold the Wanton Brown was gane,
   And eke the poor blind Harper's mare!

"Allace! allace!" quo' the cunning auld Harper,
   "And ever allace that I cam here;
In Scotland I hae lost a braw cowt foal,
   In England they've stown my gude grey mare!"—

"Come! cease thy allacing, thou silly blind Harper,
   And of thy harping let us hear;
And weel payd sall thy cowt-foal be,
   And thou sall have a far better mare."—

Then aye he harped, and aye he carped;
   Sae sweet were the harping he let them hear!
He was paid for the foal he had never lost,
   And three times ower for the gude GREY MARE.

Lullabies and Nursery Ballads.

" Oh my deir hert, young Jesus sweit,
Prepare thy creddil in my spreit,
And I sall rock thee in my kert,
And never mair from thee depart.

But I sall praise thee evermoir,
With sangis sweit unto thy gloir;
The knees of my hert sall I bow,
And sing that richt Ballua·ow !"

From " Ane Compendious Book of Godly
and Spiritual Sangs." (Published
by Andro Hart, 1621.)

———◦◆◦———

LULLABIES.

(Chambers's *Popular Rhymes*, pp. 44-50.)

HUSHIE ba, burdie becton !
Your mammie's gane to Seaton
For to buy a lammie's skin
To wrap your bonnie boukie in.

———

BYE, babie buntin',
Your daddie's gane a huntin';
Your mammie's gane to buy a skin
To row the baby buntin' in.

———

O, CAN ye sew cushions,
   Can ye sew sheets,
Can ye sing, Ba-loo-loo,
   When the bairnie greets?

And hee and ba, birdie,
   And hee and ba, lamb;
And hee and ba, birdie,
   My bonnie lamb !

Hee O, wee O,
    What wad I do wi' you?
Black is the life
    That I lead wi' you.

Ower mony o' you,
    Little for to gie you ;
Hee O, wee O,
    What wad I do wi' you?

———

Hush and baloo, babie,
    Hush and baloo ;
A' the laves in their beds—
    I'm hushin' you.

THE CATTIE SITS IN THE KILN-RING SPINNING.

(Chambers's *Popular Rhymes.*)

THE cattie sits in the kiln-ring,
    Spinning, spinning ;
And by cam a little wee mousie,
    Rinning, rinning.

" Oh, what's that you're spinning, my loesome,
    Loesome lady ? "
" I'm spinning a sark to my young son,"
    Said she, said she.

" Weel mot he brook it, my loesome,
    Loesome lady."
" Gif he dinna brook it weel, he may brook it ill,"
    Said she, said she.

" I soopit my house, my loesome,
    Loesome lady."
" 'Twas a sign ye didna sit amang dirt then,"
    Said she, said she.

" I fand twall pennies, my winsome,
  Winsome lady."
" 'Twas a sign ye warna sillerless,"
  Said she, said she.

" I gaed to the market, my loesome,
  Loesome lady."
" 'Twas a sign ye didna sit at hame then,"
  Said she, said she.

" I coft a sheepie's head, my winsome,
  Winsome lady."
" 'Twas a sign ye warna kitchenless,"
  Said she, said she.

" I put it in my pottie to boil, my loesome,
  Loesome lady."
" 'Twas a sign ye didna eat it raw,"
  Said she, said she.

" I put it in my winnock to cool, my winsome,
  Winsome lady."
" 'Twas a sign ye didna burn your chafts then,"
  Said she, said she.

" By cam a cattie, and ate it a' up, my loesome,
  Loesome lady."
" And sae will I you—worrie, worrie, gnash, gnash,"
  Said she, said she.

THERE was a guse,
They ca'd it Luce,
Was paidlin' in a pool-ie;
  By came a tod,
  Wi' mony a nod,
And bad it till it's Yool-ie.

He took her hame,
And [made her warm],
And pat her on a stool-ie;
  He singet her claes,
  And burnt her claes,
And gar'd her look like a fool-ie!

THE WEE CROODLEN DOO.

(Chambers's *Popular Rhymes.*)

"WHARE hae ye been a' the day,
  My little wee croodlen doo?"
"Oh, I've been at my grandmother's,
  Mak my bed, mammie, noo!"

" What gat ye at your grandmother's,
  My little wee croodlen doo? "
" I gat a bonny wee fishie,
  Make my bed, mammie, noo! "

" Oh, whare did she catch the fishie,
  My bonnie wee croodlen doo? "
" She catch'd it in the gutter-hole,
  Mak my bed, mammie, noo! "

" And what did you do wi' the banes o't,
  My bonnie wee croodlen doo? "
" I gied them to my little dog,
  Mak my bed, mammie, noo! "

" And what did the little doggie do,
  My little wee croodlen doo? "
" He stretched out his head, and his feet, and dee'd,
  As I do, mammie, noo!"

A NURSERY SONG.

(Chambers's *Popular Rhymes.*)

WHEN I was a wee thing,
    'Bout six or seven year auld,
I had no worth a petticoat,
    To keep me frae the cauld.

Then I went to Edinburgh,
    To bonny burrows toun,
And there I got a petticoat,
    A kirtle, and a goun.

As I came hame again,
    I thocht I wad big a kirk,
And a' the fouls o' the air
    Wad help me to work.

The herring wi' her lang neb,
    She moupit me the stanes;
The doo, wi' her rough legs,
    She led me them hame.

The gled he was a wily thief,
    He rackled up the wa';
The pyot was a curst thief,
    She dang doun a'.

The hare cam hirpling ower the knowe,
To ring the morning bell;
The hurcheon she came after,
And said she wad do't hersel.

The herring was the high priest,
The salmon was the clerk,
The howlet red the order—
They held a bonny wark.

ROBIN REDBREAST'S TESTAMENT.

(Chambers's *Popular Rhymes.*)

GUDE day now, bonnie Robin,
  How lang have you been here?
Oh, I have been bird about this bush
  This mair than twenty year!

Chorus.

  Teetle ell ell, teetle ell ell,
  Teetle ell ell, teetle ell ell;
  Tee tee tee tee tee tee tee,
  Tee tee tee tee, teetle eldie.

But now I am the sickest bird
  That ever sat on brier;
And I wad make my testament,
  Goodman, if ye wad hear.

Gar tak this bonnie neb o' mine,
  That picks upon the corn;
And gie't to the Duke o' Hamilton,
  To be a hunting-horn.

Gar tak these bonnie feathers o' mine,
    The feathers o' my neb;
And gie to the Lady o' Hamilton,
    To fill a feather-bed.

Gar tak this gude right leg o' mine,
    And mend the brig o' Tay;
It will be a post and pillar gude,
    It will neither bow nor gae.

And tak this other leg o' mine,
    And mend the brig o' Weir,*
It will be a post and pillar gude,
    It'll neither bow nor steer.

Gar tak these bonnie feathers o' mine,
    The feathers o' my tail;
And gie to the lads o' Hamilton,
    To be a barn flail.

And tak these bonnie feathers o' mine,
    The feathers o' my breast;
And gie to ony bonny lad
    That'll bring to me a priest.

Now in there came my lady wren,
    With mony a sigh and groan;
Oh, what care I for a' the lads,
    If my wee lad be gone?

* A bridge across the river Gryfe in Renfrewshire.

Then Robin turn'd him round about,
  E'en like a little king ;
Go, pack ye out at my chamber-door,
  Ye little cutty quean.

Robin made his testament
  Upon a coll of hay,
And by cam a greedy gled
  And snapt him a' away.

THE WREN.

(Chambers's *Popular Rhymes.*)

THE Wren she lyes in care's bed,
In care's bed, in care's bed;
The wren she lyes in care's bed,
In meikle dule and pyne, O.

When in cam Robin Redbreist,
Redbreist, Redbreist;
When in cam Robin Redbreist,
Wi' succar-saps and wine, O.

Now, maiden, will ye taste o' this,
Taste o' this, taste o' this;
Now, maiden, will ye taste o' this?
'Tis succar-saps and wine, O.

Na, ne'er a drap, Robin,
Robin, Robin;
Na, ne'er a drap, Robin,
Though it were ne'er so fine, O.

And where's the ring that I gied ye,
That I gied ye, that I gied ye;
And where's the ring that I gied ye,
Ye little cutty quean, O?

I gied it till a sodger,
A sodger, a sodger,
I gied it till a sodger,
A true sweitheart o' mine, O.

WHITTINGHAM FAIR.

(Child, Part iv., p. 495.)

'Are you going to Whittingham Fair?
   Parsley, sage, rosemary, and thyme,
Remember me to one who lives there;
   For once she was a true-love of mine.

'Tell her to make me a cambric shirt,
Without any seam or needlework.

'Tell her to wash it in yonder well,
Where never spring-water nor rain ever fell.

'Tell her to dry it on yonder thorn,
Which never bore blossom since Adam was born.'

'Now he has asked me questions three,
   Parsley, sage, rosemary, and thyme,
I hope he will answer as many for me;
   For once he was a true-love of mine.

'Tell him to find me an acre of land
Betwixt the salt-water and the sea-sand.

'Tell him to plough it with a ram's horn,
And sow it all over with one pepper-corn.

'Tell him to reap it with a sickle of leather,
And bind it up with a peacock's feather.

'When he has done, and finished his work,
O tell him to come, and he'll have his shirt.'

Notes.

"There was never ane o' ma sangs prentit till ye prentit them yoursel, and ye hae spoilt them athegither. They were made for singing and no for reading, but ye hae broken the charm now, and they'll never be sung mair. And the warst thing o' a'; they're nouther right spell'd, nor right setten down."

—*The Ettrick Shepherd's Mother, to Sir Walter Scott.*

NOTES.

THOMAS THE RHYMER.

Thomas of Ercildoun (Earlston), the Rhymer, was born about 1220. Professor Child points out resemblances between his adventure and that of Ogier the Dane. From many circumstances it is plain that Fairy Land here, and in *Tamlane*, is a modified survival, in popular memory, of the prehistoric Hades. Persephone, as Fairy Queen, abides in Fairy Land, as Venus does in her haunted hill. Compare Campion's refrain, "The Fairy Queen Proserpine," in Mr. Bullen's *More Lyrics from Elizabethan Song Books.*

TAMLANE.

The story is localised at Carterhaugh, just above the meeting of Ettrick and Yarrow. The ballad is peculiar to Scotland. In *Penda Baloa*, a negro ballad of Senegambia, the Fairy Lover turns into a crocodile, when once he has carried the girl into his enchanted kingdom.—(*Contes Pop. de la Sénégambie.* Bérenger Ferand. Paris, Leroux, 1885.) The converse of the plot is in *Alison Gross.* A knight, bewitched into a hideous form, is restored by the Fairy Queen to his own likeness, on Hallow E'en, "when the seely Court was riding by." —(Jamieson, *Popular Ballads*, ii., 187. Edinburgh, 1806.) The dipping of Tamlane in water or milk answers to similar processes in *Surya Bai* (Miss Frere's *Old Deccan Days*), to a Hottentot story (Bleek, *South African Folk-lore*), and to the dipping of Bitiou's heart in water (*Les Deux Freres*, in Maspero's *Contes Egyptiens*, p. 22). Also to an Albanian tale in *Von Hahn*, ii., 130. The resemblance to the story of Proteus, in Odyssey iv., has often been observed. The

version here printed was given by Burns to Johnson's *Museum*. The
version in the *Border Minstrelsy* (Fourth Edition, 1810) is in some
ways better, but has been interpolated.

The Elfan Nourice.

This pretty fragment is given in fairness to the Queen of Faery.
She has " borrowed " a nurse from " Christened land," but will restore
her safely when once the task of nursing a fairy child is ended.   Compare Gervase of Tilbury in *Otia Imperialia*.   The *Otia Imperialia*
was written about 1211.   Instead of " fairy," Gervase says *draco*.   He
declares he has seen the Fairy's nurse, *Vidimus equidem hujuscemodi
feminam* (*op. cit. ed.* Liebrecht.   Hanover, 1856, p. 38).   In the
ballad six fragmentary lines, apparently borrowed from *Thomas the
Rhymer*, are omitted.

Alison Gross.

Jamieson, from the recitation of Mrs. Brown.   Here the Queen of
the Fairies plays the part of benefactress.   This ballad is, as Professor
Child remarks, a variety of *Beauty and the Beast*.   There are Greek,
Danish, and Norwegian variants.

Kempion; or, Kemp Owyne.

A similar ballad is *The Laidley Worm of Spindleston Heughs*.   The
motive of the story is not unlike the charming old French tale of *The
White Cat*.   Icelandic, Danish, Italian, and English variants exist.
Heywood and Delira give a like tradition which is said to have existed
at Basil.   "A tailor, in an adventurous mood, chose to descend into
an obscure cavern in the vicinity of the city.   After many windings, he
came to an iron door, through which he passed into a chamber.   Here
he found, seated upon a splendid throne, a lady, whose countenance
was surprisingly beautiful, but whose shape terminated in a dragon's
train, which warped around the chair on which she was placed.   Before
her stood a brazen chest, trebly barred and bolted; at each end of
which lay couched a huge black bandog, who rose up, as if to tear the

intruder in pieces. But the lady appeased them; and, opening the chest, displayed an immense treasure, out of which she bestowed upon the visitor some small pieces of money, informing him that she was enchanted by her step-dame, but should recover her natural shape on being kissed thrice by a mortal. The tailor essayed to fulfil the conditions of the adventure; but her face assumed such an altered, wild, and grim expression, that his courage failed, and he was fain to fly from the place. A kinsman of his, some years after, penetrated into the cavern, with the purpose of repairing a desperate fortune. But finding nothing but dead men's bones, he ran mad and died."—Sir Walter Scott.

THE WIFE OF USHER'S WELL.

Often attached to *The Clerk's Three Sons of Owsenford*. The moral is that the grief of the living disturbs the dead. The dead child, in a *märchen*, has to carry vessels full of his mother's tears.

CLERK SAUNDERS.

The latter part of the ballad may be, and often is, detached from the first part. Then it is *Sweet William's Ghost*.—(Child, iii., 226.)

WILLIE'S LADY.

In Sir Henry Layard's *Early Adventures* we hear of tying the sacred knots when an Arab woman is in labour, *that she may have an easy deliverance*. This is the reverse of the effect of the "witch-knots" in this ballad. Probably when Simaetha, in Theocritus (ii., 4), says she will "bind" her faithless lover, the effect is like that of *nouer l'anguilette*, in French folk-magic.

The similar case of Hera and Leto at the birth of Hercules is well known. Child cites many European variants.

SIR ROLAND.

Communicated to Motherwell "by an ingenious friend." The authenticity of the ballad is disputed. We believe it to be, for the more part at least, genuine. That is a beautiful touch of dread:

> " O yon chamber is very dark, fair maid,
> *And the night is wondrous lown.*"

For a description of such a night, see Mr. Stevenson's *Thrawn Janet*, in *The Merry Men.*

EARL RICHARD.

Scott supposes the tell-tale candles to have been the traditional "corpse-lights;" and gives many examples of the divination by touch —*i.e.*, the phenomenon of the murdered corpse (occasionally even the whitened bones) bleeding at the approach, or contact, of the murderer. Herd, with whose copy Scott collated his own, calls this ballad *Young Hunting.* Kinloch gives another version under the name of *Young Redin.* Others exist, notably one taken down from recitation by Motherwell. There are Scandinavian variants of this ballad.

YOUNG BENJIE.

In this ballad the reader will find traces of a singular superstition not yet altogether discredited in the wilder parts of Scotland. The lyke-wake, or watching a dead body, in itself a melancholy office, is rendered, in the idea of the assistants, more dismally awful, by the mysterious horrors of superstition. In the interval between death and interment, the disembodied spirit is supposed to hover around its mortal habitation, and, if invoked by certain rites, retains the power of communicating, through its organs, the cause of its dissolution. Such inquiries, however, are always dangerous, and never to be resorted to, unless the deceased is suspected to have suffered foul play, as it is called. It is the more unsafe to tamper with this charm in an unauthorised manner, because the inhabitants of the infernal regions are, at such periods, peculiarly active. One of the most potent ceremonies in the charm, for causing the dead body to speak, is setting the door ajar, or half open. On this account the peasants of Scotland sedulously avoid leaving the door ajar while a corpse lies in the house. The door must either be left wide open, or quite shut ; but the first is always preferred, on account of the exercise of hospitality usual on such occasions. The attendants must be likewise careful never to leave the corpse for a moment alone, or, if it is left alone, to avoid, with a degree of superstitious horror, the first sight of it.

The following story, which is frequently related by the peasants of Scotland, will illustrate the imaginary danger of leaving the door ajar. In former times, a man and his wife lived in a solitary cottage, on one of the extensive Border Fells. One day the husband died suddenly; and his wife, who was equally afraid of staying alone by the corpse, or leaving the dead body by itself, repeatedly went to the door, and looked anxiously over the lonely moor for the sight of some person approaching. In her confusion and alarm she accidentally left the door ajar, when the corpse suddenly started up, and sat in the bed, frowning and grinning at her frightfully. She sat alone, crying bitterly, unable to avoid the fascination of the dead man's eye, and too much terrified to break the sullen silence, till a Catholic priest, passing over the wild, entered the cottage. He first set the door quite open, then put his little finger in his mouth, and said the paternoster backwards; when the horrified look of the corpse relaxed, it fell back on the bed, and behaved itself as a dead man ought to do.

This ballad is given from tradition. I have been informed by a lady, of the highest literary eminence, that she has heard a ballad on the same subject, in which the scene was laid upon the banks of the Clyde. The chorus was—

"O Bothwell banks bloom bonny."

And the watching of the dead corpse was said to have taken place in Bothwell church.—Sir Walter Scott.

PROUD LADY MARGARET.

A "Mr. Hamilton, music-seller, Edinburgh, with whose mother it had been a favourite," communicated this to Scott. Several other Scottish versions exist. In Buchan's, the phantom of the dead brother reproves and admonishes his sister; at the same time warning her of her probable fate should she persist in her pride.

> "In Pirie's chair you'll sit, I say,
> The lowest seat o' hell ;
> If ye do not amend your ways,
> Its there that ye must dwell."

A like incident may be found in a ballad from Brittany, where a dead mistress counsels her lover to amend his ways (Ampère, *Instructions relatives aux Poèsies populaires de la France*, p. 36), and in other French *volks-lieder*.

FINE FLOWERS IN THE VALLEY ; OR, THE CRUEL MOTHER.

" This story has its counterpart in Scott's *Lady Anne*, which is, in all likelihood, a modern composition, with extensive variations, on the theme of the popular ballad. . . . Kristensen, in the course of his very remarkable ballad quest in Jutland, recovered two versions which approach surprisingly near to Scottish tradition.—Two other Danish versions have been obtained since then, but have not been published." —(Child.) A like story is widely diffused in Germany. The version here given has been collated from Johnson's *Musical Museum* and Kinloch.

THE TWA BROTHERS.

All the Scottish versions were obtained within the first third of this century, and since then no others have been heard of. It is interesting to find the ballad still in the mouths of children in American cities,—in the mouths of the poorest, whose heritage these old things are. Motherwell was inclined to believe, and Kirkpatrick Sharpe was convinced, that this ballad was founded upon an event that happened near Edinburgh as late as 1589, that of one of the Somervilles having been killed by his brother's pistol accidently going off.—(Child.) Either supposition seems doubtful ; we incline more towards the hypothesis of primitive invention.

Compare the ending of this ballad with that of " Edward."

THE DEMON LOVER.

Mr. Motherwell could only find a fragment of this, and obviously thought that Laidlaw, Scott's amanuensis, added "the snow-white sprites," and a good deal more.

Love Gregor; or, The Lass of Lochroyan.

Compare, for a reversing of the rôles and fates of Lover and Lady, *The Drowned Lovers* (Buchan, i., 140).

The "Love Tokens" are found, in their earliest form, in the Odyssey, xxiii., 255-287. This ballad has many names and variants.

The Dowie Dens o' Yarrow.

Motherwell, in his first edition, has "Dowie Downs." The Dowie Dens have been localised between Cat Craig and Cat Slack, on Whitehope. Here are two standing stones. Scott changed Annan Street, the local name of the site, into Annan's Treat, to chime in with a legend that Annan was the murderer's name. This was quite arbitrary. He thought the slain knight was a Scott of Kirkhope, or of Oakwood, a son of Harden's, or Walter Scott, son of Scott of Thirlestane, an ancestor of Lord Napier and Ettrick. Compare Mr. Craig Brown's *History of Selkirkshire*, i., 48. Perhaps the *Dowie Dens* are really the black pools of Yarrow beneath precipitous banks, between Harehead and Bowhill.

Lord Thomas and Fair Annet.

Child gives Norse variants. In modern Greek (Fauriel), the old true love wins the day, and the new bride is rejected. A curious English variant is added from a MS. copy which Mrs. Rider Haggard has kindly supplied.

The Twa Sisters o' Binnorie.

A difficult ballad to get correctly edited. Jamieson interpolated it : Scott compiled from Mrs. Brown, and a fragment known to a Mr. Walker, who had it from Miss Brook, who had it from an old woman. Perhaps Jamieson's Fifeshire version (ii., 48) is best. The version here is from Mr. Allingham. In Binnōrie, accent the penultimate.

The *story* has two forms—a brother slays a brother (*The Twa Brothers ; Edward, Edward ; Son Davie*), with Swedish and Finnish variants ; or a sister, as here, slays a sister. For the Harp, compare *The Singing Bone* (Grimm, *K. & H. M.*, 28).

BESSIE BELL AND MARY GREY.

"They died of the plague, communicated by their lover, in the year 1645."—C. Kirkpatrick Sharpe. Aytoun says they were daughters of the Lairds of Kinvaid and Lednoch, and the "bower" (how like the bower of Nicolette it is) was on the banks of the Almond.

BARTHRAM'S DIRGE.

A pious fraud by Surtees of Mainsforth. It is not easy to say what Surtees did not write. *Lord Durie, The Slaying of Anthony Feather-stonehaugh,* and possibly a good deal of *Hobbie Noble* are his. The Nine Stane Rig is near Hermitage Castle, in Liddesdale. See *Life of Surtees,* 1852.—(Surtees Society.)

THE LYKEWAKE DIRGE.

Similar theories of the voyage to Death's land are found in most mythologies. Among the Ojibbeway, the Brig o' Dread is a fallen tree (Kohl, *Kitchi Gami*). In Arab faiths this bridge is the razor-edged bridge of Sirat. St. Boniface mentions such a bridge (Epist., xxi.); it is found in the Golden Legend, in popular rhymed prayers in France. The Hell-shoon of Scandinavian funeral rites were apparently to be useful in this emergency. Compare Jones's *Traditions of North American Indians,* i., 228; Catlin, ii., 127.

Here one is indebted to M. Edélestand du Méril, *Etudes sur Quelques Points,* p. 434 (Paris, 1862).

THE DOUGLAS TRAGEDY.

Though localised on the Douglas Burn, a tributary of Yarrow, the ballad is widely diffused in Europe. The Danish is *Ribolt og Guldborg.* Icelandic, Norse, and Swedish variants are found.—(Child. Editions of 1861, ii., 114.)

THE GAY GOSS HAWK.

From Mrs. Brown's MS., with additions from a MS. of Sir Walter Scott's.

The idea recurs in *La Maîtresse Captive* (Puymaigre, *Ch. Pop. du Pays Messin*, 1865, p. 46). Gérard de Nerval gave a version in *Filles de Feu*. As early as 1607 a version (*Belle Isambourg*) was printed.

The incident is sometimes added to *Le Père Sévère*. (Translated. *Ballads and Lyrics of Old France*, 1872, p. 65.)

CHILDE MAURICE.

The popular version is *Gil Morice*. The foundation of Home's once famous play of *Douglas*. The language is slightly modernised.

FAIR ANNIE.

An old form of the plot is in *Le Lai del Freisne* of Marie de France. There are German, Dutch, and Danish versions. The old leman wins the day in a Greek ballad in Fauriel, but is not said to be the sister of the new bride.

WALY, WALY.

Part of this is extant, Aytoun says, in a MS. of 1566. Portions have found their way into *The Marchioness of Douglas* (1670), in Kinloch's MS.

THE LOWLANDS O' HOLLAND.

A *volks-lyrik*. Date unknown.

GLASGERION.

Glascurion, in Chaucer's *House of Fame*, is where Orpheus and where Chiron are.

> "The harper Orion,
> And Eacydes Chiron,
> And other harpers many oon,
> And the gret Glascurion."

Glaskeraint was a Welsh bard, "Blue Mantle." The idea of the plot is found in German, and in Decameron, iii., 2. *Glenkindie* is a Scotch version.

HELEN OF KIRKCONNELL.

She was a daughter of Irving, or Bell of Kirkconnell, in Dumfries-shire. Her lover was Adam Fleming of Kirkconnell. Date unknown. The last verse may have suggested a verse in *Oriana.*

LADY MAISRY.

The punishment of burning a girl for incontinence is denounced by Ariosto as *l'aspra legge di Scozia, empia e severa.*—(Child.)

THE BONNY HIND.

A tale of unhappy recognition, akin to the Œdipous story. It is difficult to imagine how Motherwell could have preferred *Sheath and Knife*, as being less abhorrent in detail than *The Bonny Hind*. The first has a mournful refrain of great beauty,

"And we'll never gang doun to the broom ony mair;"

but is, in our opinion, in every other respect distinctly inferior to the ballad given here. *Lizie Wan* and *The King's Dochter Lady Jean* are Scottish ballads, which turn upon a like central idea. In the first half of the story *The Bonny Hind* closely resembles the fine Scandinavian ballad of *Margaret*, which Child says is as yet known to be preserved only in Färöe aud Icelandic. A similar tragedy is found in the great Finnish epic, *The Kalevala*. In the story of *Kullervo*, his unhappy sister drowns herself on learning the truth. (*Ka'ewala, übertragen von Schiefner*, runes 35, 36.) Professor Child, having had access to Herd's MSS., in which he found three separate transcriptions of *The Bonny Hind*, has supplied some stanzas omitted by Scott, who only had MS. No. 1 in his hands.

Two of these stanzas are restored to the version in this collection. According to Scott and Motherwell, many tales of this kind exist in the antique ballad literature of Scotland. Scott attributes the source of their existence to a low state of civilization, but owns, at the same time, the great poetic merit of *The Bonny Hind*. The savage strength and purity of this marvellously dramatic ballad are as beautiful as they are terrible.

Hynd Horn.

The idea of the gift which pales with the giver's inconstancy or danger is an old and a widely diffused one. It recurs in Indian, Roumanian, Sicilian, and Silesian songs and stories. In some versions of "Lamkin" the lord of the castle is warned of the evil that has befallen his wife by the springing in two of the rings on his fingers. The identification by an old love-token (sometimes divided between the lovers, each keeping half) may be found in old English, French, Scandinavian, Flemish, modern Greek, and Russian romances and *volks-lieder*. Boccaccio tells a tale founded on the same idea; and it is also repeated in a Picard ballad. Child gives many variants.

Lady Elspat.

Taken down by Jamieson from the recitation of Mrs. Brown,

Young Atkin; or, Hind Etin.

This ballad has been much damaged and corrupted by vulgar and prosaic transcription. The supernatural character of the hero, so distinctly marked in the Norse and German variants, is well-nigh lost sight of. The only remaining indications are the enormous strength of the etin, and the miraculous mist that surrounds the capture of the lady. The assertion that he was her father's cup-bearer is obviously absurd.

The Cruel Brother.

Dr. Prior remarks that the offence given by not asking a brother's assent to his sister's marriage was in ballad-times regarded as unpardonable. The peculiar testament made by the bride, by which she bequeaths good things to her friends, but ill things to the author of her death, is highly characteristic of ballad poetry. It will be found again in "Lord Ronald," "Edward," and their analogues.—(Child.)

Jellon Grame.

In Child's opinion the four stanzas before the last two of this ballad are not simply "modernised" (as Scott calls them) but modern. It bears a close affinity, in some particulars, to *Fause Foodrage*. The incident of the murdered mother avenged by her young son occurs also in several Scandinavian ballads.

BROWN ADAM.

A Danish ballad, where the father of a girl, whose honour is in danger from a rejected suitor, cuts off the intruder's hand, bears a remote resemblance to this.

THE LAMENT OF THE BORDER WIDOW.

A *volks-lyrik*. Scott says, "This fragment, obtained from recitation in the Forest of Ettrick, is said to relate to the execution of Cockburne of Henderland, a Border freebooter, hanged over the gate of his own tower by James V. in the course of that memorable expedition in 1529, which was fatal to Johnie Armstrong, Adam Scott of Tushielaw, and many other marauders." Its authenticity is perhaps not above suspicion.

GRAEME AND BEWICK.

The ballad is remarkable, as containing, probably, the very latest allusion to the institution of brotherhood in arms, which was held so sacred in the days of chivalry, and whose origin may be traced up to the Scythian ancestors of Odin. —(Macfarlane's MSS.)

ERLINTON.

An example of the old story of a young girl who is confined by her father in a "bigly bower," or a tower, and rescued by her lover. Le Père Sévère (Translated, *Ballads and Lyrics of Old France*, 1872, p. 65), has a less fortunate conclusion.

THE GARDENER.

Collated by Mr. Allingham from Kinloch and Buchan, and by him entitled, "A fanciful short ballad of wooing."

Lord Randal.

Known in Italy 300 years ago. There are German, Dutch, Swedish, Magyar, and Wendish versions. Poisoning by a snake also occurs in Romaic.—(Child.)

Johnie Faa.

He was King of the Scotch Gipsies in 1495.—(Pinkerton.)

The Twa Corbies.

Written down for Scott by C. K. Sharpe, from recitations by a lady. The English version is *The Three Ravens.*—(Ravenscroft's *Melismata,* London, 1611.)

The Three Ravens.

Unlike the Scotch version, the English song makes the lady true and tender.

Sir Hugh.

The superstition about the Jews is very old and tenacious of life. It caused massacres in Damascus in the middle of the present century. Matthew Paris tells the story as an event of the reign of Henry III. Mr. Newells, in New York, found a version among negro children. The Jew had become the Duke.—(Newells, in *Child's Play.*)

May Colvin.

Child gives this as one form of *Lady Isabel and the Elf Knight.* In *May Colvin* the Elfin opening *fehlt.* We are not told that the lady summoned the false lover to her side. She stabs him where he slew seven kings' daughters. In the *Water o' Wearie's Well* the lady drowns him, but not by May Colvin's *ruse.*

Jamieson found the story in oral tradition, as a kind of *cante-fable,* verse and prose mingled. Variants occur in Holland, Denmark, Sweden, Norway, Iceland, Germany (the traitor's previous victims, in the shape of doves, sing a warning song, like the "Birds of the Thorn

Country " in Zulu). Poland, with other Slavonic lands, has this ballad.
In all these the incidents vary in various versions. In France it
was first published by Gérard de Nerval. It is known in Italy, in
Spain, Portugal, and among the Magyars. Bugge finds a form of it in
the Saga of *Sampson the Fair*, where the villain is a wood-haunting
being of origin partly elfin. He looks for the "remote source" of the
ballad in the Apocryphal adventure of Judith and Holofernes. This is
looking too far afield. Grimm's *Robber Bridegroom* is a *märchen*
greatly resembling this class of ballad. The devices by which the girl
deceives her would-be murderer are like the tricks in the widely-diffused
European and savage versions of *Hop o' my Thumb*.

BARBARA ALLAN.

There are many barbarous variants, turning on the adventures of
Giles Scroggins, or Collins. One of these, from a MS. of Mrs. Rider
Haggard, is printed here :—

GILES COLLINS AND LADY ANNICE.

Giles Collins said to his own mother,
  "Mother, come bind up my head ;
And send for the parson of our parish,
  For to-morrow I shall be dead.

" And if that I be dead,
  As I verily believe I shall,
O bury me not in our churchyard,
  But under Lady Annice's wall."

Lady Annice sat at her bower window,
  Mending of her night coif,
When passing she saw as lovely a corpse
  As ever she saw in her life.

"Set down, set down, ye six tall men,
  Set down upon the plain,
That I may kiss those clay cold lips
  I ne'er shall kiss again.

" Set down, set down, ye six tall men,
    That I may look thereon ;
For to-morrow, before the cock it has crow'd,
    Giles Collins and I shall be one.

" What had you at Giles Collins's burying ?
    Very good ale and wine ?
You shall have the same to-morrow night,
    Much about the same time."

Giles Collins died upon the eve,
    This fair lady on the morrow ;
Thus may you all now very well know
    This couple died for sorrow.

EDWARD.

This is the ballad of the Bloody Brothers, as is Binnorie of the Cruel
Sister. Mr. Swinburne has translated the Finnish version. There are
Swedish and Danish variants.

ANNAN WATER.

According to Scott, these are the original words of the tune of *Allan
Water.* Annan is in Dumfriesshire. An Allan water runs into Teviot
above Branxholme.

LORD LOVEL.

This is from a broadside ballad.

THE HEIR OF LIN.

Notice a converse idea in Child (viii., 60, 1861), and the Greek
epigram (Brunck, i., 106).

JAMIE TELFER.

Sir Walter Scott fancied the Dodhead was that near Singlee, on the
Ettrick, in Selkirkshire. In that case Telfer was twenty-five miles
from his feudal protector at Stobs, and he could not conceivably have

covered the ground in the time. Besides, he would have passed Harden and Branxholme on his way. Telfer's Dodhead is near Penchrise, not far from Skelfhill, on the south side of Teviot. He was within three miles of Stobs, where Elliot treated him so badly. Turning towards Teviot, he naturally came to Jock Grieve, at Colterscleugh, thence up the water to Branxholme. Having warned the water, they set out to cut off the English, who had gone by the present Carlisle road, up Teviot till it is joined by the Frostlee Burn, then up the burn over the water-shed by the Wisp.

KINMONT WILLIE.

The gallant exploit here chanted was performed in 1596, April 13. There is a prose account very like the ballad in Satchell's *History of the Name of Scott* (1688).

JOHNIE ARMSTRONG,

Of Gilnockie, near Langholm. There is a feeble Westmoreland version.

GORDON OF BRACKLEY.

This pretty version is from Mackay's editions of Motherwell. It seems a pity to omit this form, especially as it sounds so prophetic of Charles Gordon of Khartoum.

> " *A Gordon rides out*
> *Who will never ride hame !* "

But we are not told how or why the ballad varies so much from the shapes in Aytoun, Jamieson, and Motherwell.

HOBBIE NOBLE.

This hero had taken part in the rescue of Jock o' the Side, and was but ill repaid by the Armstrongs for his services. The date is about 1570-1580. The " Land Sergeant " was an officer under the Warden of the Border. Who the Earl of Whitfield might be was much debated. See *Life of Surtees of Mainsforth.*

Jock o' the Side.

Jock o' the Side seems to have been nephew to the laird of Manger-toun, cousin to the laird's Jock, one of his deliverers, and probably brother to Christie of the Syde, mentioned in the list of Border clans, 1597. Like the laird's Jock, he also is commemorated by Sir Richard Maitland.—*See the Introduction :*

> "He is weil, Johne of the Syde,
> A greater thief did never ryde ;
> He nevir tyris,
> For to brek byris,
> Our muir and myris
> Ouir gude ane guid," etc.

Jock o' the Side appears to have assisted the Earl of Westmoreland in his escape after his unfortunate insurrection with the Earl of Northumberland, in the twelfth year of Elizabeth.—(Scott.)

Dick o' The Cow.

According to Scott, a ballad very popular in Liddesdale, and well known in England so early as 1596. Dick o' The Cow seems to have been Lord Scroope's jester. In spite of his cautious removal to Burgh-under-Stanmuir he fell into the clutches of the Armstrongs several years after this exploit, and was put to an inhuman death.

Archie o' Ca'field.

Ca'field, or Calfield, is a place in Wauchopdale, belonging of old to the Armstrongs. In the account betwixt the English and Scottish Marches, Jock and Geordie of Ca'field, there called Calf-hill, are repeatedly marked as delinquents.—*History of Westmoreland and Cumberland*, vol i., Introduction, p. 33.—(Scott.)

The Raid of the Reidswire.

This poem is published from a copy in the Bannatyne MS., in the handwriting of the Hon. Mr. Carmichael, advocate. It first appeared in "Allan Ramsay's Evergreen," but some liberties have been taken by him in transcribing it ; and, what is altogether unpardonable, the MS., which is itself rather inaccurate, has been interpolated to favour his readings ; of which there remain obvious marks. The skirmish of the Reidswire happened upon the 7th of June 1575, at one of the meetings held by the Wardens of the Marches, for arrangements necessary upon the border.—(Scott.)

ROOKHOPE RYDE.

This is a bishopric border song, composed in 1569, taken down from the chanting of George Collingwood the elder, late of Boltsburn, in the neighbourhood of Ryhope. Rookhope is the name of a valley about five miles in length, at the termination of which Rookhope burn empties itself into the river Wear : the dale lies in the north part of the parish of Stanhope, in Weardale. Rookhope-head is the top of the vale. The ballad derives some additional interest from the date of the event being so precisely ascertained to be the 6th December 1572, when the Tynedale robbers, taking advantage of the public confusion occasioned by the rebellion of Westmoreland and Northumberland, and which particularly affected the bishopric of Durham, determined to make this foray into Weardale.

The late eminent antiquary, Joseph Ritson, took down this ballad from the mouth of the reciter, and printed it as part of an intended collection of border ballads, which was never published. His nephew, Mr. Frank, was so good as to favour me with the copy from which it is here given. To the illustrations of Mr. Ritson, I have been enabled to add those of my friend, Mr. Surtees of Mainsforth.—(Scott.)

JOHNIE OF BRAIDISLEE.

Of the mournful story here sung there are several variants, in one of which the hero is called Johnie of Cockielaw. Scott remarks that he has selected the stanzas of greatest merit from each copy to form the ballad here printed.

KATHARINE JANFARIE.

Plainly Scott's inspiration for "Young Lochinvar." He states that ·this ballad was published in the first edition of *The Border Minstrelsy* under the title of "The Laird of Laminton," and was later printed, in a more perfect state, from several recited copies. He adds that "the residence of the lady, and the scene of the affray at her bridal, is said, by old people, to have been upon the banks of the Cadden, near to where it joins the Tweed. Others say the skirmish was fought near Traquair, and Katharine Janfarie's dwelling was in the glen about three miles above Traquair House."

THE BONNY HOUSE OF AIRLY.

The history is very confusing, Lady Ogilvie speaking of her gude Lord as with "Prince Charlie," not a term applied to Charles I. At this time, too, as Kinloch says, Montrose was with the Covenanters.

THE FIRE OF FRENDRAUGHT.

Given to Motherwell by Charles Kirkpatrick Sharpe. The date of the burning was October 8, 1630. The whole feud, with its ending, reminds one of Icelandic society and manners, in the age of. Njal : "About midnight that dolorous tower took fire in so sudden and furious manner, yea, and in a clap, that the noble Viscount, the laird of Rothiemay, and others were cruelly tormented and burnt to the death without help or relief. The laird of Frendraught, his lady, and haile household, looking on, without moving or striving to deliver them from the fury of this fearful fire, as was reported."—(Spalding.)

WILLIE WALLACE.

Motherwell took this version from "Gleanings of Scarce Old Ballads," Peterhead, 1825. It was derived from the recitative of "an Itinerant Tinker and Gipsie." The adventure is in Henry the Minstrel's "Metrical Life of Walays," Book v.

Sir Patrick Spens.

Child seems to despair of discovering any historical event that closely answers to the story of this ballad. But many Scotch knights were drowned on their way back from conveying Margaret, daughter of Alexander III., to wed Eric of Norway (1281).

Edom o' Gordon.

This was Adam Gordon of Auchindoun, brother of the Marquis of Huntly. In 1571 his man, Ker, burned Towie Castle, which held out against the cause of Mary Stuart. The House o' the Rhodes has been introduced erroneously by some Border reciter. It is near Gordon in Berwickshire.—(Aytoun.)

The Queen's Marie.

Scott could find no historical basis for this except an intrigue between a French waiting-woman and the Queen's apothecary. Aytoun (ii., 45) gives a text in some respects better than Scott's. The scandal (Kirkpatrick Sharpe) about a Miss Hambleton and Peter the Great can hardly have influenced the piece. The maids of other ladies, as well as of the Queen, are called "Maries" in some ballads. Sharpe had a little German almanack, with a cut of Miss Hambleton on the scaffold, and the Czar beside her, "very prettily done."

Otterburn.

The battle was in 1388. Douglas is really buried in Melrose Abbey. Douglas of Cavers has his flag, and a lady's gloves, embroidered with K. P.—Katherine Percy. The English version perverts the facts of the battle.

The Battle of Philiphaugh.

The battle was in 1643. Scott says of the ballad that its sole merit is in coinciding accurately with historical fact. It was, in his time, preserved by tradition in Selkirkshire, and is remarkable as being the last field fought in Ettrick Forest.

The Gallant Grahǎms.

The preceding ballad (says Sir Walter Scott) was a song of triumph over the defeat of Montrose at Philiphaugh; the verses which follow are a lamentation for his final discomfiture and cruel death. The present edition of *The Gallant Grahams* is given from tradition, enlarged and corrected by an ancient printed edition, entitled, *The Gallant Grahams of Scotland,* to the tune of *I will away, and I will not tarry,* of which Mr. Ritson favoured me with an accurate copy.

The Battle of Pentland Hills.

The battle was fought on the 28th November 1666—a day still observed by the scattered remnant of the Cameronian sect, who regularly hear a field-preaching upon the field of battle. I am obliged for a copy of the ballad to Mr. Livingston of Airds, who took it down from the recitation of an old woman residing on his estate.

The gallant Grahams mentioned in the text are Grahams of Claverhouse's horse.—(Scott.)

The Battle of Loudon Hill.

This battle, between the Covenanters and the Cavaliers, was fought in 1679.

The Battle of Bothwell Bridge

Followed close upon the Cameronian success at Loudon Hill. Scott supposes Alexander Gordon of Earlstoun to have been the hero of this ballad.

Mary Ambree.

A ballad of the wars of 1584, where some English volunteers, like Sir Randal, went "to fight the foreign loons in their ain countrie." History says nothing of Mary Ambree. Percy got the ballad from a black letter copy in the Pepy's Collection, "improved from the Editor's folio MSS., and by conjecture."

ROBIN HOOD.

As nothing is known about Robin Hood, much is conjectured, and in the entire absence of facts, there is abundant learning. Did he live *temp.* Richard I., or under Edward II. ? Is he a mere ideal outlaw, Robin of the Wood? Is he Woden? Is he the Sun? People have been found to maintain all these and other opinions. The ballads of his adventures are exceedingly English, long and dull.

The Comic Songs and Lullabies, with the Nursery Songs, need little comment. It may be noticed, however, that the childish tale of " bigging a kirk,"

> " *And a' the fowls o' the air*
> *Wad help me to work,*"

unconsciously perpetuates the Greek myth of the building of the first Temple at Delphi by birds and insects.

Printed by WALTER SCOTT, *Felling, Newcastle-on-Tyne.*

www.ingramcontent.com/pod-product-compliance
Lightning Source LLC
Chambersburg PA
CBHW052349110726
47901CB00005B/1423